ABANDON

AN ORC MONSTER ROMANCE

TRISH HEINRICH

CONTENTS

For that little girl who obsessively watched Indiana Jones and always
wished there was more kissing.
This one is for you kid.

AUTHOR'S NOTE

I am a huge history nerd. Some of my favorite books are about the Queens of England and Egypt, the Mongol Empire, the court of Henry the Eighth, just to name a few. I used to be able to tell you the lineage of British kings from their matrilineal line starting at Eleanor of Aquitaine and ending with Elizabeth the first (though that brain space is a bit rusty these days).

I've always been that nerd.

So when I tell you that this book was me letting my history nerd flag fly, I'm not kidding.

Now, before you continue, I'm warning you right now that there may be spoilers in what I'm about to divulge. So if you don't want that, come back here after you've finished the book and we'll geek out together.

If that's okay with you, then feel free to read on and we'll geek out now.

Ready?

Let's talk about how a Medieval mystic and polymath by the name of Hildegard and the Nazi regime intersect. (Buckle up, I'm about to go full nerd on you!)

Hildegard was an extraordinary woman who counseled some of the most influential men of her time including the Pope, the Holy Roman Emperor, and Henry the second. She wrote many books filled with visions God had given her that are poured over to this day by Feminists and mystics alike. These books also contained recipes for medicines, including safe at home abortions, as well as many other remedies and suggestions pertaining specifically to women's health, something rare indeed for that time. Pretty much all the things Luke says about Hildegard in this book are true. She really did create her own language, write musical compositions that no one had ever heard before, and establish her own religious order that survives to this day. Her descriptions of God as a woman are some of the most astonishing parts of her writing, as are the clearly female pieces of art she created. Look up Hildegard's cosmic egg and tell me that doesn't look like a woman's genitalia. (And, if you are curious about Hildegard and other fascinating women of the Medieval era, I can't recommend Femina by Janina Ramirez strongly enough. It's incredible!) Just about the only thing she didn't do was befriend a poor town of Orcs and create a mystical cure for the disease plaguing them. But hey, fictional license.

Many of her original manuscripts have been lost, though we do have reproductions and translations that are still read by many today. Two of her most famous books were the Scivias and the Riesencodex, and it's here that her story intersects with the Nazi regime briefly.

Fast forward to 1945. The two books were in a German library, mostly forgotten and only remembered by scholars. But, in his quest for mystical artifacts to lend the power of propaganda to the Nazi regime, Himmler wanted the books in a safe location. So, they were transported to Dresden, and put into a secured bank vault by the Nazis, presumably while they were on their way to Himmler's castle. While they were in Dresden, the city was bombed and the vault was broken. When officials found the vault, the Scivias was missing but the Riesencodex was still there.

This is where I inject a bit of fantasy and fiction and use this fascinating bit of history to my own devices. No one has ever seen the Scivias again in real life. But I thought, wouldn't it be so amazing, if this book was the one thing that Luke needed? And so the idea was born to make the Scivias the central artifact of this book.

But then, where has the Scivias been? Who had hidden it this whole time?

This is where, once again, I tap into actual history surrounding the Nazis.

After the collapse of the regime, many high level officers and engineers of the Third Reich fled Germany under the guise of Catholics fleeing communist persecution in Russia. Now, the role of the Catholic church in this is a bit of a hot button topic to this day. While many believe the corruption wasn't wide spread among the church, there is ample evidence that some cardinals and bishops did knowingly help high level Nazis escape to Argentina, where many of them were never found until their deaths.

Where I massaged history a bit was in the inclusion of Himmler's treasures from his castle.

Himmler really did have a castle, and yes, he really did store a ton of items there that he claimed held mystical power. The dude even had an entire room built to house the Holy Grail. Many doubt that Himmler believed his own bullshit. Instead, the man was simply creating high level religious propaganda to keep the people enamored of the Third Reich. Whatever the reason for his eccentric behaviors, he had a lot of items there that people thought were of the utmost value. As a result, Himmler's castle was raided when Germany lost the war and all those precious treasures were scattered across Europe.

When I read this, a plot came together.

I'd already established in my world that the Secret Archive and the Nazis had a shadow war going on for control of powerful artifacts. So then…

What if some of those Nazis that raided Himmler's castle also fled to Argentina?

And what if what they took were powerful religious artifacts?

And what if the artifacts destroyed them?

And what if there was one man there, who was pure of heart, who wanted to keep all of these items safe?

And, what if one of those items was the Scivias?

Now, I wanted to keep the story in Argentina, but as big as that country is, it didn't have the sufficient amount of rainforest for the needs of the story. And since Chile and Argentina share the Valdivian rainforest, I thought what if the priest fled into Chile?

And the rest…well, the rest you either have read or are about to read.

Thank you for geeking out with me for a few minutes, and for loving my Monsters & Artifacts series. I can't believe that I get to blend two of my favorite things (romance and history) into such exciting and romantic stories!

CHAPTER ONE
ANDROMEDA

"**A**re you coming home for your father's birthday?" my mother asked on the other end of the phone.

"Yes, Mom, I'll be there." I glanced at the door of the director's office.

If I'm not redacted and spending a mandatory six weeks in a mental health facility.

For the sixth time in about as many minutes I rubbed my clammy hand on my black dress slacks.

"What's wrong?" Mom asked.

"Nothing."

There was silence on the other end and I knew she was standing there, in her home office, waiting for me to tell her the truth. She always knew when one of us was lying and she could wait us out with patience and love like no one else on the planet.

I both loved and loathed that about my mom.

"I'm in London," I said as I paced in the small waiting room.

"And you're nervous about that."

"Yeah."

My parents knew about my history with the Secret Archive, about the rebellion that I, and several dozen other agents, had fought against the previous director, Francesca. They knew that I still had nightmares, that in some ways it had cost me my marriage, and that being this close to this office brought up gut wrenching fears that, almost two years later, I was still having problems handling.

"If you don't feel safe, I want you to get to Ramon and take the jet home, you understand?" Mom said, slipping into Spanish as if that would keep what she said a secret. "I don't care if it is the Archive, no one messes with a Kane."

My family was one of the wealthiest, most powerful families in America. We had our fingers in everything from entertainment, technology, weapons development and pharmaceuticals. No one fucked with us and if they did, they found out real quick that it wasn't a smart move.

But this wasn't America, and the Secret Archive was practically a country unto itself.

Outside the jurisdiction of every single government on the planet, the Archive had been around since the library of Alexandria. Every hundred years or so the headquarters moved, as did the enormous collection of dangerous mystical artifacts it kept safe from the rest of the world. Down through the ages, the Archive had grown from a small group of men and women, determined to safeguard the artifacts, to a worldwide secret organization that employed thousands, both Mundanes, like me, and Supernaturals such as Orcs, Gargoyles, Werewolves, Fae, and Ephemerals. We protected the world from the mystical artifacts that could end it. We kept them out of the hands of governments, terrorists, private citizens, and, lately, a rogue group of agents that had defected from the Archive and now called themselves the Protectors.

But that altruistic mission didn't mean that every once in a while someone didn't come along and take over that was themselves, a real life villain. Francesca had been such a person. She was responsible for the deaths of hundreds of agents and their families, for conducting experiments on Mundanes and Supernaturals alike, for degrading the trust the Archive had built over centuries. She was dead; beheaded by the woman who was currently in that position in fact. And if rumor was to be believed, the new director was the exact opposite of her predecessor.

That didn't mean I still wasn't nervous as hell at being recalled from my Archive job in Los Angeles to London. Especially when there had yet to be an explanation for it.

"Mom, you do realize they speak every language right?" I answered in Spanish, trying to keep things light.

"My love, you don't have to stay with this place, you don't owe them anything. Your father can get you a job at the CIA, FBI, even MI6 if you wanted to stay in London. Just say the word."

I smiled, knowing that this all came from a place of deep love and affection, something that most families in our income bracket didn't have. It might've had something to do with the fact that we had to be close to survive as a mixed race family among those who proudly and often talked about how they could trace their lineage to founding fathers. My mother was the only child of my grandparents, who had fled Mexico when they found out my grandmother was pregnant with her. When she was a fresh faced nineteen-year-old, she won Miss New Mexico and had come to New York for the Miss America pageant. She didn't go home with a crown but six months later she was married to the most eligible bachelor in the city; my father, Thomas Kane.

His name ensured entry into society, but not acceptance. My mother was one of the strongest people I knew and she taught us how to navigate the tricky waters of society while still managing to be ourselves. I was proud of my heritage on both sides, but it was never easy. Most people liked to put you in a box, and when you didn't fit, it meant you were a special kind of 'other'. Growing up, I learned the hard way that the only people who would accept me, who I could trust not to use me, was my family. When I got older and joined the military, then special forces and finally the Archive, that circle of trust did expand, but not by much. The Archive was my family, or it had been. And I knew my mother was right, I didn't owe them anything. But for whatever reason I just couldn't leave them.

"I appreciate that, but I'm staying for now."

"Well, if you change your mind you let me know. Ramon can have the jet ready in an hour."

"Thanks, Mom."

"Of course, my love. So, since you're at the London office, have you seen Luke there?" my mother asked innocently.

I should've been surprised by the sudden change in subject, but I wasn't. I had a distant uncle that was a Mothman, so my family already knew that Supernatural beings were real. And they were delighted that I'd eloped with a brainy, sweet Orc who had doted on me like I was a fucking queen. So delighted, in fact, that a year after our divorce, they still asked about him.

"No, Mom, I haven't."

"Don't get snippy with me. I know you haven't gotten over him. You haven't dated at all since the divorce."

"That's not true, I've dated."

"One date, one."

"Mom, I don't want to talk about this again. It's over, I haven't seen him since we signed the papers. He's probably buried in a dusty library under a pile of books."

Or under a hot, nerdy woman who can talk dirty to him in Sumerian or some shit that I never could.

It was supposed to be a good thing when your family liked your husband. But when my brothers still looped him into their fantasy football brackets, when my dad still called him for lunch when he was in London and my mother still sent him Christmas presents, it became less wonderful, and more frustrating.

How the hell am I supposed to move on when they all still act like we're married? Hell, Antony practically cried when I said we were done. I think he loved Luke more than me.

Luke and I were complete opposites, and at first that was exactly what had attracted me to him. I was the one that knew ten different ways to kill a man with my bare hands, Luke knew every obscure dialect on the planet. He was brains, I was brawn. And I loved him for how different he was, how he seemed not to care about who my family was. But then things went pear shaped. Not fast, not even noticeably at first. It was little things here and there, and before I knew it I was taking extra missions and requesting that Luke not be sent with me, just so I could get away from the fights and unspoken hurts between us.

I opened my mouth to change the subject with my mother and ask about my niece when a rich, low voice started to filter through the hallway to my right and my pulse jumped.

Was that him? Was I going to have to come face to face with Luke after all?

You can do this. Nut up, Andromeda! He's just your ex, for crying out loud.

I took a deep breath, squared my shoulders and slipped into the stone-faced mask I'd gotten very good at wearing. Underneath it, my heart was beating so damn hard it hurt, and my nails dug into the palms of my hands. There was no way to avoid this so I was going to just have to accept that and move on, like I'd done with things before.

"Andromeda, are you still there?"

"Yes, Mom, but I need to call you back."

"Alright, you better. I want to know that you're alright after this."

"I promise. I love you."

"I love you too."

But when the owner of the voice came around the corner, it wasn't the six and half foot Orc I'd expected. Instead, it was a very handsome Korean man with tattoos on his forearms and backs of his hands. His dark blue suit was a bit on the baggy side, but not in an ill-fitting way. Honestly, the way his hair seemed to defy gravity in a flopping kind of way, and the smirk on his face combined with the clothes, he reminded me of a real life Cowboy Bebop.

"Ah, Ms. Kane, we're so sorry to have kept you waiting," he said, reaching his hand out. "I'm Trey Park, Liaison to the Council."

I shook his hand, which was inordinately hot, and noticed his tattoos shifting on his skin. One look into his eyes told me that it wouldn't be prudent to ask about it, so I let it go without a word and followed him into the director's office.

The office was warm, in a very beige way; the colors much brighter at least than Francesca's with the cream walls and blue furniture. It was nice not to have a sense of terror and foreboding hanging in the air as I shook Director Dearborne's hand.

She was leaning on her desk in a dark purple and white pant suit. Her graying blond hair was cut into a bob at her chin and her eyes were sharp as they took me in, a relaxed grin on her face. Director Dearborne looked every inch the society matron with a spine of steel she was rumored to be, but that didn't necessarily put me at ease. I knew better than most that looks could be deceiving. Deadly even.

Out of habit, I took an 'at ease' position in front of her, waiting for an invitation to sit. It was comforting to slip into a military state of mind, the chain of command, the simple rules.

"Ma'am," I said.

"Agent Kane, it's a pleasure to meet you in person," she nodded at Trey as he poured her a cup of coffee. "Would you like anything?"

"No, thank you."

She nodded and accepted the cup from Trey. There was a crackle of energy between them that I recognized as attraction, but also caution.

Interesting.

"Please have a seat and we'll get down to business," she said, setting the cup on her desk. "We've called you back from Los Angeles because we have an asset that has gone missing and we need you to find him."

Unease prickled along my spine. I wasn't usually sent in for extraction. Bodyguard maybe, security detail certainly. But getting someone out of a scrape was not my specialty.

"Yes, ma'am."

"You seem confused," she said.

"Permission to answer freely?"

"Yes."

"Extraction isn't something I've done a lot of. It's unusual to have the Archive request this of me."

"And the fact that it's this office might make you especially uneasy?"

I straightened my spine further, not at all liking that Director Dearborne picked up on that.

"I understand," she continued, "and I can tell you that there are no nefarious reasons behind this. The asset is someone you know and we believe that he will trust you."

She handed me a file and that unease ratcheted up to full on nerves. The second I opened the file and saw his picture, the bottom fell out of my stomach.

"Luke," I whispered.

His beard had gotten slightly greyer, as well as the hair at his temples. His glasses were square now, and he had a bit more weight on him, which looked really good. The deep, sudden bolt of longing hit me like a strong drink and I was surprised at how much I wanted to see him again. Maybe to show him that I was fine without him, maybe to make sure he was okay without me. Or maybe just to look into his eyes again, make him smile.

And all of that is a slippery fucking slope that's just going to end in me being broken hearted again.

"We both signed a request not to be assigned together after our divorce," I said.

"I read that," Angelica said.

"We didn't part on the best of terms. So you know sending me in is a fool's errand. If you want him out of there, you need to send an actual extraction team. My apologies for the bluntness, ma'am, but it's the truth."

She let out a long breath and folded her hands in front of her. I held her gaze, determined not to look away.

"If I may be frank with you?"

"Yes, ma'am."

"This is a very delicate situation and I need someone that Professor Turner is going to listen to."

"And you believe that's his ex-wife?"

"I believe that's his former partner," she clarified. "The two of you had one of the best track records of any research team in the Archive prior to your divorce."

"So you need me to help him find something?"

"No, I need you to stop him from finding it."

I frowned at her in confusion. None of this was making any sense.

"What exactly is the situation? Because what you're telling me isn't enough information for me to understand exactly what you're asking me to do."

Director Dearborne glanced at Trey and he nodded.

"You should tell her."

My hands were turning clammy at how shady the two of them were acting. What the hell had Luke gotten himself into?

Director Dearborne nodded and took a thick file off her desk.

"What do you know about the shadow war between the Archive and the Nazis during World War II?"

Now that question definitely had my stomach starting to turn, but I kept the nerves under lock down as I answered.

"What most know. That there was one, that we just barely kept the most dangerous artifacts out of their hands and it had cost a lot of agents' lives to do it."

She nodded.

"There's a lot more to it. When high level Nazis fled Europe, many of them went to Argentina," she began.

"Yeah, I know. I have some distant cousins that hail from there. They always like to talk about how their fathers helped Israeli operatives capture a few."

"Many of them fled under passports falsely stamped by the Red Cross as refugees from communist oppression and were aided by members of the Catholic church," Trey continued. "Ones that empathized with the Nazi party. But it wasn't just people that escaped."

Director Dearborne handed me another file, older, the pages inside thin and yellowed with age.

There were black and white pictures of a dock in Argentina where large crates were being unloaded. One of the last photos was of a man in a bishop's robe and what I recognized as several high ranking Nazis that had escaped trial for their crimes.

"That's Bishop Giuseppe Russo," Trey said. "He was instrumental in helping the Nazi officers smuggle stolen artifacts out of Germany into Argentina. Many of them were fakes that we'd planted, but among them were genuinely dangerous and powerful ones. All of them had been stored in Himmler's castle. When the Nazi regime fell, the spoils were divided among high ranking officials. We were able to recover some during the chaos. Others were deemed lost in the war."

"Until a few Archive agents stumbled onto this," Director Dearborne gestured to the file. "They sent along information for a month before being discovered and killed."

I flipped to the last picture and took in a sharp breath.

It was a black and white photo, but the dark smears over the group of bodies was quite obviously blood. The bodies were covered in it. Though it was hard to see faces, and many of those that I did see looked like they'd been shredded, I recognized the bishop's robe among the civilian clothes of the other bodies.

"What happened to them?" I asked.

"Ever see *Raiders of the Lost Ark*?" Trey asked with a smirk. "Only ten times as bad. The artifacts they had in those crates didn't play well with others. As far as we can tell, it drove them all mad."

"And the artifacts?" I asked.

"Thought lost until ten years later when one of our agents claimed he stumbled onto a small village along the coast of Chile that had a story about a cave that housed the secrets of God. He believed that the artifacts had been smuggled to Chile through the Valdivian rainforest by a priest who did not agree with what the bishop had been doing. The local legends supported the theory but the agent disappeared before he could tell anyone more. When his gear was recovered, there was a map fragment among his belongings and his journal, half destroyed by water damage. It's this journal and map fragment that Professor Turner believed would help him find the artifacts," Director Dearborne said.

"Wait," I said, a pit growing in my stomach, "did you send him unaccompanied?"

"It was a research mission," Trey said. "One that was off the books, I might add. No one outside of this room even knew he'd left."

"But let me guess, someone else knew, didn't they?"

Neither of them would look at me.

"Who am I dealing with, ma'am?"

She let out an annoyed breath and had the decency to meet my eye.

"We have reason to believe the Protectors have found Professor Turner and are holding him for information."

Nerves turned to anger in a split second. What the fuck had they been thinking, sending Luke without a security detail?

Hell, Francesca wasn't even that reckless!

I wanted to rage at them, to demand what the hell they'd been thinking and then march out of here and rescue him. But I did none of that; a good soldier did not throw her CO the middle finger.

I took a deep breath, hoping it would calm my voice before I spoke, though I was sure they could both see the heat in my eyes all the same.

"So this is a rescue mission."

"Yes. But more than that, I need you to keep the professor from going after any other map fragments. And I especially need you to stop him from trying to find the cave. A cache of this magnitude, full of what is likely class five artifacts, all of a religious nature, would give the Protectors enough power to do untold damage to the world. I need that cave kept secret until I can get a proper team out there to uncover those artifacts."

I swallowed, anger still burning in me, and I found myself unable to stop the question that popped out of my mouth.

"If you knew the Protectors might be looking for it too, why did you send him alone?"

"We had thought that sending a security detail with him would be too obvious. Professor Turner was going in undercover as someone from the University of Oxford on a research assignment. I see now that was a mistake."

You're damn right it was!

But instead of letting her have it, I nodded respectfully. Losing my temper here wouldn't do Luke any good. I needed to remain level headed and get as much information as possible to get him home.

"I understand. Anything else I should know?"

"We have two deep cover agents that have been living in Chile for some time. They know the locals and the terrain of the rainforest. They will meet you at your landing zone, which will change daily to keep it secret, and the three of you will proceed to where we believe Professor Turner is being held. We need you to extract him and then get him out of the country as quickly as possible."

"Yes, ma'am, I understand."

"Here's the thumb drive with any other information you will need. Please destroy it after you've memorized the information. And good luck, Agent Kane."

I took the thumb drive and went to report for my gear, wondering how the hell I'd be able to tear Luke away from the chance of getting his hands on all those artifacts. It sounded like the kind of discovery he'd dreamed of; a once in a lifetime chance to touch and learn about things that others only knew as legends.

But I'd find a way, because there wasn't another option. Letting the Protectors get their hands on an entire cave of dangerous artifacts would be disastrous. Luke was just going to have to accept that.

I was focusing on the specifics of the mission, on the reasons for it, and literally anything else so I could ignore the way my pulse was thrumming fast at the thought of seeing him again after all this time. This wasn't a reunion, it wasn't a chance to reignite anything. It was a mission, plain and simple.

Yeah…plain and simple. Fuck, I'm in so much trouble.

"Hey, Andy, you there?" Marcus whistled and waved his hand in front of my face.

I jumped and blinked, a flush rose to my cheeks as I realized that he'd caught me letting my mind wander.

Marcus was the head of the R&D department that had flourished since Francesca's death. He had been petitioning the Archive to let him start using more nanotech combined with artifacts for several months, to no avail. But that didn't stop him from pushing the boundaries constantly with his partner in crime, Sprite, who was currently glaring at a tablet in their hand as they snapped out orders to a drone flying small crates around.

I was in one of the many warehouses the Archive used to house and test their new tech. Actually, I wasn't a fan of this area; too much stuff going on that could, and did, lead to accidents. I much preferred just getting my gear at the drop zone like a normal undercover agent, but Marcus tended to be more hands on when it came to priority missions.

Marcus' heels clacked in the cavernous space, his hair currently a gorgeous mass of tiny braids that fell down his back in vibrant pinks and blues. Usually, he liked a bit of glitter on his face, but today his flawless dark brown skin was dusted with a light pink powder across his cheeks and the bridge of his nose, with perfectly executed matte pink on his full lips. His usual flowy blouses were replaced by a midriff baring halter in sparkling blue with a flowing white maxi skirt and strappy pink heels. I'd always wondered how in the world he kept his gorgeous clothes absolutely spotless in the chaos of his warehouse considering most everyone else, except for Sprite, was wearing coveralls with grease stains on them.

Sprite was at least wearing appropriate footwear; very thickly soled fuscia Doc Martins with tiny pink spikes running up the sides. Other than that, Sprite was in pink fish nets, black and purple shorts and what looked like a ripped up black and purple band tee. Honestly, it was a bit understated compared to how Sprite usually dressed and I wondered how they were doing.

"Okay, Andy, you ready to go through your gear or is there something you need to talk about?" Marcus asked, arching a perfectly curved eyebrow.

"Nope, nothing. Gimme the goods."

"Uh-huh. Rumor has it that you're going to see a certain sexy Orc."

I pinched the bridge of my nose and let out a sigh.

"Where's the gear, Marcus?"

"A certain sexy Orc that looks damn good in those geeky t-shirts he insists on wearing."

"Marcus," I said with a warning in my tone.

"A certain sexy Orc that's put on about fifty pounds of lickable muscle since your divorce."

"The *gear*, Marcus."

"I seem to remember an entire tequila soaked weekend where I alternated between holding your head over a toilet and pouring you shots...when was that?" he cocked his hip to the side and looked up thoughtfully, index finger tapping at his lips.

I ground my molars and refused to answer.

It was the weekend after my divorce was finalized and he damn well knew it.

"It didn't seem like you were really over him then but I suppose you are now. After all, you've been dating...oh, wait."

"Get her the damn gear, Marcus!" Sprite snapped without looking at us.

"Geez, someone is testy," he groused. "But seriously, Andy, are you okay seeing him?"

He was trying to be supportive but talking about Luke like this was the very last thing I wanted to do.

"I'm fine. It's a mission, that's it. One that I need my gear for, so if you could just please run me through it?"

Marcus pursed his lips and shook his head dramatically.

"No one lies like an agent, especially when it comes to lying to themselves," he muttered.

I flatly refused to respond because Marcus could drag this out for hours until he had me back at that bottle of tequila, crying my fucking eyes out and admitting that yes, I still had sex dreams about Luke and no, in fact, none of the one night stands I'd had since him had ever made me come so hard from oral that I blacked out.

Shit, now I'm thinking about Luke's tongue. Fuck he was really good at oral too...

"Earth to Andy," Marcus said again.

"Yes, okay just..." I shook my head and took a deep breath.

"You okay?" he asked, all joking gone.

"No, but I have to be, Marcus, you understand that right? I can't go in there with all that shit in my head, I have to just do the damn job. So please, *please* stop it."

He gave me a sympathetic smile and squeezed my arm.

"Sure, honey. Let's get you outfitted. Sprite, can you bring Andy's crate over here?"

Sprite bit their bottom lip and maneuvered a small drone carrying a silver box over to us.

"Thank you, M156. You are such a good little drone," Marcus cooed.

"It's a bloody machine, you twat," Sprite snapped. "And it's a disobedient one headed for the scrap pile if I can't get it to stop glitching."

"Don't you listen to them, you're doing great," Marcus reassured quietly, as the small drone flew away.

If I lived a hundred years, I would never understand Marcus and Sprite's relationship. They both swore up and down that they weren't in a committed relationship, but they weren't just friends either. Then there was the fact that I'd hardly ever seen Sprite be anything but completely prickly to everyone including Marcus. But then again, a lot of people didn't get Luke and me either, so...

Fucking hell, Andy, focus!

"Alright," Marcus popped the top of the case and rubbed his hands together in excitement, "here's your side arm, standard Archive issue. A bowie knife for close combat. We won't be sending you with a stinger at this time because of the regulations against inflamatory devices in such a fragile eco system as the rainforest. You're also not getting an artifact because of the high chance of contact with Protectors. New regulations. This is a special sat link device that will enable you to link up with any Archive communications in any location. It's faster than WiFi and ten times as reliable. It's also not hackable and no one but us can listen in, so there's no chance of the Protectors being able to piggy back off the signal. You'll need it to communicate when you're ready for extraction, so keep it safe."

"Got it."

He pulled up that part of the case to reveal the bottom layer.

"Standard issue backpack, clothing, water purifying tablets, canteens, and ration packs. You shouldn't need more than two days worth but I packed you five just in case. I'm not sending you with any artifact bags or goop to neutralize but," Marcus pulled a small silver spray bottle out, "for emergencies."

It was dangerous to handle artifacts without taking precautions to neutralize them. Some activated with contact and could take over a person in seconds. While others just went haywire and caused rampant destruction, like in the case of an agent who accidentally touched an artifact from Pompeii and ended up causing the great Chicago fire. Because of that, the Archive developed a neutralizer that could make an artifact powerless for a short period of time. We weren't supposed to come in contact with any artifacts on this mission, but I still felt better having something.

I examined all the gear thoroughly, made sure the ammunition was in order and then signed off on it.

"We'll send this to where you're staying since I know you like to pack your stuff personally," Marcus said.

"Thanks, meet for drinks when I get back?"

"Sure. And Andy?"

"Yeah?"

"Be careful," his expression sobered and he lowered his voice. "There's something strange about this one. People are spooked, downright panicked actually. And I know the extra weird stuff is kinda your specialty, but this isn't about that. I'm hearing rumors of people protesting this mission behind the scenes. Whatever Luke went to find, it's got a lot of people either completely freaked out or salivating. I don't want to see you get hurt."

What he said made sense with what little I knew about that cave and what was in it, but knowing that this supposedly secret mission hadn't stayed secret at the Archive, that there could be some politics at play? That sent a legitimate chill down my spine. I knew that people would do anything to acquire and hold onto power. If someone higher up saw a chance to make a play, if there were fights about this, then Luke and I could definitely get caught in the middle. And if we weren't an asset, we were a liability.

The fact that the director didn't tell me any of this said that we just might be expendable if push came to shove.

And fuck that. I'm bringing him home.

"Thanks, Marcus," I said. "I'll keep all that in mind."

CHAPTER TWO

LUKE

I pushed my glasses back up my nose and repeated the phrases I was translating. The smell of trees, under foliage and wet earth hung thick in the air. Around me, rain pattered against the sides and roof of the spacious canvas tent that had been my home for the past two weeks. As far as prison cells went, it was rather posh.

True, I was chained to an enormous stake in the ground that had been spelled to not come out, no matter how hard I yanked, and the rations I was fed were sorely lacking in seasoning. I mean, how hard is it to carry salt and pepper in a rations kit? Not to mention how I would absolutely *kill* for an espresso right now. But at least I was surrounded by books, and left alone most of the day to research and think. I rarely saw another living person, unless they were pacing outside my tent with their weapons, or threatening me if I didn't work faster. It was comical how they thought threatening me would somehow make my mind fire faster.

In all truth, though, I wasn't at my peek.

Even a year ago, I would've had this chapter translated within hours. Now, it took me most of the day.

I rubbed my eyes and wished that I could get a hold of my shaving kit where my meds had been. These assholes had seized everything I was carrying, and while they'd allowed me all my books and research notes, they'd confiscated most of my personal belongings. Including my oral meds.

I just hope the eye drops are enough until I can get out of here.

All the meds in the world wouldn't cure this disease, but it would buy me time, and that was all I needed. I dug around in a nearby drawer for the drops and medicated my eyes. The drops soothed the sandpaper feeling, but they didn't do much for the joint pains. And it was taking longer for them to clear my vision when it became blurry.

C'mon Luke, you can do this! Just hang in there, milk these idiots for all they're worth and get to the cache.

My heart hammered behind my ribs and I had to do some deep breathing to calm myself. The rare disease Vanquis Bellua only affected Orcs. It had claimed my grandfather and uncle, both males dead in their fifties, who had wasted away, no memory of their life, blind and screaming in agony. Vanquis Bellua had been the bane of Orcs for centuries, especially frightening since we were immune to virtually every human disease, including the common cold.

But it seemed that fate was a cruel bitch, because the few diseases that struck Orcs were often deadly, and fewer still had cures or vaccines. As far as anyone knew, Vanquis was a blood based disease that was a cross between cancer and Alzheimer's. The first indications were always difficulty concentrating and long term memory issues, which could all be symptoms of far less serious problems. That was why it was difficult to diagnose or catch early.

Unless you were obsessed with the disease because it was prevalent in your family line and your memory was unfailingly sharp, which mine was. I knew something was wrong before the joint pains started affecting me or my eye sight began to get worse. The glamour I, and every other Supernatural, wore to pass as a Mundane and hide our true natures from the world had started to become unpredictable. Usually, adults like me could switch between the Mundane glamour and our true forms without much thought. Maintaining the glamour actually became as easy as breathing but lately, it had started to slip.

Not completely at first. Sometimes just my tusks would be out and I wouldn't realize it until people started giving me weird looks. Then my height would change from the five-eleven my glamour was to the six and half feet of my true form. These days, it was a drain on my system to hold it for more than a few hours, which was why I tended to hide at the Archive or Supernatural approved places of business. It was too taxing to walk around for very long and keep it in place. That was really the only good thing about this camp. The Protectors know about Supernaturals; they didn't care if I had my glamour up or not. So I've kept it down during my confinement, allowing me to use that energy toward research, though it hasn't seemed to make much of a difference.

I saw it as lucky that I'd been researching possible cures for years before the day I realized the disease had its claws in me. It was the only reason I'd decided to up my timetable on getting to this artifact cache. I had no hard proof that what I needed was there, just legends and hearsay. But I'd take that over slowly dying any day.

I rapidly jotted down the translation I'd been working on before my eyes could become too tired. The rain was fading, and the birds were starting to sing once again. The rainforest was temperate, not humid and hot like the tropical ones, and I was grateful for that. Not that it didn't get warm, but it was less oppressive; more like a sticky hug than a wet wool blanket. If I had more time, I would've loved to learn more about the beautiful flowers and the intricately connected ecosystem here, but that would have to wait for next time.

I read through the translation, something familiar about the phrasing. I stared at it, turning it over in my mind, but the connection that I should've been able to make kept slipping through my fingers. I tried to trace back the words in front of me to what I'd recently translated, but even that was difficult.

Was it the reference to water, or the priests' mention of Holy visions?

"Maybe the circular imagery…or the…the what?! Ugh!"

My teeth ground together and I clenched the small pencil hard enough to break it. This was ridiculous! I was a fucking genius, I had more degrees than ten people my age, and twice as many published papers. My memory was annoyingly perfect…or it had been once.

"I can do this." I took a deep breath and looked down at my notebooks spread out over a large folding table. "I can…do this. And I will…"

It would be easy to let the panic in, to let it steal my ability to think clearly and just allow myself to wallow. But I couldn't, I wouldn't. That was what my uncle had done and I'd watched him waste away quicker once he'd given up. I had time, I just had to use it wisely.

"Is everything alright Professor?" said a nauseatingly cheerful voice.

I looked up to see Kristoff Dietrich, the man in charge of this charming encampment, grinning at me from the opening of my tent. He was dressed in khakis, a white button down and a wide brimmed hat, his smile even whiter than his clothes. The man's crystalline blue eyes were colder than ice and I knew that smile was anything but friendly. I'd seen him smile just like that as he gutted a man last week for falling asleep on guard duty. He'd left the poor bastard to bleed out in the middle of the camp, then refused to allow anyone to move him all day. He'd just let any carrion birds around peck at the body until sundown.

I'd wager no one in their right mind would fall asleep on guard duty now.

My first night here, Kristoff arranged for a nice dinner under the stars, where he'd poured expensive wine from a region in France where my family used to have land many generations ago. Every bit of the dinner was chosen to appeal to any possible generational sense memory I may have inherited. I recognized at least half a dozen things from smells and tastes that had been passed down to me from my ancestors. Orcs have very developed and sensitive senses; we can detect the subtlest flavors, down to what the weather was like when something was harvested, and if the soil was acidic. We also have the ability to pass down special sense memories to our descendants. I can tell you what a pheasant's egg tasted like in the court of Marie Antoinette, or the notes in a brandy that had once been sipped by George Washington. I even knew what several extinct mushrooms tasted like. It was common knowledge that Orcs had this gift. What wasn't common knowledge was the exact memories my family might have passed down. In hitting one, much less six of them, Kristoff was sending a clear message that he knew my family. It was a clear threat, and every bite of food turned to ash on my tongue.

But he acted as if it were just any other dinner between friends. The psychopath insisted on talking about books, cathedrals and all sorts of interests of mine.

I'd thought he was stupid to give me a full cutlery set, including a steak knife and then dismiss the guards. But it was I who was dumb, thinking that a man like him would do that if I were a real threat.

Half way through, I'd stabbed him in the neck, right at the artery. He'd just laughed at me and pulled the knife out. Only a tiny trickle of blood escaped what should've been a deadly wound.

"You are so feisty!" he had said with a giggle. "I would've thought a man like you, buried in books would be pissing his pants but look at you! All fire and fight! I admire that. But you see, I have this little…oh let's call it, gift from a former colleague. And it keeps me safe from stabby professors."

He withdrew a medallion that hung on a chain around his neck and showed it off to me. I simply nodded, my mouth dry and stomach roiling with nerves.

"Now," he had said, "I am willing to excuse such bad behavior once. But," his smile faded and I felt sick, "if you try anything like that again I will tie you to a stake in the ground and carve pieces of your flesh off every hour until the animals and birds and insects have finished you off. Are we clear?"

I had nodded again, sure I would throw up.

Then he smiled again and continued with the meal, as if nothing had happened.

At the end, he told me flat out that if I didn't have answers for him in two weeks, he would cut my tongue out. He then told me to enjoy my chocolate torte before getting up and going to bed.

That very night I was escorted to this tent and the shackle went around my ankle. It was the last nice meal I'd had, but not the last conversation with Kristoff.

Now the man was standing in front of me, asking a simple question that had every alarm bell in my mind going off.

"Fine, why?" I asked.

"I just heard a shout and wanted to see if you needed help."

"Nope, just frustrated with this translation, that's all."

He nodded, a worried expression on his face.

"You know what today is, don't you?"

I stared at him, mind racing.

"Um…Tuesday?"

"Two weeks, Professor. Do you have answers for me?"

Shit, shit, shit!

"Almost, I'm very close."

"Almost? Oh, Professor, how very disappointing," Kristoff shook his head as if he were chiding a disobedient child.

Two men came in behind him; burly, huge Orcs with red eyes and silver discs at their temples indicating that they were being controlled. Something about that tickled the back of my mind but I was too panicked to figure it out. Right now was about avoiding having my tongue cut out.

"Listen," I said, backing up, "I'm almost there, I just need another day or two. Seriously, I've been trying. Why would I lie to you?"

"Why indeed, Professor. It's not as if you're a member of the Archive, right?" Kristoff laughed good naturedly, but there was a bite to it.

I swallowed, my heart racing. No one was supposed to know that. When they'd captured me, Kristoff had stuck with my cover as a Professor from Oxford. Either he'd known I was with the Archive all along, or he had just discovered it.

Images of the poor bastard that had fallen asleep during guard duty flashed before my eyes and I wondered if I was about to have more than my tongue cut out.

"Archive?" I scoffed and shook my head. "What's that? I'm a Professor at Oxford."

Kristoff sighed.

"Oh, how tedious. Well, if you're going to lie," he snapped his fingers at the two Orcs and they charged straight for me.

"Okay, hold on," I backed up as far as the stupid chain would let me, my hands up defensively. "There's no need for this!"

One of the Orcs reached for me and I ducked down. Remembering a little of the hand to hand combat classes I'd taken recently at the Archive, I punched up into that Orc's groin, expecting a groan, maybe a yell.

When the damn male didn't even flinch I knew I was in deep shit.

"Can't we talk about this?" I asked just before they both hauled me up and slammed me face first onto the table.

"I don't like punishing people," Kristoff said, handing one of the Orcs a gruesome looking knife. "But sometimes a little pain is necessary."

The Orc brought the knife close while the other one tried to pry my mouth open.

"Wait, don't get blood on the books!" I attempted to yell, half of it garbled with the way my face was being held.

The cool tip of the knife brushed against my cheek and I thought I was going to be sick. This was really happening. They were really going to cut my tongue out!

"Peese…oh!" I mumbled as one of them grasped my tongue with a pair of pliers.

An explosion shook the ground under us, punctuated by the sharp report of gun fire.

I let out a breath of relief as they let go of my tongue.

"A rescue, Professor?" Kristoff asked with a cold smile. "I didn't know Oxford had such resources. You two, go see what's going on. Professor, don't disappear, we aren't finished."

I watched them leave, my heart in my throat, body shaking. At first I couldn't seem to move but then there was another explosion and my body sprang into action. Whether or not this was about me, it was a chance to get the fuck out of here before they came back to carve me up.

It was probably the Archive out there, which under any other circumstances would've been the best news. But I had requested a solo mission for a reason. Artifacts were strictly off limits when it came to personal use. Agents were granted permission on a case by case basis to use them for missions, but that was rare. What I wanted to do was essentially steal an artifact from one of the most sought after caches on the planet. Sure, it was to save lives, mine included. But there were no exceptions when it came to using artifacts for anything outside of a mission.

"Fuck." My gaze swung around the room, mind spinning as I tried to figure out what to do.

My eyes landed on my research and I grabbed my large backpack and waterproof interior bags. I winced as I shoved my notebooks inside along with old manuscripts and map fragments sealed in plastic. I snagged my few toiletries and extra pens.

The explosions were so close they were deafening now. I could smell the coppery tang of blood on the air and strange electrical charges. I hadn't thought any of the electrical equipment from the Archive would be used here but maybe they changed it for this mission.

Maybe I *was* the mission.

It wasn't a comforting thought.

All the different smells were starting to overwhelm me, and I gagged on a particularly pungent scent of urine as I tried to carefully stow the set of papers into my pack.

One of my guards was thrown through the tent flaps and I screamed, the papers flying out of my fingers and onto the floor. As I tried to gather them up, a barrel chested man with longish blond hair, well-worn khakis and about two years' worth of dirt on his boots ran in and stabbed the guard through the chest with a very large serrated knife.

I jumped at the suddenness of his entrance and nearly scattered the papers again.

"You Luke Turner?" he grunted.

"Yes."

"Great, I'm Trevor. Now let's get this chain off you."

"It's spelled, you can't just—"

Trevor sprinkled some kind of dust over it and the chain snapped.

"Can't just what?" he asked with a twinkle in his eye.

"I have to get these papers secured."

"Nope, my orders are to get you out of here while the distractions are happening."

He tried to grab my arm but even though I spent most of my time rolling die and sitting in dusty libraries, I had an Orc's brawny physique and a tendency to lift weights when I was stressed, so Trevor's hand didn't even make it around my bicep. I skittered around the table to grab two more small books, the chain still attached to my ankle.

"Maybe work on getting that off my ankle," I growled. "I can't exactly run with that thing on."

He huffed out a breath and took more of the sparkly dust out.

"You have to stand still!"

I was walking around the table, making it harder for him and buying myself time. I couldn't just stuff the papers into the bag the way I'd done with my own notebooks. Some of these items were hundreds of years old, and others may have been only a few decades, but they'd been through hell and were still falling apart. They had to be handled carefully.

"Damn it, you oaf, stand still!"

I ignored him and continued to move when another guard ran through the tent flap. Trevor grabbed a lantern from the floor and threw it at the guard. I was so startled by the sudden movement, and the report of the guard's gun going off, that I struck out with my hand and slapped the guard across the face as he was on his way down to the ground, unconscious.

"What the fuck was that?" Trevor chuckled.

"I was startled!"

"You slapped him like some bougie housewife that was angry with a clerk at a store."

I ground my teeth together and continued to try and gather up the papers. I knew I was shit at being cool headed in the field. Because I was an Orc, it was expected that I'd be some kind of snarling warrior, smashing and punching my way through a fight like something out of World of Warcraft. But the truth was that I hated violence, the sight of blood made me sick to my stomach and I was currently fighting the impulse to scream like a small child at the explosion that just rocked the ground under me.

"Okay, that's it, let's go," the man tried to grab me again and I leapt to the other side of the table. "I'm gonna to leave your ass here!" Trevor threatened.

"Go ahead," I said. "I'll be fine now that you've dissolved my chain, thanks for that by the way."

I tried to make a run for the other side of the tent, which had a rip along a seam that I could now take advantage of since I was no long shackled to the floor.

"What the hell?" Trevor lunged for me.

I dodged out of the way, and made a run for it. I had just gotten a handful of the canvas of the tent and was ripping it to make a hole big enough for me to escape when the sound of *her* voice stopped me cold.

"What the fuck is going on? We should've been gone by now!"

I was frozen to the spot, clutching the pack to my chest like it was the treasure I sought. My heart had jumped up into my throat and all I could think about was the fact that I probably smelled terrible, and my usually trimmed goatee was grown out too much, and I really wished I'd taken my wedding ring off before I'd flown out.

"He's trying to run," Trevor complained, "and he's surprisingly difficult to corral. You'd think he wanted to stay."

"He doesn't want to stay, he wants to find the artifacts and he knows we aren't here for that. Isn't that right, Luke?"

As she spoke, the tangy scent of the ocean, mixed with vanilla and campfire, filtered to my nose. It was her scent, the strange cocktail that her hormones and the chemistry of her sweat made that smelled like home to me. I swallowed and turned around, trying so hard to not be affected by her. I knew before I turned that she was close, but I hadn't expected that she'd be in a skin tight green tank top and green cargo pants that caused me to remember how her curves filled my hands. The dark wavy hair that used to look so damn good mussed up after I'd fucked her hard was pulled up into a tight braid that was wound into a compact knot at the top of her head. Her light brown skin was luminous with sweat, and her brown eyes still reminded me of tiger's eye crystals.

Hundreds of times I'd imagined how I'd act when I saw her again, how suave I'd be, how unaffected. Maybe I'd be getting a promotion, or I'd be in one of my Versace suits, my beard freshly oiled, smelling of oranges and clove. I'd laugh at how funny it was to run into her at that one cafe and gee, are you in town long, we should really catch up! She'd be shocked at how cool and calm I was, maybe even a little sad to realize that I was over her. But I'd just give her a smile and a wave and walk away because it's not like I've thought of her every day for the past year, or woken up with her scent still floating in the air, and the ghost of her warmth in my bed.

But the only way that would happen is in my daydreams because the reality was that Andy was my Kryptonite. Always had been, always would be.

So I gave her a goofy, crooked grin accompanied by a clumsy wave and was about to say 'Hi' when shouts startled all three of us.

"Get to the asset!" the voice of one my captors howled. "Go now!"

"Time to go, Luke."

Andy didn't attempt to seize me by my arm. Instead, she grabbed a handful of my shirt and pulled me behind her like I was a dog on a leash.

"We should go this way," I dug in my heels, "there's too much going on that way, we'll get caught!"

As if on cue, two men rushed into the tent. Trevor shot the first one but took a bullet to his leg when his victim still managed to get a shot off. The second one aimed at Andy and I pulled her hard toward me without a second thought, my hand on her hip. The bullet hit the ground where she'd been standing. She plugged the man twice in the chest and once in the stomach. He went down in a wet slump.

Andy looked up at me, our chests now flush with each other and for a second everything faded and I could only think of how good it felt, how *right* to have her body against mine. Her lips parted and I thought from the way she was staring at me that maybe she felt the same. But then someone shouted close to the tent and the moment broke. Without a word, she pulled herself out of my grasp and pushed me toward the opening I'd been making.

"You good, Trevor?" she asked.

"Yeah, I'll be fine."

He tied a bandana around his upper thigh, the only sign of his pain a small grunt. I'd be lying on the ground in a panic but this guy is acting like he merely scratched himself.

"Of course you will be," Andy smirked at him as he limped toward us.

The ease with which she gifted him a smile, the playful lilt in her voice had me growling at the back of my throat. Especially when she turned to me and shoved me through the hole in the tent with a frustrated push.

"Go, Luke! You're going to get us killed by just standing around."

I glanced back to make sure I'd gotten everything and worried that I was forgetting something essential that I wouldn't realize until we were gone. But there was nothing I could do about it. I knew that the Protectors were quickly recovering from the explosions and chaos Andy and her team had wrought, and soon our escape would be cut off. If it was just me, that might be acceptable, but I wouldn't let them get Andy.

So I slung the backpack on and followed Andy out into the now destroyed camp.

There had once been orderly tents in rows, with a table and fire pit in the middle of the camp. The largest tents had been mine and Kristoff's with about half a dozen smaller ones. All of them, with the exception of mine, were now burning or half collapsed. Black smoke curled into the blue sky, heavy and wrong on the air.

Behind my tent was a narrow road on which supplies and personnel had been transported, but we didn't walk along the muddy tracks. Instead we darted into the thick trees to the east of the camp, all three of us running as fast we could.

Well, Andy and Trevor were running, I was more jogging. With my long stride I would've surpassed them in a few minutes. And if it had just been Trevor, I would've had no problem darting off into the jungle and leaving him to tell the Archive whatever he wanted. But Andy complicated everything.

Why had they sent her? There are other agents that do extraction. Andy is a bodyguard. Unless…unless they thought I wouldn't come back with anyone else.

I glanced back at Trevor, who was checking behind us as we kept up the brisk pace. I wondered which side he'd been on in the fight with Francesca, and why he was here instead of someone else. Andy trusted him, and usually that would be enough for me. But he just looked at her ass, and she had given him her little half flirty smile.

Were they a couple? Is that what was going on? Was she working with him *and* fucking him?

My hands tightened and I had to clamp down on the impulse to 'hulk out' and smash Trevor's pretty face in.

I was so preoccupied with thoughts of Andy moving on with someone who was clearly far more suited for her than I ever was, that I ran into her when she stopped at the jeep that was waiting for us.

"Sorry." I said, my hands on her hips to keep her from toppling into the car.

Her hands went to my chest and I had the crazy thought that she'd just wanted to touch me when Andy pushed against me.

"I understand you're panicked but let's keep hands to ourselves," her voice sharp.

"Oh, yeah, sorry."

I let her go like she'd burned me, and stepped back.

"I think we've got minutes before they find us," Trevor said, securing his knife to his thigh. "Good work out there."

Andy gave him a smirk and shrugged.

"You were the one that rigged those explosives perfectly, made it look like there were a dozen of us instead of just two."

"Well, you held them off pretty good, took down three at once."

"Yeah, but if you hadn't been able to just weave through all of that so fast, we'd still be back there," she said with a dimpled grin.

I'm in hell. That's what this is. I've already died and this is hell.

"Could we maybe go?" I asked.

"Well, someone is in a sour mood," Trevor said, punching me on the arm. "Didn't get all your books out of there?"

"You didn't," Andy said as she stowed her rifle. "You delayed the op to get your *books*?"

I opened my mouth to defend my choice when bullets pinged against the jeep. I flung myself at Andy and tackled her to the soft ground.

"Stop shooting, stupid. We need him alive!" we heard Kristoff order.

"We have to get out of here," Andy said and wiggled out from under me.

Another round of bullets hit the jeep. Andy went around to the other side and pulled on the neck of my t-shirt. If I hadn't been so terrified I would've complained about her stretching out the material.

"Trevor, you have eyes on the assailants? Trevor?"

I peeked around and saw the agent laying on the ground, a dark puddle steadily growing under him.

"I'm down, Andy," he grunted as he half sat up and started to drag himself toward the jeep.

Andy tried to go around and help him, but this time I yanked on her clothes.

"What are you doing?" she demanded.

"Stay there," Trevor commanded. "I can give you a little cover, but not much from this vantage."

"We need to get you to base camp," Andy said.

"Not gonna happen. You need to get that asset back, now."

"I'll leave you the jeep," she said, snagging her bag from the back, "you can get back easier."

"Sure, thanks."

For the first time, Trevor sounded like he was really hurt and I realized that, if he died, it would be saving my ungrateful ass. So, in a moment of stupidity, I crouch-ran around the back of the Jeep and snagged him under the arms.

"Luke, what the hell?"

A spray of bullets hit the ground where Trevor had been sitting just as I pulled him into the Jeep. His shoulder was covered in red that ran in thick rivulets down his arm. Bile raced up my throat and if I hadn't already been green, I would've been turning that color.

"Thanks, man," Trevor said, slapping a wet hand to my arm.

Apparently he'd been putting pressure on his shoulder with the other hand, which was covered in blood. The warm stickiness coated the skin of bicep that wasn't covered by my shirt, which was now also bloodied, and the thick smell invaded my nostrils. It was too much. I turned away and threw up in the foliage.

"Oh, fucking great," Andy said under breath before handing me a canteen.

"I'm pretty sure they're circling around behind us," Trevor managed. "You two need to get out of here now, before they outflank us."

"Are you sure you're going to be alright?" she asked.

Trevor waved a bloody hand and I almost lost it again.

"Yeah, fine. Seriously, I've had worse."

"I'm sure you have," Andy said with a grin.

And now I'm rethinking the whole saving his life.

Andy adjusted the bag on her back, took her side arm out of its holster and gave Trevor one last concerned look.

"Go, Andy, don't make me pull rank," Trevor said, smiling at her. "They'll assume you took the Jeep so I'll race out of here and see if I can pull them off your trail long enough for you get away."

He was still good looking even covered in sweat and blood.

"I owe you drinks," she said to him, then she smacked my chest and motioned to the forest, "stay close and no wandering off. We need to move fast to lose these guys."

I spared Trevor one last glance and he gave me a sardonic smile that made me want to punch him, wounded or not. Instead, I flipped him off and followed my ex-wife into the rainforest.

CHAPTER THREE
ANDROMEDA

I was rusty, instincts spoiled by being in cushy jobs stateside instead of out in the field. That was evident by the fact that my mind was a jumbled mess the second I saw Luke.

His glamour and true Orc appearance were actually quite similar but there was something about that dark green skin, the small tusks that used to scrape against my thighs when he would go down on me, the sexiness of those damn forearms of his. I froze up when he'd pulled me against him in the tent. He'd always been in good shape, but Marcus was right; those new fifty pounds of muscle were indeed, lickable. The firmness of his pecs alone was enough to have me forgetting for a second where we were. But then I remembered, and I was kicking myself for how much I had let myself be affected by a single brush against Luke's body. Even now, running for our lives, I was having a hard time reigning in the instinct to tear off his pants and climb him like a fucking tree.

We'd gotten together on a mission, had gotten married on a whim after another mission. Our hottest moments were always in the field, usually running for our lives. We'd burned so damn bright and hot in situations like the one we now found ourselves in that I was fighting my desires with every step. Fortunately, I had a good distraction in the fact that we needed to get as much distance as possible from the Protectors.

I had no idea if Trevor would be successful in getting them to follow him. And even if he was, how long before he passed out from blood loss? I picked up the pace, running at full speed with the pack on my back. The rainforest wasn't one of those cloyingly humid ones, thank God, but there was moisture in the air nonetheless and it coated my body in a fine mist that was starting to get uncomfortable.

"Andy," Luke panted from behind me. "I-I think we lost them."

I stopped and glanced back with a smirk.

"Someone has gotten soft sitting in libraries."

He squared his shoulders, pushed up his glasses with his finger, and glared at me.

"Not soft just…tired."

"I want to put a little more distance between us before we stop for rations," I said. "Can you handle a brisk walk?"

"Yeah, of course I can."

I eyed him, something itching the back of my mind. Besides the additional gray at his temples there wasn't much else visibly different. So why did I feel like there was something off about him?

"What?" he asked, looking down at his clothes. "Do I have— Aw man! There's a hole in my shirt! They don't even sell this one anymore."

I couldn't stop my lips from twisting into a grin. Luke was the biggest clothes whore I'd ever met. I had to keep my clothes in the spare bedroom closet when we were married because he couldn't stand to part with any of his clothes. Whether it was vintage suits or his collection of geeky T-shirts, Luke treated his clothes as preciously as his books.

"It's a little hole," I said, trying to make him feel better. "And, also? There are more pressing issues, like surviving."

"I know," his voice was a touch pouty and he sighed. "Well, lead on."

I gave him a quick once over, searching for an injury he might've been unaware of and Luke stiffened under my gaze.

"Is that pack too heavy?" I asked, locking onto the only thing I could think of. "You know it might be easier if you got rid of some of those books."

He adjusted the straps and stood up straighter, a silent refusal. I knew he wouldn't budge about his books, but I couldn't help poking at him. It was so natural to give him grief, to draw him out and see how long he could resist before he either laughed or snapped at me. It wasn't lost on me that it was a slightly juvenile way to interact, but it had been our way. We'd poke and prod one another until we exploded with either passion or ire.

And at the end it had been much less passion and more ire…and it wasn't playful anymore either.

"I'm fine Andy. I might not be as obviously capable as Trevor, but I can handle a walk in the rainforest."

I tried to say something but all that came out was a strangled laugh.

"Wait, are you jealous of *Trevor?*"

"No," he looked away.

"Yes, you are. Unbelievable! He came here to help me rescue you."

"And you two have a connection, that's obvious. Look Andy, who you've moved on with since we divorced is none of my business."

The way he said it, all imperious and sophisticated, as if he were so much more mature than me, as if I was making more of this than there was, it sparked my anger fast. I was reminded of every time he did this to me in a fight. While I was the one that came from a powerful, rich New York family, I hated all the posturing and staring down noses. Luke's clan lived on gorgeous acres of farmland in the Midwest, hours from any city and he always felt the need to put on this attitude, as if to prove he was just as cultured as me. It felt like a silent commentary on who I was and how I made him feel, and I hated it.

My hands curled into tight fists and I shoved past him.

"Thanks for your permission," I shot at him. "Now, if you can stop being the jealous ex, we might just survive this."

I swallowed down the unexpected lump in my throat and picked up the pace. Luke's strides were long and I had to work double time to keep him from overtaking me. In no time, his normal walk was my brisk walk and I was breathing a bit hard.

"Going a bit soft with those cushy office jobs?" he asked with a chuckle.

In answer, I turned and punched him hard on the upper arm.

"Ow!" he rubbed the spot.

"That answer your question?"

"I was only joking. You can give me shit but I can't give it to you?"

"When you have to travel across the world to rescue my ass, then you can give me all the shit you want, deal?"

His face fell and he shook his head.

"I didn't ask them to send you. In fact, I told them not to bother sending anyone, that I was perfectly capable of doing this."

"And then you got captured," I spat as we trudged on.

"That could've happened to anyone."

"But it didn't. It happened to the one guy who could lead them to a treasure trove that could tip the balance of power into their hands. Do you even understand the danger you've put all of us, the entire world in?"

He snorted.

"Half of those artifacts aren't even real."

"But some of them are! And that *should* worry you," I shook my head and shoved foliage aside. "Same as always. So focused on your books and being *the one* to make the discovery, to prove to the academic world that you're something, that you can't see how it affects everyone else."

"That's not true," his voice turned hard. "It was never about the academic world or proving anything. You were the one that was always more concerned about your job than anything else. Always chasing the next commendation, the next exciting battle, never mind what it was doing to us."

I stopped and turned around, even though I knew I should let this go. It was perilously close to the source of our final fight, the last nail in the coffin of our marriage. We never really finished that fight, unless you count signing divorce papers. But despite the control I usually exercise in my career, Luke could always get past all of that and bait me into things I'd regret. Like what I was about to say.

"And you had no responsibility in what happened to us? No, it's all my fault because I had *one* drink with my partner one night."

"After being with him for a month!"

"You weren't home!"

"You could've called me!"

My body was buzzing and I felt sick. This could *not* be happening, we could *not* be having this argument again, not in the middle of a fucking mission.

"No," I turned away and started walking again, "nope! I'm not doing this with you again."

"Running away, classic you."

"I'm not the one that ran that night, *you were,*" I said through gritted teeth.

I had to move this into less dangerous territory but I'd be damned if I lost this fucking fight. So I changed the battle ground we were fighting on to something better.

"And maybe," I continued, "some of the times I wasn't home was because I needed a break from your annoying habits! You ever think of that? That maybe I just needed a fucking break?"

"You needed a month or two break every two weeks, Andy?"

"Maybe."

"Oh really?" he crossed his arms over his chest and I ignored the way it flexed his biceps and pecs.

Do. Not. Look at the muscles. Do. Not.

"You mean annoying habits like humming when I chew?" he challenged.

Heat rushed to my face as Luke imitated me eating and humming at the same time.

"It was one time!" I shouted.

"Every time you ate something you really liked and *every* time you drank your coffee."

"And I'm the only one with a singing problem?"

"Oh no, don't you even—" he started.

"Of all the bands out there, you have to sing *Nickleback* at the top of your voice, and you don't even know all the words!"

"First of all, they are a severely under rated band. And second, I had my headphones on so you wouldn't have to hear them!"

"But I did *because you were singing them!*"

"Well at least I knew how to put my socks into a damn hamper."

I let out an indignant grunt, suddenly rethinking my strategy.

"All over the house," he continued, flailing his arms around him to emphasize his point, "on the stairs, between the couch cushions."

"And what about you, mister can't use a plate for his toast? Every fucking morning, crumbs and jam on the counter. It's not rocket science Luke, you get a plate out of the cupboard and put your damn toast on it!"

"I didn't do that!"

"Oh, was it some toast gnome living in the cupboards?"

"No, it was *you*, all messy with your morning toast because you're half dead for an hour after you wake up!"

"And I suppose you're also going to tell me that you didn't eat my last box of Thin Mints too?"

Luke pulled his hair with both hands, eyes wide.

"You mean after you *left me*?"

"I came back to get them when I came for the rest of my stuff."

"You can't claim ownership of *food*."

"They were *my* fucking cookies, Luke! My favorites. You don't even like them frozen, which by the way is pure sacrilege."

"Well then, how do you know I ate them?"

"Because there were crumbs all over the fucking bed and DVD cases of all three special edition Lord of the Rings movies scattered around," I poked him in the chest, hard. "I know how you binge when you're upset."

Luke opened his mouth to speak when the tree to my left exploded in a hail of bark. I screamed and Luke pulled me to him to try and shield me, but I pushed away from him and yanked on his wrist.

"Time to go," I snapped as I took off into the forest.

"That was an electrically charged weapon," he said as we ran. "I can taste the ozone on the air."

"Get in front of me," I pushed him ahead and unholstered my sidearm.

"What? No, I—"

"I've got the gun, you've got the big brain, we go through this every fucking mission, Luke!"

"Ya know what—?"

"Yes I do, now keep running!"

When he finally stopped fighting me, Luke's long legs propelled him into a sizable lead ahead. I looked behind me as the sound of something large barreling through the forest accented the whirring sound of the weapon recharging.

What fresh hell is this?

My eyes widened when I caught sight of what pursued us and I aimed my sidearm, partially in a panic.

It was an Orc, bigger than Luke. His eyes were red, his tusks were huge, and he was foaming at the mouth. His muscles strained the skin of his body and I swear he roared like an animal. I'm an excellent shot, so I know he took at least one of the bullets I aimed at him. But if not for the jerk of his body when it impacted him, I would've never known he'd been hit.

The Orc just kept coming as if it was nothing, just a small pebble.

"What in the— ?"

"Oh, shit," Luke breathed. "I remember now. We have to go faster!"

"What is it?"

"Explain later, run now!"

"Oh *now* you're down with the plan to just shut up and— hey!"

He yanked on my arm and threw me over his shoulder like I was a carpet.

"Put me down, you asshole!"

"We need to go faster!"

"I'm in better shape than you."

"We need speed not endurance."

He was already breathing heavy and I was positive that he didn't have enough speed *or* endurance to get us far enough away from that thing.

Luke veered to the right just before another tree exploded from the impact of the energy weapon. I screamed as bark flew at me, the splinters cutting my face. The grunting sound of the feral Orc was gaining on us as Luke's panting was growing heavier. Our only saving grace was that the scary Orc was lumbering in such a way that slowed him down, almost as if he were fighting against himself. Still, if Luke tired out too fast, it wouldn't matter how slow the others were, we'd be caught.

"Put me down, you're wearing yourself out."

"He'll…kill you," he said through heavy breaths. "They need me…alive. Not you."

I *hated* being saved with a fiery passion. Probably from having five older brothers and a father that was protective as fuck, but right now it didn't matter. I was furious with Luke for just tossing me around and assuming he could save me. I was here to save him for fuck's sake, and I could feel him slowing down, so fat lot of good this was doing us.

But maybe I can use this.

I couldn't run and fire in this foliage very well, but from this height I might be able to find a weak spot in the mega Orc behind us.

I brought my sidearm up, trying to aim as Luke jostled me around. But as I worked to line up a shot, I spotted a strange distortion around the Orc, a shimmering of the plants. Then, right before another energy blast hit the ground, I saw the shooter and the cannon they wielded. One of the lesser Fae, a Leprechaun possibly, sat on the Orc's shoulder with the cannon. As soon as the cannon fired, he and the weapon disappeared again.

Oh fuck, cloaking, really? How the hell do they have this tech?

"I have an idea…" I reached down and smacked Luke on the ass.

"Not really…the time. But if you're a good girl—"

"No, you horny asshole, I'm trying to get your attention."

"Oh, well, you did."

"I need you to hide us around the next large tree you come to. I know how to slow them down."

"Got it."

I breathed a sigh of relief that even though we couldn't go half an hour without fighting, he at least still trusted me when we were on a mission to know what I was doing.

Luke darted around a massive tree with a trunk surprisingly wider than him. I shook off my pack and put it on the ground so I could have better mobility for this. Luke was bent in half, hands on his knees for a moment before clutching his side. I longed to say 'I told you so' but that could wait until after I saved our asses.

"It's cloaked," I whispered, "the energy cannon."

Luke nodded.

"I…thought so."

"Well, I can see it a second before it fires. When I do, I'm going to shoot it. Hopefully they're arrogant enough to not have shielded it. Whoever has it is on the Orc's shoulder."

"So when…it explodes—"

"It should take him down."

Luke shook his head.

"Best we can hope for…is stunning him."

"You are going to explain mega Orc when we have a moment."

I expected Luke to correct my geek reference, something he had done constantly when we were married that annoyed the shit out of me. And if not that, I thought he'd at least join in naming the feral Orc chasing us. Instead his jaw clenched and he squeezed his eyes shut.

"Luke? What's wrong?"

"It's nothing….I just…can't joke about that poor male. It's…what was done to him is something horrific. I'll tell you once we're safe. But just know, Andy, that Orc isn't in control of himself. He can't help what he's doing."

I put my hand on his arm and squeezed to comfort him and immediately had to remind myself that he was my *ex*, because *damn*, Luke was still a thick boy, and those guns of his were still perfection under my hand.

I got lost in the fight against my libido and ended up running my hand up and down his arm. Luke stared at where I touched him, his green skin turning dark around his cheeks.

"Sorry," I yanked my hand back like he was a hot burner and cleared my throat. "Okay, we need to do this."

"Yep, yep," Luke said and fidgeted with his glasses.

And we are just gonna ignore the way I was stroking his arm. Awesome.

I peeked around the tree and saw the Orc getting close, his snarling breath almost hid the buildup of the cannon as it charged. I closed my eyes, trying to focus just on the sound of the weapon, and when I found it, I blocked out everything else.

I didn't acknowledge the fact that the Orc was getting dangerously close.

I didn't pay attention to how Luke was practically vibrating with nerves behind me.

I refused to be annoyed by the sweat and moisture from the rainforest coating my skin.

Nothing existed but that metallic whir.

"It's getting stronger," Luke whispered. "I can taste it."

With my eyes still closed, I nodded. There was another sound, barely audible as the Orc drew perilously close; a small wheezing sound, likely coming from the Imp that held the cannon.

Just as the electric whirring reached a fever pitch I took a deep breath and stepped out from behind the tree.

"Andy!" Luke reached for me but I was beyond him.

The Orc roared when he saw me but I wasn't looking at him. I was focused on the blur over his shoulder and the tiny being that suddenly became visible, holding the silver and blue cannon.

"Oh, shit," the Leprechaun squeaked.

I aimed and fired three shots into the weapon he held.

The explosion was instantaneous, with a pulse of energy and heat that knocked me back several feet. I fell on my backside, the wind knocked from my lungs.

"Andy!" Luke screamed again.

My ears rang and the smell of ozone and burnt foliage stung my nostrils.

"Are you alright?" Luke stood above me, eyes wide.

I stared at him at first, my mind swimming with what had just happened.

"Did we get him?" I asked as I clumsily sat up.

"Yeah, the Orc is down for now, and that poor little Leprechaun is toast."

"So that was a Leprechaun? I've never seen one in person."

"Yeah, they're generally mercenaries for hire. Well, some, not all. There's a nice family in Ireland that make this delicious white cheddar. I subscribe to their cheese boxes."

I snorted and shook my head at him. A bit of a mistake, since my stomach reeled as the world spun.

"Whoa there," Luke's huge hands captured my shoulders and steadied me. "You alright? You got really pale and…you're, ah…you're bleeding."

His voice got thin there at the end, and I knew he was trying very hard not to breathe in the smell. I let him help me to my feet, knowing we had to get out of here, and didn't hold it against him when he stepped back.

"We have to, ah," he coughed and covered his mouth, "get out of here before he wakes up."

I wiped some of the blood off my forehead. The wound throbbed but I wasn't nauseous and my vision was fine. There was an annoying ringing in my ears but I was pretty sure that was going to clear up in a few hours.

No concussion, maybe a bit of affected hearing.

I gave the rest of my body a quick internal scan and with the exception of some aches and pains, as well as tiny stinging cuts on my face from the splinters, I was fine.

Much better shape than the Leprechaun, poor guy.

I picked the pack up from the ground and dug around for the sat link device, only to find it in pieces at the bottom of the pack.

"Shit," I hissed as the pieces slid through my fingers.

"Sprite is going to kill you."

"Yeah, that and I have no idea how to get to the extraction point. Trevor was the one with the internal GPS in this place."

"I've got my compass and a map," Luke said, glancing back at where the Orc was still a heap on the ground.

"You should get it out now, so we're not wandering around and wasting time."

"We should get away from him first."

"He's got you pretty spooked, why?"

Luke swallowed and pushed his glasses up his nose with one finger at the bridge piece.

"Francesca had done…experiments on Supernaturals during her tenure as director. She'd figured out how to unleash some kind of latent berserker quality in Orcs. But the catch was that it turned Orcs into essentially rabid animals, uncontrollable. Until her head researcher developed a neuro device that allowed someone to mentally link with the Orc and control them. If I'm not mistaken, that Leprechaun was controlling the Orc and you killed him so—"

"When he wakes up he's going to be out of control."

"Yep. A real life Hulk. So we don't want to be here when that happens."

I gave him a short nod, doing my best to keep my brain from panicking from that information.

"Right. Get your compass out and lead us southwest. That was the general direction of the small town where Trevor's partner was waiting for us with a plane."

Luke looked like he was about to say something when he snapped his mouth shut and nodded. The compass was miraculously fine and he turned until he found the direction, which was thankfully in the opposite direction of the unconscious Orc.

It wasn't until we'd been walking for a while that my mind was clear enough to wonder how the hell the sat link device had gotten that smashed.

And why Luke seems…off for some reason.

I glanced at him as he guided us with his compass to keep us in the right direction. He gave me a grin, his tusks brushing against his full upper lips, backpack bulging with books and papers. I smiled back at him and kept walking as I observed him out of the corner of my eye.

It's something about the way he's moving…he keeps wiping his eyes. Maybe he's got dry eyes?

I shrugged it off and tried to focus on just getting us to that plane but it was hard to ignore the nagging at the back of my mind that there was something big I was missing about my ex-husband.

CHAPTER FOUR

LUKE

Seeing that Orc was like stepping back in time to right before the previous director of the Secret Archive, Francesca, had been assassinated and I was living in constant fear. Even now, as I tried to forget about the poor male back there, I could practically smell the dank underground lab where Francesca had taken my cousin. She'd acted like she was showing me something exciting, a project that I would find fascinating. But really, she'd been giving me a warning; if I didn't stop trying to undermine her, I'd be in the cell next to him.

I swallowed and tried to push the nightmarish memories aside.

He had been a quiet one, my cousin. Always kind, gentle even. He liked to garden and had been attempting to cross breed certain types of tomatoes. But the male I'd seen in that lab was wild eyed, foaming at the mouth, and his muscles unnaturally bulging against his skin as he strained against the chains that held him to a wall like an animal.

How had I forgotten that? The second I saw those two Orcs with Kristoff sporting neural discs at their temples I should've known!

I tried to tell myself I was just tired, that I'd been scared at the prospect of getting my tongue cut out, that it wasn't the Vanquis. But I knew that it was, and that it was progressing too fast.

"Are you alright?" Andy asked.

I glanced back and gave her a forced smile.

"Fine, why?"

She shook her head and frowned up at me.

"You seem distracted. Is it the Orc or something else?"

I was relieved she'd asked directly about the Orc and not why my lungs weren't as strong as they had been or how her sat link device had gotten smashed. Truth be told, I'd panicked when she'd been so focused on hearing the cannon charging and smashed it far more than I'd intended.

It was a shitty thing to do, and I felt terrible about destroying such a gorgeous piece of tech, but I had to find that cave. And if Andy had that device there would be no reason for me to guide us.

She's going to kill me when she finds out that I'm leading us in the exact opposite direction she wanted, but better her than this fucking disease.

"The Orc," I admitted with a shaky smile. "My cousin was experimented on by Francesca and…"

"Oh my God, Luke, I'm so sorry. Why didn't you ever tell me?"

"I was going to but she was dead a week later and everything was chaos. By the time I was able to get back to where she'd been holding the Orcs she'd experimented on, my cousin was dead, along with most of the others. There was so much ugliness from that time…I guess I just wanted to forget."

Not to mention how our marriage collapsed not too long after that.

She took my hand in hers and the contact sent a jolt of electricity through me. I always forgot just how much smaller Andy was than me. She was so confident, her personality and ability to command a room made her seem larger than life. But my hand swallowed hers, the long bones in her fingers so delicate even though I'd seen her kill more than one assailant with them.

I've also seen her do wonderfully dirty things with them too.

My face heated but I didn't let her go. She wasn't fighting with me, or judging me with her eyes. This was the Andy I remembered from

Venice, when we'd first gotten together. And I wanted to bathe in the sensation of her warmth, store it up for when she was gone.

But then her forehead wrinkled in a frown and she looked down at my hand. I did too, wondering what she was seeing and my stomach dropped.

"Is that your wedding ring?" she asked, her fingers now clutching mine so she could examine the gold band with tiny carvings of vines and thorns.

"Uh, yeah. Well, I knew it was a family heirloom of yours and I, uh, didn't feel right just sticking it in a mailbox. Who knows what would happen to it. And I didn't want to leave it in my apartment because you know, robbers," a nervous chuckle escaped my throat. "So, um, just to be safe, I just kept it on until I saw you again."

She stared up at me, mouth open just a little as if she wasn't quite sure what to say.

"Okay," she drew it out slowly. "Well, I'm here and so…do you want to or…do you want to keep it."

"No, it's yours I just…" I stared down at it, the last physical vestige of our time together and my heart cracked.

It was only right that I return it. The ring really was an heirloom, but there was something so damn final about taking it off and handing it back.

She'd left hers on the dresser when she moved out, as if it had meant nothing.

An oily slick of anger bubbled in my gut at the memory of coming home to find her clothes and toiletries gone, her rings on the dresser with a simple note: "I'm sorry, I just can't anymore." Two weeks later I was served with divorce papers and once I signed them, that was that.

At least for her.

"I, uh," I ran my forefinger over the band and swallowed, "my fingers are a bit swollen right now, can I…do it later?"

"Sure."

Her voice was soft, not a hint of judgment or anger. I looked into soft eyes that held only compassion and shit ton of questions. Before, she would push a bit, try to get me to open up. And I would, to a point. It wasn't that I didn't like talking about my feelings, I actually did and I wanted to share everything with her. But there had always been this impulse in me to hold back when it came to Andy. She was so strong, and the men around her were the kind that I could never picture being touchy feely, the kind that I always felt intimidated by because they had far more in common with Andy than I did. So I felt like I had to show how strong I could be too, even though, as she so deftly pointed out a few minutes ago, I was the brains, not the brawn. It didn't come naturally to me, and eventually all the shit I bottled up would spill out and we'd be in a fight about something stupid.

Like her socks, or my singing. Fuck, I can't do this anymore, I can't play a part, I don't have the energy. I'm already barely holding myself together between the stress of this mission and the disease. Besides, it doesn't matter anymore. She left, no matter how perfect I tried to be, so what's the point in trying again?

Still, while I wasn't going to paste a false smile on my face, I was also not going to dump out my purse and let her see how fucking devastated I still was. I had *some* pride left. So, I pulled my fingers out of her grasp and turned my back on her to keep walking. The way she was staring at me tempted me too damn much.

We walked on in silence after that, the conversation hanging thick between us with all the things we'd left unsaid, unexamined from our failed marriage. I once thought that if I could just get her in a room and get her to tell me what I'd done that I could fix it. But after a while, I realized that, for her, it had been over long before she'd disappeared from my life. Dredging up the dead corpse of our relationship wasn't going to fix that now. All it would do was hurt us both, and I didn't have the stomach for it.

It must've been a few hours before we heard a distant, familiar crashing through the underbrush. It was far enough behind us that we still couldn't see the Orc, but close enough to hear him.

"Oh shit," Andy breathed, "we gotta run."

My body couldn't handle carrying her again, that had been a mistake that still had my joints aching. Even just a year ago I could've done it no problem, so the fact that it hurt even a little bit now was frightening.

I shoved those worries aside to focus on the hurdle we currently faced and seized Andy's hand.

"C'mon, we gotta get some distance, hope that he doesn't pick up our scent through the plants."

She didn't fight with me, even though she had to work double time to keep up with me as we ran through the brush. I batted branches and plants out of the way in a frenzy, desperate to get away from the crazed Orc.

We burst through thick plants to come to the banks of a calmly meandering river. I let out a relieved sigh. This would be perfect, it would mask our scent and put the water between us and the Protectors, making us harder to track. I looked back at Andy with a grin, only to be met with her wide eyed stare as she shook her head violently.

"No, no way! There are *fish* in that river, I can see them! I'm not getting in there. We can run along the bank, the smell of the water should mask us."

"The bank is muddy, our footprints will give us away. We might as well shoot a flare into the sky."

She stepped back from the water just as the telltale crash of something large coming at us reached my ears. He was still far enough back not to see us, but I had no idea how refined his sense of smell was. If he'd gotten our scent, then he was going to catch us unless we got in the river.

I was just about to ask her what the hell was wrong with fish when I remembered something she'd admitted to me one drunken new year's eve.

We'd been playing Truth or Dare by ourselves after we'd drank everyone else under the table. She'd picked truth and I'd asked her to tell me about something strange she was afraid of.

"I'm 'fraid of fiss," she'd slurred.

"Fiss?"

"Ya know," she wiggled her hand in front of me and shivered. "Creepy ash thingsss."

I'd thought she must be joking. Andy was legit one of the most bad ass people I'd ever met, and the thought that she was afraid of something as harmless as fish was laughable, so I'd just forgotten it.

Until now.

"Okay, Andy, look at me," I put my hands out like I was calming a scared animal because she looked like she was about to bolt.

"I can't," she shook her head again, voice breaking, "I can't. Y-you don't...I can't, Luke."

I'd seen this woman face down things that would've made most piss themselves. Mummies? She'd simply lit torches and incinerated their asses while I screamed in terror. Zombie pythons? She had a pair of snake skin boots that glowed in the dark after that mission. Four to one odds? She wielded a fountain pen like a dagger and had them bleeding out on a library floor.

And here she was, terrified of *fish*.

I wasn't exactly sure how to handle our roles being reversed all of a sudden but I had to think fast because that Orc was closing in on us.

I looked at the river, then back at her as tears tracked down her cheeks and an idea hit me. I moved the backpack to my front and approached slowly.

"Okay, climb on my back, that way you won't have to be in the water."

"Are you crazy? No! Besides," she pointed at the backpack, "you'll get those books wet. Yeah! You don't want to do that, do you?"

"They're in a waterproof bag, I've learned my lesson over the years. Now, Andy, get on my back or we will be torn limb from limb by that thing."

My voice was low but firm and she whimpered with terror. The sound was like a fist around my heart and I reached out, cupping her cheek in my hand.

"Hey, I'm here, and I'm not going to let anything happen to you. I swear it."

"I'm sorry, it just…"

"I know." A loud crack and crash made us both jump and I took a deep breath. "You can yell at me later for this."

"What…? No!"

I flung her over my shoulder again and she screamed in panic.

"Andy, shut up!"

"Put me down!" she beat my back with her fists and then screamed. "No no no! Don't get in the water!"

"If you don't want to look at it head first, climb on my fucking back!" I said as I began to wade in.

She scrambled like a primate and managed to maneuver herself onto my back. At first she was in the traditional piggy back position, with her arms around my neck and legs around my waist. Her arms were a bit tight around my throat and she whimpered. I thought it would be okay. Sure she was strangling me a bit but this would be fine, nothing too terrible until we made it across.

But the further I waded in the more she shrieked and screamed, her legs climbed higher up my torso the further we moved.

"Andy," I gagged and coughed, "you're…gonna strangle me!"

"Don't you dare drop me!"

"Then loosen…grip!"

"No way-ah! I saw something in the water. Leeches, I bet there's leeches in here!"

And that's all it took for her start climbing me like I was some kind of tree, and not in the sexy way.

Her core was grinding against my back as her legs worked her further up my body. I like a good, hard massage as much as the next guy, but the combination of digging and slapping of her knees, booted feet and hands was not restorative in the least.

"Stop…I can't…" she kicked my side and I yelped.

"Andy, you need to calm the fuck down."

She screamed bloody murder and pointed at the water as I did my best to keep moving while she wiggled all over me.

"That's an eel, right there!"

"It's a stick."

"Eel!"

"Eels are not in this part of the world! Will you just settle down?"

She climbed her way up my back with flailing limbs until she was sitting on my shoulders, her fingers digging into my face. One snagged the side of my mouth and she pulled it open so that it gaped painfully on that side.

"Ow…ow…Ow! Andy!"

I pried her fingers off my face but that only made her wobble to the side. With more flailing arms that almost smacked my glasses off, Andy ended up hanging off my left shoulder, fingers now around my throat in a death grip. I wondered if I really would need to just dunk her so I could take a breath when she let out another blood curdling screech.

"Fish! Giant fucking fish!"

She scrambled until she was once again on top of my shoulders and I took a deep breath as I looked down where she was still pointing.

"It's a leaf, Andy."

"It's wiggling!"

"Yeah, with the current, it's a fucking leaf!"

She whimpered and clamped her thighs tight to the side of my face and her arms wrapped around my forehead. Now, any other time, Andy's thighs around my head was a fucking dream. But as I tried to traverse a river with a feral Orc starting to chase after us in said river? Not so much.

I took off with long strides, my hands holding her ankles, not to try and keep her on my shoulders as much as to try and keep her still. Even so, she was trembling so hard that it was shaking my head in a weird way, making my teeth clatter.

Behind us, the Orc was struggling, even in this gentle of a current, his arms waving out to the sides. I stopped for a second, trying to concentrate on him even as Andy screeched about how she swore she saw another eel.

It was after a second or two that I saw the wounds across the Orc's face, particularly across his eyes. That blast had not only severed his neuro-link with his handler, but it had blinded him too.

"Andy, sidearm," I demanded, my mouth dry.

I knew what I had to do.

"Great idea, shoot the fish, slimy bastards."

I didn't quite catch onto what she was doing because I was focused on keeping the Orc in my sights. But suddenly, right next to my fucking head, she discharged her weapon into the water, sending a spray up at us.

"Andy!" I reached up, snagged her hand and ripped the gun from her grip. "What the fuck are you doing?"

"You told me to shoot the fish!"

"No, I asked for your gun."

"Yeah, to shoot the fish. Now get moving!"

One foot tapped my back and I got the distinct impression she was trying to get me going, much like she would a horse. I ground my teeth together. Whatever humor I may have found in this situation died out somewhere around the first stick she mistook for an eel.

I wasn't as good a shot as Andy, but throughout our marriage I'd accompanied her to plenty of shooting ranges and learned how to handle a firearm. I could shoot. I could even hit things if they were close enough. And, as it turned out, I wasn't close enough to put the Orc out of his misery.

And Andy is no condition to do this so…fuck.

I turned and started back across the river the way we'd come and Andy let out a wail of panic.

"What are you doing? We need to get out of the water-ah! Another fucking huge fish! Luke, please get me out of here!"

I patted her leg, trying to give her a little reassurance so that she might calm down enough to let me do this.

I took a deep breath, swallowed back the sick feeling that began to well up, and aimed. There was no coming back from what had been done to him, and chances were, the Protectors would force him to remain in their service, blind or not. He'd been weakened by the explosion, burns covered his torso and exposed the skin underneath, making him vulnerable. And I was about to take advantage of that.

This is the right thing to do.

Still, as I lined up the shot and emptied the gun into the Orc, I felt like a murderer.

"Holy shit," Andy breathed, the first time since getting in the water that she'd sounded remotely like herself.

I blinked away tears, unable to watch his body crash into the water and handed her the empty gun. Without another word, I started back across the river. Even without him following us, we needed to get distance from the Protectors and cover up our direction as best we could. It wouldn't take them long to figure out something had happened to the Leprechaun and the Orc, which would likely lead them here. If they were smart, they'd figure out we crossed the river. But there was a whole lot of land on the other side, and if we were quick enough, we could put enough distance between us that they wouldn't catch us in time.

I moved faster, which splashed water up at Andy, who started to mutter something under her breath in a terrified voice. Whatever it was managed to keep her still enough that I no longer had to wrestle her and the river together, so I made good time. Once across, I made sure to get us far enough into the thick cover of the trees and the plants that even if someone were to come to the bank at that moment, we'd be sufficiently hidden.

I expected Andy to immediately jump off of me the second I stopped moving but instead she still had me in the vice grip of her thighs and arms.

"Andy?" I patted her thigh.

She flinched and whimpered, the sound so damn pitiful that my anger was fast bleeding away. Poor thing was fucking terrified.

Of fish…I'm not sure if I'm scared to hear the story behind that or intrigued.

"Andy?" I tried again. "We're out of the water."

"No-no-no-no-no…"

I sighed and took the pack off of my front and set it on the ground. Then I pried Andy's legs from my head first before reaching back and swinging her around to my front. Her legs kicked and clamped around my middle before I could set her on her feet. In this position, her front was pressed tight to mine, her arms around my neck while she buried her face into my shoulder and shook. It had been so long since I'd had her body against mine, in my arms. The feel of her, soft and yet also strong all at the same time, her heart beating out against my chest, it was so familiar and as the seconds ticked by, I had to swallow back the emotions that were fast bubbling to the surface.

I realized too late that holding her was a mistake. For the first time in so long, I didn't feel that yawning emptiness that she'd left me with and I didn't want to let her go because the second I did, it would come rushing back. But I also didn't want to be 'that guy', the one to take advantage of a situation like this but it was really hard to peel her off me when she was clinging to me like I was her lifeline.

"Hey," I ran my hand up and down her back while my other arm had circled around her. "It's okay, baby, we're safe."

I almost told her that she could let go, but the words stuck in my throat. I didn't want her to leave my arms, I wanted to let myself go and sink into the comforting warmth of her body against mine, savor this moment as long as she'd let me. Not only was it like a piece of my soul was back in my possession, but her very presence soothed the pain of taking that Orc's life. Even if it had been the right thing, my heart was raw from the act. Andy's touch, her chest rising and falling against mine, and the way her fingers had started to run up and down the back of my neck, it all told me that I wasn't a murderer, I wasn't a monster for what I'd done.

Her trembles slowed and then stopped and I couldn't help tightening my arms around her, not ready to let go yet. I let out a long breath, my hand cupped the back of her head where her bun had come loose.

All too soon, Andy leaned back so that she could look at me, her legs and arms still wrapped around me. She was so close like this, I felt her breath, saw the faint scar on her forehead, the gold flecks in her brown eyes. Without thinking, I brushed some stray hair from her face and she leaned, ever so slightly into my touch.

"You okay?" I asked, my voice husky and low.

She nodded and licked her lips.

My gaze zeroed in on that pink tongue of hers, knowing what things she could do with it, longing to taste her. I was grateful that her cuts had stopped bleeding; there was only a faint scent of copper and I could ignore it while I took her in. Even covered in sweat and cuts, smudges of dirt on her cheeks, she was still the most beautiful woman I'd ever laid eyes on.

"Are *you?*" she asked. "What you did…it was mercy."

I swallowed the tears back.

"Doesn't feel like it. It wasn't his fault what he'd become," my voice caught and I shook my head. "I wish there had been another way."

Her hand came up and cupped my face, her thumb brushed my cheekbone and this time it was my turn to lean into her. I closed my eyes and let out a long, shuddering breath.

Andy's thumb ran along my eyebrow, down my temple and back up. Over and over the way she used to do it when I couldn't sleep. It was so familiar, so easy and all the questions that had haunted me since the day she left rose to the surface. I wanted to ask what I could've done differently, how I could've made her stay. To know why I wasn't enough to keep her.

These questions had festered within me, eating away at my self-confidence and ability to trust anyone. I'd hidden away in my books, in my online games and only let myself have surface friendships. I could blame her for it all. But really, it had been my choice not to deal with it, to pretend that everything was fine when really I was eaten up with pain and self-doubt.

"I miss that," I rasped, nuzzling the palm of her hand. "It's so calming."

"You should've let me shoot him."

I opened my eyes to see her gazing at me with naked concern and something else. It was there and then gone in a flash, quick enough that I told myself I imagined the raw longing.

"You mean in between shooting leaves in the river?" I asked with a grin.

Andy flushed and looked down, her lips tense like she was fighting her own smile.

"I know that at least one of those was a fish."

"I think we need to agree to disagree on that one."

She lost the fight and looked up at me with a self-conscious grin on her face.

"Deal. And I'm sorry," she whispered. "I…I am really afraid of fish."

"I hadn't noticed."

She lightly slapped my chest and shook her head.

"Don't, I'm already embarrassed."

"My lips are sealed."

"Thank you. I hope I didn't hurt you."

"No, I'm alright. Nothing a drink and a good meal won't fix."

She tilted her head to the side.

"Are you asking me out on a date?"

"I'm not that smooth."

"No, you're not."

"But," my fingers found the edge of her tank top and I ran my index finger along the sliver of skin I found, "if I were, what would you say?"

Her smile faltered and I realized my mistake, heart dropping to my toes.

"I mean," I gave her a snorting laugh, "you don't have to…it's not a *date*. It's a, uh, friendly little…um, event."

That brought her smile back in full and she laughed.

"You are still really bad at this."

Only when it's you, Andy.

But out loud I shrugged and laughed again.

"You know me. Awkward as fuck."

"How about this," she disentangled her legs from around me and landed on her feet, "I take you out for a beer and some dinner and you don't tell anyone about this little *incident*."

"Or," I put my pack on, "we just decide to be friends and go have some food and drinks. As friends."

I stuck out my hand and she shook on it, her hand retreating far sooner than I wanted. It was a terrible fact that contact with Andy was like a drug. Being away from it as long as I had been, I was fine. But one hit, one moment and I was addicted to the smell of her, the feel of her. My mouth watered as my sense memory brought up the exact taste of her coming on my tongue, the sweetness of her skin, her mouth.

It was pure fucking torture to have the ability to recall these things in exact detail. And perhaps I was a masochist; I knew that I'd be bringing them up for a while after this because where she was concerned, I couldn't help myself.

CHAPTER FIVE
ANDROMEDA

As we walked on in silence, I hoped that Luke didn't notice the effect his touch had on me. The last thing I needed was to give him the wrong idea. I wasn't here to rekindle anything, just get him the hell out of this damn rainforest and back to HQ. But the moment his arms went around me and I buried my face in the crook of his neck, I was transported back to those early days, when we couldn't keep our hands off one another. His smell was mostly the same spicy, male scent that had always meant home, no matter where we'd been in the world.

My chest had tightened the longer I'd let him hold me and I wanted to just stay there, legs and arms holding us both in place, in such a simple, perfect moment. There were no pet peeves under our skin, no jealousy tearing us apart. We were always so good when we were able to keep it simple and for us that was usually on a mission. The adrenaline of running for our lives always ended in us fucking hard and long. It was when we were at our best, no 'real world' shit to come between us.

But nothing lasted forever. Not a mission and, apparently, not a marriage, as I learned painfully when I'd left him. It had been the hardest thing I'd ever done. I left my heart behind, along with my rings. I never told him how hard it had been to leave him, or why I felt like I had to, because I was a coward. Which was ironic since, besides fish, there was very little that scared me. But having to look into Luke's eyes and have that final fight, have to tell him that it was over…It would've killed me.

It still took about a dozen tries to write that damn note and in the end I stuck to the very basics. *"I'm sorry, I just can't anymore. It's over."*

Guilt gnawed at me because I know it had hurt him deeply to be left like that. Especially with that lame non-explanation.

Ugh, this is why I didn't want to be around him again! One hug and I'm a mess. Stupid fucking fish.

It's funny how, even when you're married to someone for almost five years, you can still find things to be embarrassed about. I had a very fuzzy memory of telling Luke about my fear of fish one new year's eve but when he didn't bring it up the next morning I thought maybe I'd imagined it and swore I'd never, ever tell him why.

And then we just *had* to traverse a fucking river.

I knew that Luke would never tell anyone about it, he was good like that. But still, I was so used to being the bad ass, the one that was in control and level headed in these situations, that it was a serious blow to my confidence to be the one in need of soothing.

It struck me as we walked on in silence that I couldn't really remember ever letting Luke be the one I leaned on. Oh sure, there were times when I needed some help with something, or that I confessed my worries to him. But let him be the strong one, the one that saw all the places in me that were frightened and fragile? I was having a hard time coming up with more than a few examples. And even with those, I had closed up pretty damn fast; showing any kind of vulnerability wasn't just scary, it was the kind of terrifying that made me want to flee.

By the time Luke led us to a good spot to camp for the night, I was one hot mess of regrets and self-recriminations. I sighed with frustration as I set my pack down and stretched my muscles.

"You okay?" he asked as he stowed his map.

"Yeah, just a little sore. There should be rations in my pack. Not tasty but good enough."

He nodded.

"I don't know if we can afford a fire, the smoke will be too obvious."

"Agreed."

"I know you probably weren't planning on being out after dark so if you need something to keep warm, I've got this," he held up an old sweatshirt that I knew well.

In an attempt to do 'normal' couple things, Luke had dragged me to a *Buffy the Vampire Slayer* trivia night at a pub. I went because I had enjoyed the show once upon a time. However, I was not prepared for the insanity that met me. Most of the competitors were in cosplay, all of them were serious as a heart attack about this game, and more than a few people had qualms with how the organizers decided to honor certain answers. I had been useless most of the night other than as someone to go get drinks for our team. But then, on a sudden death tie breaker question, I pulled the answer out of my ass and we won. There was a huge prize package for the team, and all of us got sweatshirts. Mine is somewhere in my closet, never worn. But Luke, because he's the cutest fucking geek out there, kept his.

So I was now staring at a black sweatshirt, way too big for me, that had a stake dripping blood on the front with the immortal words "In every generation a slayer is born..." across the front.

"You kept that thing?" I asked with an arched eyebrow.

His chuckle was low, rough and I had a visceral memory of that laugh rolling over my skin as he kissed his way down my body. I took a deep breath and turned away, hiding the flush to my skin with taking out my ruined bun and attempting to rebraid my hair.

"I had fun that night," he said behind me, voice so tender. "You remember the question we won for?"

I smiled in spite of myself.

"What was the name of Buffy's favorite stuffed animal. The only answer I knew."

"But hey, we won."

"Yeah," I glanced back and met his gaze.

There was a spark of heat there under the innocent joy and I found myself wanting to fan that flame until his control snapped and he held me against a tree and…

"Here," he held it out, his voice ragged.

I wondered if he could smell the arousal that I couldn't seem to control right now no matter how hard I tried, but chose to ignore the possibility. Hey, if I ignore it, then it will go away, right?

C'mon Andromeda, get it together.

I took the sweatshirt from him and our fingers brushed. Electricity shot through me and I bit the side of my mouth to keep from letting loose a gasp. I pulled the sweatshirt over my head, and it swallowed me. The hem hit me mid-thigh and I had to roll up the sleeves three times and the cuffs still hit my knuckles.

"I feel like a little kid wearing their dad's clothes," I said with a laugh.

But when I looked up at Luke he was staring at me like I was prime rib and he was starving. His Adam's apple bobbed in the thick column of his throat and his eyes raked down my body. I knew exactly what he was thinking because it was playing like a greatest smutty hits reel in my head at the moment.

I used to put his shirts on after sex, prancing around wherever we were and eventually tempting him so that we ended up back in bed, or against a wall, or on the floor or…

Luke startled, realizing what he was doing and cleared his throat as he turned away.

"Uh, I, uh, I'm gonna get those ration packets."

I nodded, not trusting my voice. The ration packs were freeze dried nutritional powder that reminded me of MREs, only these were a bit more disgusting. All we had to do was add water. Hot water created a kind of stew whereas cold water made a paste that was very similar in consistency to peanut butter.

I hated peanut butter but I'd learned in the military that you eat whatever is in front of you even if you have to choke it down, like I was doing right now. In truth, I was grateful for the distraction as I sat next to Luke on a nearby log, both of us digging the paste out of our packets with our fingers and licking it off in silence. I made the colossal mistake of watching Luke dig some of the paste out with two of his fingers and suck it off his fingers slowly. It was exactly how he used to lick *me* off his fingers after he…

"How about a little light?" I said, my voice too bright and loud.

"Um, ok," Luke replied with a slightly confused grin.

I rummaged in my pack and tried to hide the deep flush on my cheeks. I had to get a fucking grip. Sure, Luke had been insatiable when it came to going down on me and sucking me off his fingers, he used to act like it was the best thing he'd ever tasted and dear God that was sexy!

No! No it wasn't! And even if it was, he's my ex-husband. Ex, not current so…oh my God, does he have to keep sucking on his fingers like that?

I was so distracted that it took me a lot longer than it should have to find the small battery powered lamp in my pack. When I finally turned it on and set it on the ground, Luke was done with his rations and I devoured mine in a few minutes as he guzzled some water.

I flatly refused to stare at the way his throat worked while he drank the water, or remember the way he used to groan when I bit his jaw.

"You want some?" he asked.

"Hm, what?" I jumped, eyes wide and then I saw the canteen he was holding out to me. "Oh, yeah, thanks."

Luke gave me another frown full of questions but thankfully didn't voice any of them. I forced myself to steady as I washed the nutritional paste down with some cool water.

As the sun disappeared behind the horizon, my mind slowed, calmed by the beauty of the forest around me. There were colors here that I hadn't seen in a long time, not since I'd been stationed state side with the Archive. So many different shade of greens on the trees and plants, flowers that were so vibrant that I swore a few of them were glowing in the dark. There was a scent of wet earth and plants on the air, not cloying but crisp, clean. I breathed deep and sighed as the night time creatures chirped and buzzed in the trees around us. The clearing gave us an unobstructed view of the sky and even with the lamp on the ground, I could see millions of pin pricks of light in the darkness.

"I never tire of this," I whispered. "Being somewhere and looking up at the sky at night. It's the same but so different, so beautiful."

To our left, the horizon was a jagged wound across the sky, bright red and fading to pink and then purple, until finally it was the black of night. Something about that bothered me, the sunset on our left…

"Oh wow, look," Luke nudged me, interrupting my train of thought.

I followed where he was pointing and saw a huge full moon rising just above the tree line. It was so big I felt like I could reach out and touch it. Luke bent down to turn off the lamp and we were now bathed in the simple light of the moon. We sat there, Luke's body heat warming me even through the thick sweatshirt, and stared up as the night became both brighter from the moon and darker as the last bit of sunlight faded. Peace wrapped itself around me like a blanket and I leaned my head against Luke's shoulder, letting this moment sooth me. Luke hesitated for a moment and then he laid his cheek against the top of my head. I almost reached for his hand to wrap around mine but this was already dangerous enough, no need to further confuse things.

Besides, I just want to have this. I don't want anything to taint it.

"It's been a while since I was out in the field like this," I said eventually.

"Really?"

"Yeah, I'm mostly in cities these days. I got promoted to head of West Coast security."

If I didn't know him so well, I would've missed the way his body stiffened.

"That's great, Andy," his voice was tinged with sadness.

That confused me, because while Luke hated how much I worked when we were married, he never begrudged me my success. He'd always been proud of me, never sad about it.

His tone added to the sense that something fundamental was off about him. The lack of endurance, the way he was rubbing his eyes incessantly, and now this.

I looked up at him to ask and realized my mistake immediately. He was so close, his breath feathered against my face, I could see the tiny divots in his tusks from use, notice a hairline crack in the right one from when someone had attacked us in the catacombs of Paris. The silver in his goatee bright in the moonlight, the fine lines around his kind eyes. As I stared into his familiar face, it was like glimpsing a place I hadn't realized had been so precious, so missed until it was no longer available to me. A sudden hollowness opened up in me, and I wanted to go back in time to wherever we'd fucked it all up and stop us. But the terrible truth was that it hadn't been a single moment, or action. Our relationship had died by a thousand cuts gone unrecognized until we'd bled it dry.

I should look away, should protect myself, and Luke, because no matter what happened, I knew how this ended and neither of us needed any more bruises on our souls. But that was the thing about Luke, he always had been my one weakness. And damn if I couldn't just walk away now that he was here.

"You always wanted that job," he whispered, his deep voice rumbled in the small space between us.

It took me a moment to remember what the hell we'd been talking about before, but when I did, I swallowed and nodded.

"Yeah, it was…it was a nice surprise to get it."

He swallowed too and I was mesmerized by the way his throat worked. Honestly, Luke's throat and forearms were fucking porn all on their own, even without his beautiful dick…and sculpted ass…and his firm abs…his chest…Okay, his whole fucking body.

Around us, the night air closed in and the moon rose above, shedding silver light on us even as the forest on either side was pitch dark and echoed with the sounds of night creatures waking up. Distantly, I wondered about predators, but when Luke's hand tentatively cupped my cheek, I could think of nothing but the rough warmth of his palm. I leaned into it and closed my eyes.

How did he always manage to disarm me and reduce my body to a quivering mass of lust that was wholly under his command?

"I've missed you," he whispered, forehead leaned against mine as his fingers wound behind my head tentatively. "I never thought I'd see you again and then here you are, rescuing me."

I chuckled.

"As usual," I said with a smile.

"Yeah, as usual."

The sadness was back, thicker this time and I pulled away, searching for the source of it. Was it only that he missed me, that he was morose over the fact that we weren't together anymore? It was entirely possible, it even made sense. But my instincts were firing, and I just knew that there was more to this than he was letting on.

"Someday," he said, eyes tracing my lips, "I'm going to save you."

"You did."

He frowned at me and I motioned back the way we came.

"From the fish."

Luke threw his head back and laughed, a deep throaty sound that had me giggling right along with him.

"Just call me Luke, defender of those with ichthyophobia."

He flexed and I gave him a confused look.

"Ichthyophobia. Fear of fish."

Now it was my turn to belly laugh.

"Of course you would know the name of my fear."

"It's fascinating actually."

"Oh really? Well do NOT enlighten me."

He opened his mouth to say something and there was a sudden blank look in his eyes, followed closely by panic. He looked down and shook his head, covering the whole moment with a wide grin, but I saw it.

"What's wrong?" I asked, all humor drained out of me.

"Nothing. I'm just tired. Haven't really had a good night's sleep since I was captured," he got off the log and began to rummage through our packs.

But his motions were stilted, and the moment he turned from me I saw a glimpse of that same anger and fear.

"Luke," I walked to him and knelt beside him, "you can talk to me you know. If something is wrong."

He glanced over and gave me a crooked smile.

"Thanks, Andy, but I really am just tired."

I didn't really believe that but I also knew better than to push Luke when he didn't want to talk. We began to set up camp for the night in silence. I stashed my pack up on a stake that Luke pounded into one of the trees and then helped him with his. Then we both strung up the enormous sleep hammock he had with him.

"Do you want the hammock?" he asked.

"What are you gonna do?"

"Well, um…we could both sleep in it. Looks big enough."

"You want to share that?" I asked. "Kinda tight isn't it?"

His grin took on a playful note and he cocked his head.

"I don't mind. I mean, we *are* exes but we're also adults and all that. Unless you don't think you can control yourself?"

I crossed my arms over my chest because if I were perfectly honest, the idea of being smashed against Luke in a very tight space brought up every single thing I'd been trying to distract myself from. But he just threw down the gauntlet so I couldn't *not* take the bait. That just wasn't an option.

So I walked up to him and ran my eyes up his body, from toes to the tip of his thick black hair. Outside, I looked unruffled, calm and unconcerned. Inside? Well, let's just say I really, *really* hoped that he was still too concerned about smelling blood off my cuts to take a big inhale because these panties were damp.

"Oh, I can control myself," I taunted. "The question is, are you going to be good or will there be wandering hands in the night?"

"These hands? These very polite, very large, very talented hands?"

And it's on!

"Yes, those hands of moderate talent and size. Can you assure me that they won't wander over this," I ran my hands down my torso, "body?"

Luke swallowed hard the only sign that he was starting to realize his mistake. I knew this little game well; we used to play it all the time…and I always won.

Always.

"Honestly Andy, I told you I'm very tired. Now, it sounds like you're not sure you can handle being in the hammock so maybe…" he shrugged and ran a hand down the back of his head, flexing his bicep.

And fuck me, I had a crazy desire to bite him right there. But I kept it together and narrowed my gaze so he couldn't detect the way I'd zeroed in on his muscles.

Is it really just lifting all those heavy books or is it just that Luke is some kind of demi-god sent to seduce unwitting women like me?

The idea that anyone else would have their hands on him made me a little grouchy but I stamped that down. I had business to attend to.

"Yes, I can control myself," I said, "and yes, I'll share the hammock with you. But I don't like to be too warm while I sleep so…"

I pulled the sweatshirt off and dropped it onto the log we were sitting on with a wide grin. Then, I proceeded to yawn and stretch my arms overhead, arching my back so that my tight tank top stretched even more over my tits. When I finished I put my hands on my hips with a very satisfied smile. Point and probably match to *moi*.

"Okay, great," he said too brightly and nodded. "That's great. I was hoping you wouldn't be too uncomfortable sleeping that close to me. I am a little hot though so…"

He took the hem of his shirt in his hands and made a bit of a show of pulling it over his head.

Son. Of. A. Bitch!

Luke's broad green chest was speckled with fine, wiry hair that was now turning a bit gray, somehow making it even more sexy. He never had that V that some males had, but instead, there was a teensy bit of overhang over the waistband of his shorts that I knew was one of his ticklish spots. His abs weren't washboard but his tummy was just the right kind of tone with a little plump to it. And his shoulders? Dear God in heaven. They were that perfect combination of toned without being a body builder's mass, and Luke was a big male, no doubt. But he had just a little pudge mixed in with the muscles that always sent me over the edge and before I knew it I was usually licking him like a frozen treat.

I thought it was bad when we were married, but being away from him all this time and seeing him again, like this, had me salivating. I hoped like hell he hadn't heard the small inhale I took without thinking, or that he couldn't see the flush that I knew I was wearing.

"Is this going to be ok with you?" he asked, a sexy little smirk around his short tusks.

Well, this might not be smart but in for a penny…

"Absolutely," I said. "In fact, I'm pretty warm myself so I think I'll just…"

He surged forward and seized my wrists before I could yank my tank top over my head. I was so surprised that I let him bring my hands behind me so that my back was arched and I was mere inches away from our bodies touching.

"Andy." All playfulness was gone as he stared down at me with a look that was hot enough to set this entire forest on fire. "We've been playing around, but if you take that shirt off, you're waving a red flag in front of a bull and I *will* take it that far."

My mouth turned dry as a desert and I stared at him with parted lips. Luke had never been this aggressive when we'd been together. Oh sure, he'd said what he wanted to do to me, sometimes took control in sex but there was never this threat, like a caged beast that was on the edge of erupting. He was warning me with a dangerous growl in his voice that had me wanting to do crazy things. Like take my shirt off and see just what Luke was like when he unleashed.

"Are you saying I win?" My voice was wrong; all breathy when what I wanted was confident and unaffected.

The grin he gave me was downright feral and my knees shook, threatening to give out with just a look.

I know it's been a while but for fuck's sake, why is he affecting me like this?

"If you want to look at it that way," his voice dropped and he pulled me until our bodies were flush, "or you can test me and see what happens."

Holy hell, what was happening? Was Luke, my bookish, sweet ex who had always approached sex with a certain amount of fumbling joy suddenly a bona fide sex god, or was I just too horny for my own good?

Both maybe?

He transferred my wrists to one hand and let his fingers run along the waistband of my pants with the other. As he did, Luke brought his mouth down to my ear, skimming my jaw on his way there. I shivered as cold fire worked through my body at the contact, and my eyes closed of their own accord as I melted into him. I did not imagine the low growl he made that vibrated in his chest, or the hard bite of his teeth that sent warmth blooming at the apex of my thighs.

Definitely both.

"I know this is just the mission adrenaline," he whispered. "I know that it doesn't mean anything more. But damn if I care right now, Andy. I've missed you," he brushed his lips against the skin at the base of my ear. "Have you missed me?"

I groaned low in the back of my throat and twisted my hands out of his grip so I could bury them in his hair. Luke's other hand gripped my hip, grinding me against his hard length.

This was dangerous for so many reasons. Luke wasn't the type of male to love 'em and leave 'em. He became attached and I didn't want to play with his heart. But the more he trailed kisses down my throat, the more his hands savored my skin, the more lost to good common sense I became.

We never said good-bye after all. What's the harm in one more time, just one more…

I took in a jagged breath to tell him that yes, I'd missed him. Missed the way his hands trailed sparks up my skin, the drag of his tusks against my throat as he kissed me, the joy he had in pleasing my body.

But I never got the chance because at that moment something wet and thick splattered on my face.

"Oh my God, *what the fuck?*"

I jerked back and saw a splatter of white on the top of Luke's head right before he pulled back too, eyes wide behind his glasses. I started to reach up to touch the thick gooey texture on my forehead and Luke stopped me.

"Uh, that's…shit."

"What, what is it?!" I screeched.

Luke's mouth tensed as he fought back a smile.

"It's shit."

And that's when it hit me. Some fucking bird cock blocked us by doing a fly by shitting.

"I have body wipes, hold on," Luke said, running to where his pack hung from the tree.

I walked over to him, afraid to straighten my head and have the sludge drip into my eyes or, God forbid, my mouth. So I had my head back and at an angle as I tried to run to where Luke was holding a package of wipes. I imagined I looked like Phoebe from *Friends* when she ran through the park, and I had to swallow back a belly laugh.

He took a handful of wipes out and then handed me the package just before his deep, rumbling laugh started to shake his shoulders.

"It's not funny," my voice wasn't convincing as I cleaned the mess off me.

"It's kinda funny," he said, eyes twinkling at me. "I mean, how many times can you say that the mood was interrupted because a bird shit on you?"

I tried to stop myself from smiling and failed.

Then I tried to stop the bubble of laughter that was building in my chest, but the longer Luke chuckled, the funnier this actually became and I couldn't hold it back any longer.

We were laughing so hard that I doubled over at one point and leaned on Luke, who was also gripping his stomach as he leaned against the tree and belly laughed.

"Oh my Gods," Luke wheezed, wiping his eyes behind his glasses. "Here, lemme help, you've got a bit still in your hairline."

I cringed in spite of the fact that I was still trembling with laughter and let him clean up what I'd missed. That's when I noticed all the spots he'd also missed and I snagged a couple more wipes.

"Kneel down, you've got some in your hair."

Luke knelt at my feet and I cleaned the last bit from his hair as we both let out the last few gasps of laughter.

"Okay, you're good," I said and looked down.

Luke was staring up at me, naked adoration burned in his eyes just for a moment before he locked it away but it was enough to strike a weak spot deep within me. If that bird hadn't interrupted us, I'd have my back against one of these trees while Luke fucked me within an inch of my life, I had no doubt about that.

But I would've regretted it because this was *Luke,* not some bar hook up after too much tequila and self-loathing. This was the man who had once skipped a research trip to Peru to stay with me when I had my appendix out. This was the guy who watched every *Friday the 13th* movie with me, even though he hated horror movies. This was the man who held me for hours as I cried when my *abuelita* died. For all our troubles, for all the reasons why I believed we couldn't work, Luke deserved better than to be used and tossed aside.

So I started to lock away the parts of me that were still tempted to pick up where the bird had interrupted us. I took a deep breath and reminded myself of why I'd left in the first place, the reasons that we didn't work.

Luke pulled his shirt back on and handed me the sweatshirt with a lopsided grin. He was nervous, thinking about the same thing I was probably. Of how good it had felt in the moment, of what we would've done. But was he thinking it would've been a mistake, or was he wishing we'd done it anyway?

The unspoken, unfulfilled desire between us was about as comfortable as a wool sweater and I needed something, anything, to break that tension. So I pulled the sweatshirt on and laughed.

"That must've been a big ass bird," I said.

"There's some large ones around here," Luke said, brushing dirt off his knees.

"Hopefully they stay away while we sleep."

He chuckled.

"I think we'll be okay. The hammock should cover us a bit."

Oh…right. The hammock.

I glanced over at the thing and realized that we were going to smashed together all night in a very, very tight space.

Not exactly the set up to avoid temptation.

"If you're uncomfortable I can—" he began.

"No," I said with a smile, "it's fine. We're adults and…look, things happen on missions, we know that. And we have a history so it was bound to be a risk."

"Right," he said in a voice that was a bit shaky, a smile that was too wide. "Absolutely, it was just a moment of…weakness."

"Yeah, exactly," I agreed, my own voice too loud to my ears. "We almost slipped into old habits but it doesn't mean we can't be friends, right?"

My chest was tight as I realized how bad I needed Luke to not only *not* be weird about this, but also not run from me. I knew I'd missed him, but being here with him, feeling his hands on me, his mouth, hearing his voice, it all exposed just how much of a hole his absence had left in my life. And, whether or not it was smart, or right or fair, I just couldn't let him go again.

"Friends, sure, yes!" he nodded, but it was off. "Friends sounds…good."

"Good, great!"

We both stood there for a second nodding, not looking at one another until Luke broke the moment.

"We should probably sleep."

"Yeah, good idea."

Luke held the hammock for me so I could climb in and then got in himself. It took us a few minutes to get comfortable and when we did, my back was to his front. The tension was like a heat wave between us, knowing that all it would take is for him slip my pants down, hike my leg over his hip and…

Danger! You can't think like that. Distract, distract!

"You know what this reminds me of?" I asked, my voice warbly with nerves.

"Alaska?"

"Yes!"

Luke chuckled behind me.

"Oh my God, what a disaster! I still can't believe that no one thought to test the snow for mutant amoebas."

"Well, who really knew that Tesla's radio would have that effect on simple water amoebas?"

"Or that they'd start chomping on the power lines like an all you can eat buffet?" Luke laughed.

"God, that was a cold night. We had to double up on clothes and then zip ourselves into that giant thermal hammock. If not for the Archive sending techs out, that poor town would've been without power for a week."

"It was cozy though," he said, wistfully.

"Yeah."

While a part of me still wished Luke would just rip my fucking clothes off, the trip down memory lane had sobered me a bit. Because what we didn't talk about was how that had been one of our last missions together. How I'd started requesting to go alone after that. And how we'd had one of our biggest fights in Alaska.

Luke shifted behind me and I looked back to see him trying to figure out where to put his arm.

"You can put your arm around me," I said. "I'm not sure where else you're going to put it and it's just gonna go there anyway."

"Are you preemptively accusing me of groping you in the night?"

I smiled in relief at the playfulness in his tone.

"Maybe."

"I've already gotten my grope, I'm good."

I snorted and closed my eyes, relishing the warmth of his body around me.

I've missed you…

I didn't want to admit how comforting it was to have his body at my back, the familiar scent and feel of him. I wanted his arm around me more than I should, especially after almost tearing his clothes off a mere half hour ago.

But Luke was trying to be a gentleman, as always, and he wasn't going to do it on his own. So I grabbed his hand and pulled his arm around my waist.

"I'm cold," I murmured, instead of telling him the truth.

That I needed his arm around me, that I hadn't realized how much I'd missed him until that blazing hot moment against his body.

"Ok," he whispered in my hair. "Good night, Andy."

"Good night, Luke."

CHAPTER SIX

LUKE

Andy never believed me when I said she snored like a lumberjack with a head cold, or that I thought it was adorable. It was the kind of snore that was both cute and a little shocking. She used to wake herself up with it, her eyes shooting open in shock to find me smiling at her. Then she'd deny that she was snoring and blame me, which I let her do because I didn't really care. She was so fucking cute and sexy, beautiful and untouchable, even by me sometimes.

But the times she had opened to me during our marriage? The times when I stripped her of everything during sex, when I had her under my control? She was wanton; a blazing fire that trembled in my hands with absolute trust. *Those* were times I'd never forget.

Unless I do.

I swallowed down the fear that threatened to smother me. Andy was picking up on my illness, all her questions, the way she looked at me sometimes. I should've known I wouldn't be able to hide it from her. I wasn't ashamed, but I knew her. She'd want to be with me, helping me with everything, nursing me. And I wouldn't be able to handle that. If we'd grown old together and I was ninety something, that would be different. We'd have earned those final intimacies of caring for one another in the last days of our lives.

But I was young, and it wouldn't be her taking care of me as her husband, but out of pity, obligation, guilt. And that I would never allow.

It was only a matter of time before she figured out that I wasn't taking her to the extraction and then I would have to either come up with a lie good enough to convince her to let me go, or tell her the truth.

Or, I could get out of this hammock, and leave her.

That was likely the best option, even if it did rip my heart out. She'd see it as a betrayal, and I'd be leaving her stranded in the forest with dangerous people after us that wouldn't hesitate to torture her to get to me.

No, I can't do that. Andy isn't helpless but she has no way to navigate to safety. We should reach the town tomorrow and all I have to do is find the church Father Juarez built there, the final clue to where he hid the cache. Then I can leave her there. She'll be able to find her way safely. I just need to keep her from figuring out what I'm doing until then.

It was a shit plan but the only one I had. And if Andy figured out what was wrong soon, I'd have a decision to make.

Right now, though, I needed to sleep.

I hesitated before putting my arm around her waist. There wasn't any room in this thing and she was right, my arm was going to do it at some point, might as well make sure it's not across her chest.

Damn, why did I think of that.

My dick wasn't getting the message that fucking Andy was a very bad idea. It wouldn't fix what was broken between us any more than it ever did. In fact, it would probably make everything worse because I'd want to keep her. Hell, having her in my arms right now was already breaking my damn heart.

I caught a glimpse of the band still around my ring finger and my chest squeezed tight. She knew I'd never gotten over her, and the bullshit about the ring was just that: bullshit. I could never bring myself to take it off, even when friends told me I had to move on, that it was unhealthy to pine after her. They were right, but I just wasn't ready.

So now a year later here I was, pressed up against the only woman I wanted and hadn't been with in over a year, and I was expected to just what? Not be mentally wrestling with my libido?

I let out a long breath and began to recite the periodic table backwards. Then I did it forwards and then backwards again. Before I knew it, I was drifting off to the sound of Andy's snoring.

I'd like to say that it was a deep sleep, that I wasn't kept in a state of half dreaming as my body reacted to the soft warmth of Andy's, but that would be a lie. It was torture, waking up just enough to be painfully aware of my hard dick nestled against Andy's ass. And it wasn't like I could go to the other side of the bed either. This hammock had us snuggled up tight. So the only thing to do was distract my mind and force it to drift off again. I did this for hours until I couldn't take it any longer and decided to just get up.

When I peeked my head out of the hammock, I was surprised to see that the sky was beginning to lighten. Apparently I'd gotten more sleep than I thought, though whether or not it was restful was debatable.

Andy groaned when I clumsily got out of the hammock, swinging it a bit.

"What's...wrong?" she mumbled.

"Gotta pee, go back to sleep."

She flopped her head back down and was snoring before I'd even taken my pack down from the peg on the tree.

I found my reading light and got out my journals, along with the map and compass. I needed to be sure I wasn't forgetting anything about the location of the town or the church. There were legends about both, how the priest had somehow been able to protect them from evil men that would plunder its secrets. While I suspected that there were booby traps in the cavern where the artifacts were hidden, I couldn't remember if there was anything we needed to be wary of before we got there.

I got lost in my reading, underlining things so I could find them easier and then making more notes in my current journal. It was obvious in my last two months of writing that something was wrong with me. I repeated information, and left out some information that I now remembered so there were theories that weren't correct. I crossed those out and made better notes in my current journal, trying not to panic.

If I hadn't done this, I might have led us in the wrong direction and I definitely wouldn't have known what I was looking for in the church, which was more of a small chapel than the cathedral style I'd assumed before.

I took my glasses off and let the tears flow down my face. What if this was progressing faster than I thought? What if instead of years, I had mere months? These notes proved that I was losing my capacity for logical thought at times, that I was losing memories of things that should've been stuck firmly in my mind. What if I woke up tomorrow and…

"Luke?"

Andy's voice jolted me out of my pity party and I looked around to notice that the sun was just starting to break the horizon.

I wiped my eyes and slipped my glasses back on.

"What's wrong?" she asked.

"Nothing, I didn't sleep well."

She waved her hand through the air to wipe away my lie.

"Stop. I know you're keeping something from me and I'm sick of it. What is going on? And," she looked to the horizon and my stomach dropped, "why is the sun…and last night…Oh, you son of a bitch!"

"Andy, I can explain," I said, holding out my hands as she advanced on me.

She smacked me in the chest, then the arm.

"Are you fucking *kidding* me?" her cheeks flushed, eyes blazed with fury. "You lied to me so you could go find that cache, didn't you?"

"Yes, but—"

"Did you break my sat link too?"

"Andy, if you'll just let me explain—"

"Explain what? How this is the find of a lifetime and how you just can't pass it up? How you thought I'd understand so you lied to me, led me in the opposite direction of the extraction point, putting us and the entire *world* at risk?"

"That's not it! I have my reasons, you're just going to have to trust me!"

"*Trust you?* You lied to my face and did exactly what I told you we can't do! Not to mention, I know something else is going on with you but you keep lying about that too!"

"I know, I'm sorry. It's complicated."

"What's complicated? I've seen you get tunnel vision on a project before but I have *never* known you to be so reckless."

"Exactly, so just trust me when I say I need to do this, that there's a lot more going on than finding some cache of artifacts. Please, Andy."

I could see her mind working, going over the options, over what she knew and what she'd seen. And I saw the exact moment when she decided to refuse me.

"No," she shook her head. "I'm sorry, this is too big. You need to tell me right now. What is *so* important that you'd risk the entire world for it?"

I gave a grunt of frustration and turned away.

"God damn it, Andy! Why can't you just fucking trust me?"

"We aren't married anymore, Luke! I'm not just going to roll over and trust that you know what you're doing!"

That was like a shot to the chest and I spun around, eyes wide.

"What the fuck is that supposed to mean?"

"It means that I let you get away with a lot on missions because we were together, because…because I was afraid to rock the boat. But I'm not willing to do that anymore. So you gotta give me something, or I'm taking that fucking compass and I'm taking us to the extraction point."

"Let me get away…what are you talking about?"

She opened and closed her mouth, tapping her foot on the ground as she tried to figure out how to answer me.

"The Grail, Luke," she finally said.

I closed my eyes and sighed.

"Fuck, that was an accident."

"You almost gave it to the man who is now running the Protectors, because you were so desperate to be the one to find it."

"So that Francesca didn't get her hands on it!"

"No," she shook her head, "you wanted the recognition, Luke. I could see it."

"If you're saying that I wanted to be the first person at the Archive to hold the Grail in five hundred years, then yeah, you're damn right I wanted to find it. I'd devoted years of my life to that project, it had taken over everything."

"Exactly! And now there's a whole cave of Grail-like artifacts for you to find. Luke Turner, the legend of the Archive."

"Fuck you, Andy," I advanced her this time, my body shaking with rage. "It was always easy for you! All you had to do was shoot a gun or punch a face while I had to think of *everything*! Every clue, every possible pit fall, every contingency if it turned out not to be where I thought it was. You go on a mission and it's a few months and then you go on to the next, mission *accomplished*. You have no idea what it's like to fight with everyone, including yourself, for years to find *one* thing, to feel like you achieved the aim."

She swallowed, eyes wide with shock that I'd challenged her.

"It was never easy for me," she rasped after a second. "You have any idea how frightening it is, to be a shield? How terrible it feels to take a life? I don't just shoot a gun or punch a face. I kill, I injure, and I protect. I convince myself, before and after every mission, that the lives I take are in service to something greater, something that deserves it. And when…when I was with you, it was easy to convince myself in some ways, because I was protecting *you*. But don't stand there and tell me it was always easy, because it wasn't. Not even a little. I don't get to just forget about it all at the end of a mission. I carry that around for months, sometimes years. Don't you *dare* diminish what I do and the price I pay to do it any more than you want me to diminish *your* sacrifices."

I wanted to take her in my arms and hold her, or shake her, or kiss her breathless, or maybe all three. But instead I just stood there, staring at her, our chests heaving with the force of our emotions.

"I'm sorry," I said. "I didn't mean to make you feel like your job wasn't hard."

"Well, you did," she shook her head and murmured, "You always did."

I was taken aback by that and frowned.

"What the hell does that mean?"

"Nothing, I don't want to get into it."

"You opened this fucking can of worms!"

"No, Luke, *you* did! Now if you want this fucking cache so badly you have exactly thirty seconds to make your case before I march your ass to the extraction point."

She wasn't going to let this go, and I knew that I didn't have a choice. It was tell her the truth about everything, or lie again and risk her making the situation worse by taking my only way of finding this stupid town.

But when I opened my mouth to say the words, they stuck in my throat. I had only admitted to myself that I had Vanquis Bellua, no one else. Andy would be the first person I told, the first time I said it out loud and I found myself completely unable to do it, as if saying it would seal the deal and I'd end up condemned to suffer through it no matter what.

"Luke, c'mon, just tell me!"

"I'm trying!"

"What could be this hard to say?"

"I'm dying, Andy!"

The words flew out of my mouth, cracked with panic and anguish.

She stared at me, mouth open as if she were about to say something and froze.

"What?" she breathed after a moment.

"I...I have Vanquis Bellua. I'm...I'm dying."

Andy just stared at me, the truth coiling between us, a fearful specter that had changed everything in a moment. She knew exactly what this disease could do; she'd gone with me to say goodbye to my uncle. He'd been in the final stages, sedated in a twilight state to help with the pain, half blind and not recognizing anyone. I knew she was envisioning the same end for me, just as I had done hundreds of times.

I could see her mind trying to process it all as her mouth opened and closed. She reached for me and then withdrew and then reached again, this time clasping my fore arms in her hands.

"W-when did you find out?" she choked out.

"About a month after you left."

I didn't think her eyes could get any wider but they did, and her face flushed with emotion.

"Why didn't you tell me?"

I frowned at her and shook my head.

"Seriously? You left, Andy. I wasn't going to bring you back into my life out of guilt. If you weren't there because you loved me then I didn't want you there at all."

It came out far harsher than I'd intended, loaded with all the feelings of abandonment and heartbreak I'd carried around for so long. The words stung; I could tell by the way she wouldn't look me in the eye.

"You still should've told me."

"And what then? You come back so you can watch me slowly deteriorate? No thanks."

"Maybe I wanted to be there."

I pulled my arms free and put some distance between us. I didn't want to tell her how much I'd wanted her with me since I found out, how many nights I'd spent shaking with fear and crying alone. But I was so tired of being the vulnerable one that she had to save, the one that enabled her to hide her own pain and fear behind the excuse of needing to be my shield.

I should've said some approximation of any of that. But I couldn't stand the thought of being that damn vulnerable with her right now.

"You left," I finally said, turning my back to her, "and when you did, you forfeited any right to know this. You're going to have to accept that."

She made a choking sound behind me and I turned around to find her hand clamped over her mouth, tears streaming down her red face as she sobbed. I could count on one hand the amount of times I'd seen Andy really, truly cry so the sight of her completely overcome hit me like a punch to the gut.

I didn't think, just reacted and pulled her into my arms. Andy clung to me as she sobbed into my chest.

"I-I'm sorry," she gulped. "I'm s-so sorry, Luke."

I sighed and ran my hand up and down her back, unsure exactly what she was sorry about. Was she sorry I was dying? Was she sorry she'd left like she had? Or was it something else, and did it really matter?

"Don't feel sorry for me," I soothed. "I don't want your pity."

"Not pity," she looked up at me, face red and tear streaked. "I wasn't there this whole time because…because of how I'd left. If I'd just…"

She shook herself and clenched her jaw. Classic Andy for when things got too real and she was having a hard time handling it. I'd always let her do it too, figured it was just her. But what if it was one of the things that had torn us apart? What if I'd pushed to see those parts she hid and proved to her that she could trust me with them? Would it have made a difference?

"If you'd just what?" I asked.

"Nothing."

I let out another long breath and released her.

"Yeah, sure."

Andy's lips parted and she frowned up at me, confused by my reaction and I just didn't have it in me to push. Like she'd said before, we weren't married anymore. Just as I didn't need to enable her to avoid her feelings, so I didn't get to dig into them either. So I stepped back and began packing up my notes.

"There's an artifact that has a cure for Vanquis," I said. "If I can find it, and convince Director Dearborne to reopen the Medical Research Department, I know I can help create the cure."

Andy sniffled and wiped her palms up and down on her pant leg.

"Okay," she took a breath, squared her shoulders, the perfect picture of a soldier compartmentalizing for the mission.

"I know you have orders," I continued, "so I'm not asking you to help me. I need the compass to reach the town that has the last clue to where the cache is. Once I'm there, you can take the compass and go to the extraction point. Tell them you lost me or whatever. I'll go along with whatever story you create."

I looked up after a minute because she hadn't said a word. Andy was rebraiding her long hair, her face a mask of determination.

"I'm going with you," she said. "I'll help you find this thing and get you home."

I stood up, shock barreled through me.

"Andy, you don't have—"

"I'm doing it, Luke. I know you probably think this is guilt for not being there and maybe it is a little. But…you're one of my best friends, no matter what's happened in the past. If there's a chance in hell that there's something that will save your life, then I'm helping you find it."

"What about your orders? What about keeping the world safe from the Protectors getting their hands on those artifacts?"

She swallowed, a war waged in the way she avoided my gaze and spent too much time tucking in her tank top. When she looked at me her brown eyes swam in tears that she scrubbed from her face when they fell. Her mouth trembled, throat strained as if she were holding something back.

Finally, when she spoke, I knew that it wasn't what she really wanted to say, and a jolt of disappointment hit me, even though it shouldn't have. Andy didn't owe me anything, much less her truth.

"You let me worry about all that," she said, the words hard. "You concentrate on finding the damn thing."

I could only stare at her, speechless. In all the time I'd known Andy, the mission, her orders were sacrosanct. It was one of the reasons she'd had such a hard time working with me and the rest of the Agents that were trying to overthrow Francesca. For Andy, being a good soldier was part of her inner compass. She'd only ever broken it when it had become absolutely clear that Francesca was a threat to the world and needed to be eliminated. Now here she was, going directly against her orders. For *me*.

Maybe…maybe she still has feelings for me.

I shook those thoughts right out of my head and started to help Andy stow the hammock. As much as I still loved her, Andy was the one that walked away in the first place.

Besides, do I really want her to start up anything with me just because I'm dying? Do I want a pity fuck?

I hated the way my body responded to that question, my dick answering very much in the affirmative. But I clamped down on such thoughts because it wasn't going to help anything. Andy said this was about friendship, and even though I had my suspicions that there was another reason, I highly doubted it was because she wanted to fuck my brains out one more time.

Stop thinking about fucking…think about the booby traps waiting for us…boobies, God I miss her tits…nope! Stop it!

"You want some?" she asked.

"Huh, what? No!" I gave her a nervous snort and shook my head. And then realized that she was holding out a ration pouch.

"Um, are you sure?" she asked with a confused frown.

"Sorry, I was just, um, thinking about other…things. Yeah, food sounds good, thanks."

Andy handed me two of the ready mix ration pouches. They were grainy and one note, not at all appealing in any way. But I was grateful for the distraction nonetheless because Andy seemed far too preoccupied with her rations to figure out why I'd been acting so weird.

In an effort to keep my own mind on task, I took out the map and started to let Andy in on where we were going. We sat down on the nearby log we'd used last night and I spread the map out between us. The mission was safe, somewhat neutral ground now that the truth of it was out there. I could retreat to this with her, like I always did, and all the problems, the messy debris of what we never said didn't matter. It was both a relief and something that was starting to chafe, like sand in a clam. Only I was certain whatever happened, we weren't going to be able to turn this into a pearl.

"The priest that hid the cache founded a small town that should be right around here," I said, refocusing and pointed at the map. "It's not on any map and many believe God hid the place from any who would seek out the artifacts for selfish reasons."

"So that would mean that the cache is near the town."

"It's possible. All the clues so far lead me to believe that it's in a cave, but which one? There's an intricate network of them near the town, both in the mountains and on the coast. We'd spend months searching and probably still not find it. Also, there's an indication that the priest constructed booby traps in places that were false entry points to further confuse people."

"So, the town has the clue that will narrow it down then."

I nodded.

"That's what I think, yes, specifically the chapel in the town. There's very little written about the priest, but both times the chapel is mentioned it's described as his heaven on earth. And, there's one account of a woman who went to the chapel with her dying child asking for a miracle. When she left, her child was completely healed and neither of them ever had any illness again. I tried to find other stories of miracles at the chapel, but wherever I look, there tends to be a dead end. Which leads me to believe that people have been covering up its existence all this time."

"And why do that if there's nothing there to hide?"

"Precisely! Now," I dug around and pulled out a plastic covered map, "these are all the map fragments I've been able to find in books, on tomb markers, and other places. The priest left clues to find the cache but only for the faithful, the truly pure hearted. There's one piece missing and I think it's in that chapel. In fact, I think it was buried with him."

"What makes you think that?"

I flipped through the pages of one of my journals until I came to the drawing I was looking for. It was a small wooden carved cross, the size that someone would have on a rosary.

"This is a cross that many believe was carried by Galahad himself when he and the other Knights of the Round table went in search of the Grail."

"Was it really carried by Galahad?" she asked.

I shrugged.

"The number of artifacts that are attributed to Galahad is enormous. There's an entire sub-basement for them, and most are only powerful because someone believed them to once belong to Galahad. But, in this case? Yes, I think this is a Galahad artifact. Now, look at this." I dug out a cloudy, almost destroyed photograph and handed it to Andy. "This is the only picture to survive from the archive agent that found the town. That's the priest and it's hard to see, but the rosary he's holding—"

"Has the cross on it," Andy gasped.

"Yes! I think he was buried with it to ensure that no one found his remains or the final piece of the map unless they had a true, pure heart."

"And that's you," she smiled at me.

I ran a hand up and down the back of my head, and heat rushed to my face.

"I don't know about that. The level of pure heartedness we're talking about here is, frankly, legendary. But I have hope that because I'm not seeking it for myself alone, it will make all the difference."

"I know it will, it has to," she said, a slight tremble in her voice at the end. "So let's get moving. You need to tell me what clues we're looking for in the chapel and also what artifact you're looking for. I need the details if I'm going to help."

She started pulling on her pack and I put my hand on her shoulder, my throat tight as I realized just what she was risking to help me and my people.

"Andy," I said, "thank you for this."

She didn't meet my eye, but she did grab my hand and squeeze.

"You never have to thank me, Luke. Not for this."

CHAPTER SEVEN
ANDROMEDA

I don't know how I managed to keep the tears at bay as I followed Luke into the forest.

If someone had stabbed me with a knife in the gut, it would've hurt less than hearing that Luke had Vanquis. He wasn't mine to lose anymore, I'd shut that door when I'd left. But the thought of the world spinning and Luke not being a part of it nearly sent me to my knees with grief.

The nutritional paste was threatening to come back up and I had to bite my cheeks to keep a sob from escaping. I'd known, the second I could think past the panic, that there was only one choice in front of me. I'd spill my own blood and burn this fucking world down before I let him die. It didn't matter that we couldn't be together after this; all that mattered was that Luke lived a long, beautiful life.

"So," I said, clearing the clog of emotion from my throat, "tell me about this artifact. What are we looking for?"

Distract me from my guilt and terror. Let me listen to that big brain of yours, you gorgeous green hottie.

Luke's grin was so delighted it hurt. He always loved spilling knowledge like wine when we were together. I'd sit and listen to him gush for hours about ancient Sumerian burial practices, or the journey of this object or that object through history. Half of it I didn't quite understand, especially when he started speaking Latin, but I loved the way his face lit up like a kid on Christmas, with unabashed joy.

"We're looking for a book," he said with an eyebrow waggle.

I couldn't help laughing.

"Don't you have enough of those?" I asked with a nod to his pack.

"This book is special. It was written by the Medieval mystic and polymath Hildegard of Bingen."

He stopped and smiled wide, his eyes even wider, clearly so very excited about a woman I'd never heard of.

I nodded, giving him what I hoped was an equally enthusiastic grin.

"Wow," I said somewhat sarcastically, "that's great."

"You don't know who that is do you?"

"Not a fucking clue, no."

Luke took a deep breath, but not out of frustration. This was more like someone who was about to dive into their absolutely favorite thing in the world and they wanted to make sure they had enough air to get through it.

"Hildegard was so many things - a linguist who invented her own language, a counselor to kings and popes, the founder of an abbey devoted to a life of service, a prophet and politician, mathematician, scientist. Modern day feminists, musicians, new age practitioners, they all hold her up as a wonder, reading her works even today! She lived into her eighties, which, in that time, was incredibly long. She wrote several important religious works. Most were her visions that she believed God was giving her. Oh, Andy, it would take me hours to tell you about her life! The fact that she escaped being branded a heretic when she constantly gave God female pronouns and form in her visions is astounding! But not just that, she was a visionary for my people too. At a time when we were in hiding because glamours hadn't been perfected yet and so many of us were being killed because everyone thought we were demons, Hildegard saw us as something else, she saw us as blessed by her God. Of course, that's not true, but it afforded us protection in the area around Disibodenberg where her original abbey was founded. She even took some of us on as servants or nuns and monks."

Luke was waving his hands around as he spoke, the wedding ring catching the light, and I tried my best not to let the guilt rise up again. He needed me focused, sharp. Wallowing in what I'd fucked up wasn't going to help the situation.

"Okay, so she was smart and courageous, saw visions and the female side of God. What does this have to do with Vanquis?"

He nodded enthusiastically.

"So, since she was close to the Orcs that lived in the settlement near Disibodenberg, she saw Vanquis Bellua first hand. There are even some who say she gave the disease its name. She prayed, sought counsel and did experiments to figure out different treatments. According to what I've been able to find, Hildegard believed she had a vision from God about how to cure the disease. When she and her fellow nuns created the 'potion' and blessed it in a specific way, it cured the disease."

"That's incredible," I said, "but how do you know it's in this book? And why isn't it better known if this Hildegard is so well known?"

"Her visions were…well, *poetic*, I suppose you could say. Like most prophets, different people could interpret what she was writing different-ly. And since my people were so reviled, and Hildegard had to constantly guard against being branded a heretic, she likely had to code the cure within her prophecies and art. Of all the books she wrote in her lifetime, few originals survive, but there are two that are quite famous. I believe that the cure was hidden in a copy of her work called Scivias, one of two extremely rare books that had illustrations done by Hildegard herself. Now, her books have been copied hundreds, even thousands of times, but throughout history, her works have been caught up in book burnings and religious purges. One of the last known copies of the Scivias was locked in a vault with a rare copy of one of her other books, the Riesencodex, in Dresden during the second World War. The city was bombed soon after, and when the vault containing the books was found unharmed, it was discovered that the Scivias had disappeared."

He paused, letting me digest all of that. While I didn't have Luke's gift for sifting through mountains of books, clues and archaic languages to find the answers to mysteries most had given up on, I was just fine taking the clues he found and working with him to see the bigger picture.

Something he'd taught me over the years.

The thought hit me right in chest, and a warmth spread through me. I'd never considered myself stupid, but certainly nothing close to the intelligence of the Orc walking next to me. Yet, I realized that his patience and belief in my intelligence had given me the ability to develop this skill. Luke had made me a better agent and I hadn't even realized it until this moment.

I swallowed the now constant lump in my throat and focused on the information he'd just gushed about.

"If it was in Dresden, does that mean the Third Reich could've possibly stolen the Scivias?"

"That's my thought. Though, why take one and not the other, I'm not sure. The Riesencodex was in a very heavy, large box for its own protection, so perhaps it was more about opportunity since the Scivias is much smaller. All I know, is that from what I was able to uncover, the Scivias somehow made it into the cache of artifacts that the Nazi officers brought with them to Argentina."

"Do you think you'll be able to find the cure if it's in code or in some of her art?"

"I've been studying her works nonstop since I first had the theory of the cure in the Scivias, so yes, I'm confident I can. But I'm also fairly certain that there was a religious artifact involved in the creation of the cure. Which is why I need the Archive to allow me access to their warehouse."

"And to reopen the Medical Research Department."

Luke nodded.

"It's a long shot," he admitted, his enthusiasm tempered. "I know that Francesca used that department for unconscionable things, but I also have to believe that it can be remade into something better, something good. And I know I'm doing this for somewhat self-serving reasons but I want to take what I can do and apply it to something that will make so many lives better."

I snagged his thick fingers with mine and pulled us both to a stop. I couldn't stop the burn of tears as I looked up at him.

"You're not selfish for wanting this." My voice was thick with emotion. "I know you can do this, that you're the right person to make that department what it always should've been. We're going to find that book and fix this."

My face crumpled and suddenly I was pulled against him just like this morning. I nuzzled against his chest, breathing in his scent, while my hands clutched at his back. I wanted to memorize all of this, imprint it so hard that it was always with me, no matter what happened.

"I know something is eating at you," his voice rumbled under my ear. "I know you were hiding it this morning. You can trust me, Andy. You always could."

He said with so much sincerity that I just wanted to take a leap of faith and spill the ugly truth to him. Even with all the things I'd tried to hide from him, Luke still saw more of who I was than anyone in my life, even my family. It was one of the things that simultaneously made me hold onto him so long, and made me feel like I had to leave before he did.

I looked up at him, that handsome face with the perfectly bitable square jaw, the kind eyes behind glasses that made him look like a sexy Clark Kent.

Luke brushed some hair back from my face, thumbed away the stray tears and looked at me like I was a treasure. It disarmed me and I found my defenses melting by the second.

"I just…I hate the guilt lingering from the way we…the way *I* left everything. Luke— "

At that moment, the tree next to us splintered, and dirt flung up into our faces from gunfire behind us. That's when I heard the deep motor of some kind of rugged terrain motorcycle, three of them, closing in fast. The sharp report of another gun sent us both running.

We'd both been so distracted by this conversation that we hadn't heard the motorcycles as they'd crashed through the forest.

Stupid, stupid! I need to focus or neither of us are getting out of this alive.

We both ran blindly toward the cover of some thick foliage in front of us. It was futile, we'd never be able to out run those vehicles, but if we could make it there and hide…

That was when a military motorcycle with wide tires, front and back, with a dark green, slightly wider than average body out flanked us and cut us off from the cover. I turned, only to see two more behind us. All three riders wore motorcycle helmets and gloves, and green fatigues, which was strange since the ATVs weren't exactly stealthy. They leveled their guns at us and we put our hands up.

"We only need him," said one of the riders.

"You shoot her and I'll never go with you alive," Luke warned.

I gaped at him but didn't say a word.

"Yeah, right, no pussy is that good," said a different rider.

Luke let out a feral snarl and took a step forward.

"Can it!" said the rider that had cut us off. "We'll take both."

"We only have one set of cuffs," complained the rider that was currently getting off his motorcycle.

"Then cuff them together! Jesus! Do I have to think of everything?" said the one behind us.

Okay, they're a little incompetent, that could work for us.

When the rider grabbed Luke's left hand and my right and started to click the cuffs in place, I fell to my knees and clutched my stomach like I was hurt.

"Andy?" Luke asked.

"What's wrong with—ah!"

I leveled a punch right at the guy's dick and he collapsed. It was enough of a distraction for me to draw my gun. I spun to the one that seemed to be the leader and shot him twice in the chest before he could get a shot off.

"You bitch!" said the only one still upright.

He came at us, which was dumb since he had a fucking gun, but good for us. Luke swung back and punched him hard. And for what Luke may lack in panache, he more than made up for in brute strength.

The guy did a comical spin and landed on his ass on the dirt, his helmet cracked across the face plate. I turned to shoot the one I'd dick punched and the gun clicked. I was out of ammo.

"Fuck!"

"Come on!" Luke yanked on our joined wrists and pulled me to the motorcycle of the only rider I'd been able to shoot.

I managed to snag the gun on the ground before Luke and I both tried to get onto the seat, only to realize that with the way we were cuffed it was not going to work. The other two goons were getting to their feet and if we didn't get the hell out of here, it was going to get ugly.

I shoved Luke onto the seat and climbed on behind him, side saddle style. I'd seen Luke ride ATVs and motorcycles with his family, and I knew he was a much better driver than I was when it came to a vehicle like this.

"Go!" I shouted as I turned and shot the gun with my left hand.

Luke took off like a shot and my ass slipped on the sliver of seat it was on. I looked back and saw the other two pursuing us. I was a decent shot with my left hand, but I couldn't keep my balance the way I was sitting. I needed more stability, not slipping every few seconds while Luke jerked on my cuffed right wrist.

"I need to change positions!" I yelled.

"How?"

An idea flashed in my head, and while it would definitely put the two of us in a compromising position, I really didn't have a choice.

"Keep driving, I'm gonna move."

"Okay— oh, shit! What are you doing?"

Trying my best not to get knocked off the bike by branches and giant ass leaves, I set both feet on the foot plate, then slipped one leg in front of Luke, sliding myself under his arm and in front of him, chest to chest, crotch to crotch. Once my ass was settled on the saddle in front of him,

I wrapped my legs around his waist, ankles crossed. Like this, my cuffed hand was back where he was gripping the clutch and I held onto his wrist while my left arm wound under his arm so I could get a shot off a little steadier.

It was all very logical, very much in service to taking these goons out and not getting killed. In other words, it was necessary.

And it was also fucking *hot*.

The adrenaline was shooting through my system like a strange aphrodisiac that made me hyper aware of every place we touched. The delicious stretch of my inner thighs as my legs wrapped around the girth of Luke's hips.

And speaking of girth.

My crotch was lined up perfectly to his, though, because I was sitting up so I could look over his shoulder, it hovered just above the Jolly Green Giant's pants. But my breasts? Those were smashed tight against his hard chest and I couldn't miss the way his breath hitched. I met his gaze as he glanced at me, our mouths so damn close that it wouldn't take much to press my lips to his. But then his focus snapped back to navigating the rainforest, and the bullets hitting the trees around us caused my libido to cool.

The mission Andy, focus on the mission. We need to not die here, so get it together.

I sat up as tall as I could, thighs clenched tight around his waist. I suppressed every memory of what it felt like to have him driving into me like this as I raised the semi-automatic and fired.

CHAPTER EIGHT

LUKE

I'd be fucking lying if I said that this right here hadn't always been a fantasy of mine.

Okay, maybe not the fleeing through the forest with bullets zinging past me part. But the part where Andy was straddling me on a motorcycle?

Oh, hell yeah.

She kept doing these little pulses up and down, her thighs clenching around me and conjuring up memories of the times they were around my face as I drank her orgasm from the source.

Or when I'd fuck her against a wall.

Or in bed.

Basically any time I fucked her that wasn't from behind.

Okay, getting a semi right now is pretty messed up. Focus! We are running for our lives…and now she's brushing up against the tip of my dick. I don't know if this is heaven or hell.

It wasn't just the physical position, it was Andy with her game face on, the way she turned from sexy every day woman to avenging goddess. It always made me want to worship her on my knees, my mouth on her pussy, sucking her clit between my teeth while she pulled my hair.

I hit a rough spot that I would've seen if I hadn't been distracted by the press of Andy's body against mine and she screamed.

"Sorry," I offered.

"I got one," she shouted, "but the other one is still back there. I'm running out of ammo."

Bullets pinged against the back of the bike, and I swerved as Andy cried out.

"Are you hit?"

"No, it was close though."

"We gotta lose this guy!"

I was well practiced at maneuvering these kinds of motorcycles but my joints were starting to ache and I worried that if they weakened, I'd lose reaction time and hurt Andy.

"I have an idea, you gotta trust me though!" she shouted.

"Okay."

"Get more distance between us if you can. When I say, I want you to stop and turn the bike so my left hand is facing out. I need to get a steady shot, he's squirreling."

With anyone else, I'd say they were crazy. But not Andy. I trusted her with my very life, as evidenced by the fact that even though it was going against every bit of what my instincts were screaming at me, I did exactly what she said.

There was a clearing ahead of us, and the moment I broke the tree line, I gunned it, putting stress on the engine that made me wince. I was just at the edge of the clearing when I pulled up fast and turned the bike so that Andy was able to swing her arm around just as we came to jerky stop. She lined up her shot as the other guy came into the clearing and also brought his gun up. My breath stalled in my chest as I waited and at the last minute, Andy fired her last two bullets into the goon. He fell with a thump as his motorcycle veered wildly and crashed.

We let out a long breath of relief, and Andy slumped against me. I pressed a kiss to the top of her head and for a moment, I just relaxed into the feel of our bodies against one another. I curled an arm behind her and pulled her closer, the thud of our hearts meeting against our rib cages.

"That was close," she whispered.

"Yeah," I whispered gazing down at her.

Andy's legs were still wrapped tightly around my hips, her hot center pressed against my now fully erect cock. The sounds of the forest faded to the back of my mind; the fact that we were being hunted, that we'd just narrowly avoided being captured or killed was a distant worry as my entire body lit up against hers.

This is how it had always been for us. Run for our lives and then fuck each other's brains out because we were so damn grateful to be alive and have one another. It was also one our problems because we'd thought we could build a marriage on that adrenaline.

There was a mountain of reasons why I should push her away, why I should get off this motorcycle, or at the very least get the hell out of here. But Andy's bright eyes locked onto mine, her panting breaths mingled with mine, and every single one of those reasons seemed to pale in comparison to the raw need that raged through me.

She'd leave at the end of this.

It would kill me to lose her again.

This wouldn't fix anything.

In fact, it would make it worse.

I'd be a damn fool for giving in.

But...

"Fuck it," I breathed and took her mouth in mine.

I kissed her like I'd been wanting to every moment since she left: with a hungry, savage instinct that would suffer nothing short of everything she had. I scored her lips with my teeth and thrust my tongue into her mouth, imprinting myself on her, punishing her for depriving me of the taste of her for so long. My tusks scratched along the outside of her mouth, and a spark of delight hit me at the thought of her wearing those marks for the rest of the mission, signaling to everyone that she was mine.

Mine...mine...

It sang in my blood as I yanked her hips tighter to me and started dry humping against her. We were fully clothed in the middle of a forest, with a dead body cooling a few feet away, but I didn't give a shit. Andy was giving it as good as she got, her body grinding in tandem with me. I was wound tight enough that a few more minutes of this and I'd be coming in my pants.

Too soon…I haven't had enough yet.

Her cuffed hand yanked against mine as she tried to bring it up to touch me. But that ember of lust fueled anger was quickly building to a full blown inferno and I didn't want to give her control just yet.

So I pulled her hand behind her back with my arm, pinning it there, while my other hand went to the button of her pants. I needed the tight heat of her pussy around my fingers, to feel the moment I made her come apart.

"Luke," she gasped as my lips bit and sucked down the perfect column of her throat. "Please…"

"That's right," I breathed against her skin, "beg me, Andy. Beg me for what you want."

I may have been filthy when we'd fucked in the past but taking control like this? This was new, and if the glitter of fire in her eyes was any indication, Andy liked it.

I slipped my hand into her unbuttoned pants and past the waist of her panties, but I hovered just above her clit, and drew little circles on her mons while she swirled her hips. The little mewling sounds she made while I left marks all along her skin and teased her was almost too much for me and I started to buck, desperate for my own friction.

"Put your hand on me," I commanded, "jack me like a good girl."

Andy took in a sharp inhale and stared at me, mouth swollen and gaping in shock.

"You want me to play with this pussy?" I asked, almost not recognizing my own voice. It was harsh, deep and dark, filled to the brim with anger and need. And she heard it, and wasn't afraid.

I slid one finger between her soaked folds and Andy's eyes rolled back. But a taste was all I gave her. I devoured the tiny sob that escaped her lips as I withdrew back to her mons and played with curls there.

"Do you?" I asked.

"Yes," she whimpered.

"Then you know what I want, Andy."

"You're not the only one."

I chuckled as she fumbled with one hand to unbutton my shorts. It probably would've helped if I could take my mouth off her for a second but the moment my tongue grazed her skin, Andy's taste exploded on my tongue and I was ravenous for more. I'd dreamed of her skin, craved her for so long that if this was it, my last chance, I was going to suck and bite every exposed inch I could find.

I was mid bite when her strong fingers closed around me and I groaned hard against her throat.

"Andy…Andy."

Her grip tightened as my fingers slid down to her supple pearl. I loved playing with her, so sensitive and swollen against the pad of my finger.

We fell into a familiar rhythm with no effort, our hands working one another as our hips thrust in tandem. Our groans and gasps rose into the damp air and I never wanted it to end even as I chased that finish alongside of her. I was home, for the first time in a year. There was no gaping hollowness in my chest, no sense of loss. Here, in this impossible moment, in this impossible place with this beautifully impossible woman, I was whole again.

"Andy," I moaned again.

"Yes…there…fill me, Luke…"

Incapable of denying her, I plunged two fingers into her tight cunt and curled them as the heel of my palm pressed against her clit.

Her mouth popped off mine and she let loose an obscenely low, drawn out moan that ended on a series of syllables that were complete gibberish. I wanted those sounds, the breath they rode on. They were mine and I would not be denied. I worked her harder as I crushed my mouth to hers and thrust my tongue into her in time with my fingers.

I was on a hair trigger, so fucking close just from the way Andy was reacting to my touch, that when she seemed to remember that I was in her hand and began to stroke me roughly, I saw stars and lost my last thread of rational thought.

Our hips ground and thrust in erratic patterns as we savagely spurred one another on to a finish we both desperately needed. When Andy's inner muscles contracted and a rush of wet heat hit my fingers, her scream echoed through the clearing and I wasn't far behind.

I came with a raw cry of her name, my body convulsed against hers as I painted her hand and my stomach with a release that had me seeing stars. It was impossible to know how long I sat there, my fingers still inside of her, head resting in the crook of her neck as the two of us panted and slowly came back down to reality.

"Andy," I whispered against her skin, a holy benediction on my lips.

Her lips grazed my ear and temple, breath coasted in warm flutters against my skin, cooling the sweat there.

"We should…get cleaned up," she whispered.

I nodded but neither of us moved for another few minutes. I was reluctant to break the post climax haze that had settled over us, obscuring the broken shards of our marriage that lay between us.

But then Andy pulled back and I had to raise my head from her shoulder. The moment was gone, and now it was back to business.

My chest felt like it was caving in, but I managed to get my pack off and find the package of body wipes. We didn't say anything, and Andy avoided my gaze as she wiped me off her fingers. I wasn't sure what she felt about this, other than she'd been as keyed up as I'd been. But what about now? Afterwards we would usually joke, hold each other or something. This tense silence was new and unnerving.

Mentally, I retreated to the safe space of the mission, just like before at our camp site. It was empty and unsatisfying, but it was also safe and that's what I needed right now. A place I could secretly nurse my disappointment and broken heart without her noticing.

"I want to see if he's got the keys to these things," Andy said, gesturing to the body on the other end of the clearing with our cuffed hands.

"Sure," I nodded and followed after her.

The smell of blood hit me before we were within range and I clenched my jaw against the immediate bile that flooded my throat.

"Puke over there if you have to," Andy smirked at me as she bent down to search the guy.

I could only nod. If I opened my mouth, I would vomit for sure. Andy made short work of searching the dead man's clothes and the small pouch at his waist.

"Oh, thank God," she said, holding up a small set of keys.

I nodded again and turned up wind, taking a long inhale of the crisp forest air.

"He's also got a gun…some ammo and…holy shit."

I turned to see a small black box with a few buttons and a knob in the middle.

"Is that a sat link? It looks like…erm…" I burped and turned away.

"Come on, let's get minimum safe distance from that blood."

Again, I nodded, grateful that she didn't sound put out, and followed her back to our motorcycle and my back pack. Once we were there I took several big breaths, concentrating on the individual scents of the bike, the soil beneath our feet, the foliage around us, and Andy, whose smell still lingered on my fingertips.

She went to work with the keys and unlocked the cuffs, which she stuffed into her back pocket and then looked at the small box.

"This might answer how they found us," she sat, a deep frown wrinkling her forehead.

"Other than the fact that it looks an awful lot like the one Sprite made for you, how so?"

"Is it possible the Protectors put a tracker in your stuff?"

"Shit, I hadn't thought of that."

We went through my pack, careful of the delicate map and other pieces of paper I'd managed to pilfer from the Archive library and my captors. There was nothing in my books or pencils. Nothing in my glasses or clothes. But when Andy started feeling around the lining of my bag, she found a small cylindrical device.

"How did they get that in there?" I asked.

Andy's lips pressed together and she shook her head.

"This is Archive made. I recognize Sprite's handy work anywhere."

I frowned, a sick feeling spread through me, cold and oily.

"Why would the Archive be tracking me?"

She stomped on the device and ground her foot on top of the remnants.

"The director knew where you were, it was too precise and I should've questioned it more," her voice was hard, distant but I recognized the anger underneath it. "Where did you get this pack?"

I swallowed.

"Sprite gave it to me with supplies. If they've been tracking me, then they must've had their doubts about me."

"It also means that the Protectors might have figured out how to piggy back off our signal and are using it track us."

"Oh, shit," I gasped, eyes wide. "Andy, if the Archive was tracking us—"

"Then they know that we're not going to the extraction point. They're coming for us. We gotta get out of here, now."

I grabbed her arm before she tried to get back onto the motorcycle.

"You can't stay with me, they'll know you're helping me. Disobeying orders with possible consequences of this magnitude will end your career."

"I don't care about that."

"Andy—"

She reached up and yanked my face down to hers. With a whimper, her mouth claimed mine. Fire shot through me at the contact and I pulled her against me as I plundered her mouth. The moment she yielded her lips to me, opening herself to my tongue, everything rushed through my mind on a tidal wave. Her taste, vanilla and campfire, burst on my senses and I was dragged out of that distance I'd just established in my mind, pulled helplessly into her orbit. My hands trembled as they raced down her spine, cupped her ass one moment and then her hips, up the side of her body to her face, where my huge hands framed her beloved features.

I'd just been knuckle deep inside of her and I was still ravenous, as if I hadn't touched her at all in ages.

I haven't, not really. One quick finger fuck isn't going to do it. I need her.

When she pulled away, her lips were pink and swollen, and there were new red marks on either side of her upper lips from my tusks. A possessive jolt went through me and I wanted to lick and bite every inch of her, wipe away anyone else's touch until she was covered in *me*. My scent, my tusk marks, the bruises from my teeth.

"You are more important than my career, Luke. If they don't like it, they can kiss my ass."

"Andy—"

"Come on, we need to get to this town, get the next clue."

I wanted to yank her back to me, and try to convince her to leave but she was right; we did have to get out of here before the Archive or the Protectors found us.

I straddled the bike and Andy's arms went around my middle as I started it up again, her front pressed into my back. I couldn't help it, I took one of her hands and pressed a hungry kiss to her palm. She gave a hissing gasp and shuddered behind me.

"Later, big boy," she said with a breathy chuckle.

Relief swept through me. She wasn't going to keep her distance, she wanted me too.

"I'll hold you to that," I said, and rode out of the clearing.

CHAPTER NINE
ANDROMEDA

The throb of Luke's heart against my palm was a constant reminder of how he had pulsed in my hand as he came. I'd locked away so many memories of us just so I could move on that I'd forgotten how powerful it felt to make him come apart like that. His dick was a fucking work of art, thick and hot when it was hard. A long vein ran along the underside and his foreskin hugged the dark green tip so perfectly. I remembered all the times I'd ran my tongue along the edge of his foreskin, lapping up his precum and driving him to the very edge in minutes.

I was hungry for that and a thousand other things that were now flooding my mind.

My lips stung a bit from the scratches of his tusks and I reveled in it, proud of how he'd marked me. But then I remembered that all of this was temporary. The mission would end, they always did, and what then? We'd go back to our lives, me likely to being fired and Luke to possibly being censured for stealing what the Archive thought of as their property.

Real life is what waited for us.

The everyday life that we'd been so fucking imperfect at navigating together. Hell, I was bad at it on my own; with Luke I'd felt like a disaster. Even when he'd seemed happy, I'd worried that I was somehow falling short, that he was keeping things from me the same way I was from him.

After the divorce, my therapist told me this was 'projection'. I hadn't really been invested in the therapy though since it was Archive mandated, and couldn't quite remember what she'd advised for it.

Guess I should've actually paid attention to the woman.

Was it too late to change? I'd already destroyed our marriage, broken his heart and mine. Was it possible to get a second chance at us, to actually air out everything and make it right? With the exception of how this mission had started, what was developing between Luke and me felt good, it felt *right*. But did that mean I should reopen all our wounds and ask him to try again?

I hugged him tighter, as if I could delay all these questions by just holding on to him. But that was just like a kid, closing their eyes to try and hide from a nightmare.

Besides, there were more important things to worry about at the moment. Namely why the fuck the Archive had been tracking him, and how the hell had I missed out on that fact.

The answer to the second question was simple if I was being honest with myself. I'd missed the obvious clues because Luke had been in trouble and no matter how professional I'd been, the second I'd known that, nothing else mattered.

But the first question, that was the one that had my instincts on overdrive. Francesca had created such a hostile, fearful environment that it was a constant game of Russian Roulette when it came to trusting anyone. They might be on your side today, but tomorrow could be a different story. The only allegiances I'd been sure of during that time had been Luke and Derek Dearborne, the current director's son who had spear headed the rebellion. Everyone else was suspect, kept at arms' length.

Marcus did tell me to be careful, that there was something else going on here. But what? What is the director's angle in all this? If she wanted the artifacts, why tell me to extract Luke before he can get to them? Or maybe she knew

I'd fold. Maybe that's why she sent me, because she needed someone to blame if this whole thing goes tits up.

That set my blood on fire, and not in the fun way Luke had a few hours ago.

I'd had enough of being used. And I'd definitely had more than my fair share of trying to find the angles in every single order. Staying at the Archive after Francesca hadn't been easy, but it had felt like the right choice. What if it wasn't? What if I was getting set up to take the fall for something?

The director better not try that shit with me. I'll bury her.

My quick willingness to go after my CO was startling but also felt *right.*

What the fuck? I'm not that kind of person, but then again here I am, rebelling again.

I sighed and pressed my forehead into Luke's back. Everything felt jumbled and broken. Usually, a sense of duty was a security blanket for me. It simplified everything, gave me a clear goal and path. But now I was starting to wonder if Francesca had eroded that simple, pure drive of mine.

Or maybe it's just life. Nothing is black and white, going against Francesca had taught me that. So maybe I need to go with my gut on this mission. Do the thing that feels right instead of what the mission, and the Archive, deems as right.

"You okay, did you fall asleep?" Luke asked.

I looked up and hadn't realized that we'd stopped. Behind us, the forest stretched out, dense and beautiful in so many shades of green accented by bright yellows, oranges and pinks from the flowers that bloomed. I thought I could hear a waterfall in the distance and my gaze swung around to what was in front of us. We were on a small hill; the forest had given way to a pristine beach in the distance to the left and below us was a tiny town, the buildings stretched out in a grid from what appeared to be a town square of some kind. At this distance, it was hard to tell. But north of the town, just barely visible, was a lone building with a cross at the top of what could've been a bell tower.

"Are we here?" I asked.

"I think so. I need to get closer to tell but from everything I've discovered, all the clues, I think this is it."

I expected him to charge forward. This was the last stop before we found the one thing that could save his and so many others' lives. But Luke sat there, the bike rumbling beneath us. I sat up, my butt coming off the seat and leaned over Luke's shoulder to try and see his face.

"What's wrong?"

"This is it," he whispered, "if I can't find what I'm looking for here, I've got no other direction. What if I'm wrong, Andy? What if I've dragged you into this, killed your career and put you in danger and it's for nothing?"

My heart squeezed at his words, the naked vulnerability in them. In all the years I'd known him, I'd never heard Luke so afraid that he'd made a mistake of this kind. I realized then that the disease was either frightening him to a level that had Luke completely doubting himself, or this was just one more thing he'd kept hidden from me while we were married. The thought made me angry, and a little betrayed.

He'd always pushed me to open up, telling me I could trust him when…Calm down, Andy. You don't know that for sure. And besides, different things need my attention right now.

I slid off the bike and then back on so that I was sitting side saddle in front of him. He curled one arm around me and pulled me tight against him, taking a deep breath of my hair as I wound my arms around his shoulders.

"You're the smartest person I've ever met," I said, "and no matter what is going on with you, no matter the difficulties you've faced, I believe in you. This is it, I can feel it. We are going to find what we are looking for and we are then going to find that book."

He let out a long breath, some of the tension bleeding out of his body.

"And the Archive? The Protectors?" he asked.

We were under a ticking clock, we both knew it. But I didn't want to reinforce that pressure on Luke; he was putting enough on himself.

"If they find us, I'll handle the Archive. But I think we've got enough of a head start and they may know what direction we're going in, but they don't know the destination. That gives us an edge."

"Yeah, that's true. I know the answer is in the church. If I can find his tomb… Andy, thank you. For sticking by me, for everything."

"I told you," I leaned back and forced a smile, "you never have to thank me. Now, let's go find that tomb."

Luke chuckled.

"Just like old times."

That coaxed a genuine laugh out of me.

"Yep, only this time there better not be snakes."

Luke shuddered as I took my seat behind him.

"Where did those snakes even come from?" he asked as we made our way down the hill.

"Right? And what did they eat? I mean, there was no vermin around, that's for damn sure."

"Do you still have those zombie python boots?"

"Uh, *yeah*," I said. "You think I'd just give those away? They're sitting right next to that big stick I used for the Nepal mission."

"It was just a stick though, nothing special."

I missed the baiting sound in his voice and walked right into his little trap.

"Excuse me, it was *the* stick that I fought off a half dozen demon cows with, thank you very much."

"So you're saying it's a bad ass stave?"

I groaned. The Great Stave Debate was something that had begun on our very first mission together and continued throughout our entire marriage. It wasn't that I didn't think it was a good weapon, obviously a Bo staff is a good weapon. But superior to all others? I didn't think so. We'd cleared entire rooms at dinner parties with this argument, and I was still in it to win it.

"I use a staff *once* and suddenly you think that means that they're the superior weapon."

"Did your bullets harm the demon cows?" his voice was thick with amusement.

"One situation, Luke, *one* does not make a sound basis for victory in this argument."

Our back and forth continued all the way down the hill until we reached the outskirts of the small town. My assessment from a top the hill was more or less accurate. There was a wide road that led down the center of the town to a fountain in the town square. People milled around outside of homes on the outer edges and then, as we got closer to the center, the homes gave way to shops. Most of the walls were the same white washed kind of brick and stucco with red or green tiled roofs. Bright pots of plants sat outside, and there were a few vegetable gardens that looked like they could've been community plots. Bright awnings flared out in the front of some of the shops, with dried herbs and peppers hanging and filling the air with their aroma. The people stared at us and I checked to make sure Luke had raised his glamour, which he had. We were very obviously strangers and I gathered from the looks and whispers that they didn't get a lot of outsiders around here.

Luke pulled over in front of what looked like a large two story house with a beautifully carved wood rail balcony that wrapped around the upper level. Three sets of French doors were open on the second level, exposing a hint of red and yellow tiled floors and white walls. The lower level had a beautiful garden out front with a small fountain gurgling away.

"It's an inn," he explained as we both climbed off the motorcycle.

"Yeah, I can read the sign."

My legs protested as I walked timidly from the bike, muscles stiff and achy from the time on the back of it. I took in a bit more of our surroundings and realized that I'd entirely missed the floral garlands strung up around the town square, along with the brightly painted booths. There was the mouthwatering scent of cooked meats, breads and pastries in the air and my stomach let out a long gurgle.

"Are they getting ready for a party of some kind?" I asked.

"Not just any party," his voice was low but filled to brim with excitement. "I think they're celebrating the anniversary of the priest's death."

"Weird thing to celebrate if he was their protector."

"Not if they believe in such a thing as a celebration of his life, of his accomplishments. If they looked at him as a holy man, it would be like celebrating a saint's day."

"And I'm assuming that's a good thing for us?"

"It's very good. This is also the second night of the full moon. The intersection is exactly what we need."

I smiled up at him.

"Well then, all we have to do is wait for nightfall and get the goods."

"Yeah, but to blend we should get a room and join the celebration."

"A room?" I asked with a playful quirk to my eyebrow.

"Uh, I mean, *rooms*. We should get rooms and, um, shower and stuff."

"Relax, you dork," I slapped him on the arm and giggled. "You think after what we did on the motorcycle, one room would be a problem?"

Luke about killed me when he blushed and rubbed the back of his neck, grinning at me in that nervous yet down right sexy way of his.

"I was hoping you'd say that," he admitted.

A thrill shot through me and my stomach did a funny little flip. I'd hoped he would be open to the idea too because, while I knew that continuing what we started in the forest was a bad idea, I was apparently incapable of saying 'no' when it came to being with my ex-husband.

Just like always.

No matter how hard I'd tried to fight it when we were just friends, Luke had managed to wear me down until I'd let him fuck me hard and thoroughly on the mission to discover the Holy Grail. That had been the beginning of our whirlwind. But was this a new beginning or one last good-bye?

That question rattled around in my mind, sapping some of the playfulness out of me, as I followed Luke into the quaint, beautiful hotel.

CHAPTER TEN
LUKE

The inn was a converted plantation style house with only a half dozen rooms. I had limited cash on hand and wasn't about to use my card since the Archive was tracking us. That fact had my stomach in knots, though I was doing my best to hide it from Andy. She shouldn't have come with me, I should've made her stay away.

Yeah right, when have I ever been able to make Andy do anything?

I smirked and glanced over to where she was leaning over a flower pot, smelling an orchid. The small entry way was flooded with the scent of flowers, as well as the earthy aroma of the leaves on the garlands strung around. Andy's round bottom was hugged tight by her pants, the curve where her waist met her hips just visible as her tank top rode up. I wanted my hands on her naked body, to cup the soft mounds of that ass. Staring at her now, the guarded expression she'd worn so much during the last few months of our marriage and the beginning of the mission had melted away, exposing the tender heart and easy smile she hid so often. I never understood why she didn't show this side to more people, but then again I hadn't exactly been Mr. Forthcoming during our marriage either. I'd hidden plenty from her, in spite of how often Andy had asked me to share.

The petite woman behind the check in desk with a graying bun and bright smile held out a key for me to take.

"Here you are, a beautiful room for you and your wife," she said in quick Spanish.

"Oh, we—" I began.

"Are so grateful for your hospitality," Andy cut me off and plucked the key from the woman's hands. "Aren't we sweetie?"

I stared at her for a second, glanced at the woman who was began to frown at me in confusion and then pasted on a wide grin.

"Yes, thank you. We're very excited about the festival tonight."

The woman's expression brightened.

"Ah yes! It is a special feast to celebrate our dear protector. You are both welcome to join us, the festivities begin at sundown."

"And the chapel? I've heard so much about the beautiful mosaics in there," I said. "Any chance we could take a look?"

The woman's smile became tense and she straightened as if trying to put a little distance between us.

"The chapel is closed for now, renovations you see."

"Ah, yes, well, maybe next time."

She nodded and turned to the small doorway behind her and disappeared.

"That was bullshit, right?" Andy asked me in English.

"Yep. They're protecting the chapel. Which means I was right. He's buried there, along with the last piece of the map."

We started walking through the entry way to the small staircase when I stopped Andy with a hand on her arm.

"Why did you let her believe we were married?"

Andy shrugged.

"I figured if they were super religious it might get us in their good graces to pose as a married couple rather than a divorced one."

"Oh, yeah that's…good idea."

A strange stab of disappointment hit me in the chest and I turned away from her as I started to climb the stairs. I must've looked upset or worried because Andy felt the need to reassure me, even though that wasn't the problem at all. I wasn't even sure I wanted to look too closely at why I was feeling this way.

"Relax," Andy said with a short laugh, "not like they're going to check up on it."

I nodded, but I couldn't relax. This mission had been fraught with emotion even before Andy had been a part of it, but since she'd shown up, everything felt tangled and complicated. We were silent as we walked down the hall of bright blue, red and green tiles on the floor.

The sound of a bird squawking jolted me out of my thoughts and Andy laughed, a full throated sound that I couldn't help smiling at. The bird was brightly colored and imposing, sitting proudly on its perch inside a large enclosure to our right. It was like a giant bird cage, with the roof of the inn open above it, bright green plants growing in pots around the perimeter. The enclosure was a beautiful and odd interruption in the sequence of doors along the wall. To our left, across from the enclosure, the wall opened to reveal a courtyard below with a fountain also in blue, red and green tiles. Patio furniture sat around the space with more plants and flowers in pots scattered around. The roof was open over the courtyard too, and I realized that the interior of the inn was a square around this hollowed out space.

"This is gorgeous," Andy breathed, staring down at the courtyard.

Afternoon sun streamed in and hit her just right, bringing out the subtle shades of red in her dark hair, the caramel gleam in her brown eyes. We were both in desperate need of showers, and there were smudges of dirt on her forehead, not to mention a bit of dried blood on the hem of her tank and pants. But none of that mattered. Andy was and always would be the most stunning woman I'd ever seen, especially when all of her walls were down and it was just *her*. Not Agent Kane, not Andromeda Kane, heiress and socialite. Not special ops Lieutenant Kane.

Just *Andy*.

My Andy…

I shut away the small voice that told me that she wasn't mine anymore, that this mission changed absolutely nothing about our history or the gaping hole she'd left in my heart when she'd left me without explanation. I should be guarding myself, should be furious with her, but I wasn't. Maybe it was knowing that I was dying, and the clarity it provided, that lessened my need to cling to those feelings that had haunted me since she left. Maybe it was a kernel of stupid hope that she'd change her mind after all.

Or maybe I just *needed* her in that way that I always had, the way that defied all logic and all the reasons why we would never work.

It didn't really matter. The only thing I could think of was getting those lush lips under mine again, to feel her body under my hands, to lose myself in her embrace, even if it was as hollow as a mirage in the end.

I may be a genius, but I never said I was smart when it came to who I loved.

I reached out and hooked one of my fingers under her chin, turning her to look at me. Her eyes widened when she took me in. I knew she was seeing the fire in my eyes, the desire in my stuttered breath and shaking hands, as I cupped her face with both my hands on either side and ran my thumbs over her cheekbones.

This time, I didn't slam my lips to hers. This time I would savor her.

My lips feathered over hers, light and barely touching. When she strained to deepen the kiss, I pulled away; the sunlight bathed her in gold, a celestial spotlight illuminating the treasure that I'd once held and lost. The only treasure I really wanted.

I once again skated my lips over hers, letting my tongue dart out, asking for entry. She opened to me and I groaned as I drank deep of her. My fingers reached around her head and I tilted it to take her deeper, slowly plundering her mouth, savoring every shared breath and sigh.

When I broke the kiss, Andy's eyes drifted open, hazy and lust drunk. I ran one of my thumbs over her bottom lip, then up to the fading scratches from my tusks.

"All of my travels," I whispered, as my eyes devoured her, "every wonder I've ever seen, and nothing has ever compared to you."

"Sweaty and dirty as I am?" she asked with a dimpled smile.

I ran my lips over her forehead, down the bridge of her nose, across one cheek to her temple and down to her jaw line. The salty, earthiness of her exploded on my tongue and I licked the small spot under her ear then sucked it into my mouth to prove how much I wanted her.

"Does that answer your question?" my voice rasped against her skin.

Now that I'd started, I wasn't sure I could stop.

"I want to devour you," I backed her into a wall. "I want to leave my marks across your skin…a map of where I've been and where I want to go."

Andy's fingers tangled in my hair and she gave a little tug but not to stop me. One long leg hitched around my hip, her little mewling cries in time with the grinding motion of her hips.

"Room," I breathed. "Now."

"Damn right."

She tugged on my hand and we ran down the hall to the end where our room was. Andy was struggling to get the key in the lock as I pressed hungry kisses to the back of her neck and tugged her flush with me. Her arm wound up and around my neck until she was pulling my hair again as I swirled my hips so my cock dug into her ass.

When she finally got the door open I didn't even wait for her to walk in. I swung her up in my arms, bridal style, and claimed her mouth once again as I walked in, dropped my glamour and slammed the door with my foot. The entire world could be burning around me and the only thing I'd see, the only thing I'd feel was Andy.

She was everything to me, but I wasn't convinced that was true for her. At least, it hadn't been when we were married. I always knew she was holding pieces of herself back, but I accepted it, told myself that some was better than nothing. And even though I'd been hollowed out without her this past year, I knew that what I needed wasn't the pieces she doled out.

No, I wanted all of her.

All of her fear.

All of her joy.

All of her worries.

I wanted her very soul.

And even though I knew I'd never get it, I also knew that I'd shatter myself here and now for a chance that I might be wrong.

When my shins hit the edge of the bed I finally came up for air and set her on her feet. But my hands stayed on her body, the ends of her tank top in my hands as I pulled it over her head. A moment later, Andy had my shirt in her hands and I pulled over my head for her, sending my glasses to floor with it.

The sharp intake of her breath had me preening in delight as her eyes took me in. She left sparks in her wake as her fingers skated over my skin. It had never ceased to amaze me that I could be desired so completely by this incredible woman, that I was the one she wanted when Andy could be with anyone. It didn't matter that this was temporary, that in a day or two she wouldn't be coming home with me. I chose this moment's delights, and accepted the pain that was to come, small by comparison.

I unhooked her bra and cupped her breasts when it fell from her arms. They filled my hands, the nipples already pebbled and sensitive. I pinched them and Andy gasped, her nails biting into my shoulders. Bending down to take one stiff peek into my mouth, I laid her back onto the bed and stretched beside her. My tusks would leave scratches on her tits just like I did on her mouth and the thought only made me press my mouth harder to her skin. God how I'd missed her tits! So responsive, so full. I took my time with them, the appetizer to the feast I was working my way toward.

Andy's hands threaded through my hair and she arched her back, her breathy cries demanding that I take my mouth lower but I stayed there for a bit longer, relishing the way she panted for me. My hands ran over the soft planes of her body, familiar and new all at the same time. The motorcycle had been a feverish rutting, a desperate need to feel one another in the wake of almost dying. But this was different, this was awakening the part of me I'd often tried to keep leashed outside the bedroom. That primal part that demanded my scent, my marks all over my mate. I could feel the beast clawing at its cage, the bars getting weaker the more Andy begged me to give her release, the more I laved her breasts with my mouth. I barely managed to keep it at bay, needing to stretch this moment out, to savor it just a little longer.

Gentle breezes came through the window nearby, stirring the pale curtains as our mouths and hands rediscovered one another, the afternoon sunlight casting gentle illumination on the marks I was leaving on her. All the contours of her skin were precious, familiar, and I explored them anew, lingering, memorizing.

"Luke…" My name fell from her lips, full of lust and longing.

By now I'd gotten her pants off, and my fingers slid along her inner thigh, teasing little circles that had her panting. I could smell the salty tang of her arousal, and my mouth watered. I wanted that taste on my tongue, to lap it up and make her beg for more.

I kissed my way down her torso, leaving a trail of red scratches in my wake until I came upon her mons covered in dark curls. I loved that she didn't shave all of it away, loved the way it ran wet with her and eventually with me. I bit my way along her inner thigh as my thumbs ran along the outside of her pussy lips. She bucked her hips, searching, begging and I laughed against her.

"You want me to eat this pussy?"

"Yes," she breathed.

"How bad do you want it, Andy?"

"So bad. Please, Luke, please."

"Please what, this?"

I bit her thigh harder than usual and her eyes shot open.

"Or this?" So very slowly, I plunged two fingers into her soaked cunt and pulsed them just inside of her.

"More…more…"

I went deeper, but just a little.

"I want to hear what you want, Andy."

"I want you to fuck me with your fingers while you suck on my clit. I want your mouth on my pussy and I want to come down your throat."

"Fuck," I groaned just before I pumped my fingers all the way to the knuckle and pressed my mouth to that swollen little pearl of hers.

Another obscene moan, deep and rolling, came from me as her taste flooded my mouth. After that, I was as lost as she was. My mouth and fingers worked in tandem as she writhed under me, begging and crying out as I sucked her clit between my lips. A moment later, wet heat rushed from her onto my fingers. I pulled them out and pressed my mouth to her opening, my tongue replacing what my fingers had been doing, as my thumb massaged firm circles on her bundle of nerves. I drank my fill as she sobbed and shuddered out the last of her release.

But that had only been the first course. I was ravenous now, savagely so, and I wanted more. I wanted it all.

CHAPTER ELEVEN
ANDROMEDA

I had forgotten just how transcendent the experience of Luke devouring me was.

Oh, I remembered that he liked it, but I'd not had the mind melting pleasure of his mouth on me in far too long. I didn't even care that I hadn't showered in over two days and was fucking his face with unrestrained need, that the sounds he coaxed out of me were wet and obscene.

Instead, I wanted more of it. I wanted him to keep breaking me into pieces. Being with him was always the most exquisitely torturous pleasure of my life. He could unravel me completely, lay me bare to my soul, and I knew that I had nothing to fear from him. I was safe, always.

I looked down at him gazing at me from between my thighs, his mouth still pressed tight onto my cunt, hand cupping my mons. Those eyes, so intense and beautiful, missed nothing of my reaction. It wasn't just the eyes of a male that wanted to please me. This huge, intelligent Orc was on his knees for me, and these were the eyes of a supplicant longing to know that they were pleasing the one they worshiped. It was frightening and exhilarating to be the object of such complete adoration. I could tell myself that this was just the mission adrenaline, that this was being in close quarters with an ex that I never fully got over.

But as I reached down and ran my fingers along his forehead, down the bridge of his nose, I knew that wasn't true.

And while giving him up at the end of all this might just kill me, there was no way in hell I wanted him to stop.

Unfortunately, there were limits to what my clit could handle, and when the enthusiastic attention began to make me convulse I pulled on his hair to stop him.

"I-I can't take…anymore," I panted.

"Yes you can. Give me one more, baby, one more taste before I fuck you hard."

Oh my dear God in heaven, the power of Luke Turner's filthy, talented mouth!

Those words sent me over the edge once again and I screamed as I came apart, my very bones on fire from the intensity of the pleasure.

"There," Luke grinned and pressed a kiss to my inner thigh, "such a good girl."

I sat up as he did and yanked him to me by the back of his neck. He tasted of me and somehow that circumvented the way he'd over stimulated me, and I was plundering his mouth. He gave as good as he got, his gifted tongue sliding along mine as his hands found my breasts and he pinched my nipples tight enough to bring me to that toe curling edge of pain and pleasure.

"Pants off," I panted, "now."

Luke chuckled against my mouth.

"So bossy when you want cock."

"I missed the Jolly Green Giant." My hands fumbled with his button.

"I didn't miss that nickname."

He slid the shorts and underwear down and the aforementioned giant green cock sprang free. I hadn't had the chance to get a good look at it on the motorcycle, but now it jutted out from him. The skin strained to contain his girth, and the dark crown that peeked out from the foreskin was bathed in glistening white pre-cum that dripped onto my mons as I watched.

"Fuck," Luke groaned, rubbing it into my curls. "I missed painting your body with me."

I whimpered as his hands strayed too close to my still over sensitized clit, but I didn't want him to stop. Luke's eyes turned positively feral as I reached out and swiped a finger through the white fluid. He watched me with a predatory intensity that had my cunt aching for him.

"I missed it somewhere else," I said, and as he watched I slipped my finger between my lips and sucked him off me.

Luke growled low and deep and I shivered, knowing that with that one act I'd pushed him onto a very thin ledge. I loved watching my studious Orc turn downright feral, sometimes brutal, with his fucking. But there was something I needed to do first, something I'd missed so much that I felt like I'd die if I didn't get that thick, green, weeping cock into my mouth.

I slid off the bed and now it was my turn to kneel as Luke stood up, fist around himself at the base. I unwound his fingers and replaced them with mine, even though they didn't make it all the way around him.

"So many choices," I purred. "Do I start here?"

I moved my fingers so I could lick around his base. His exhale was stuttered, hands curled into fists at his side.

"Or maybe I play here a bit?"

I cupped his balls and squeezed just a little.

"Oh my fuck…Andy, I'm not gonna last if you keep doing that."

"Good," I said with a devious grin. "I want you to fill the back of my throat, I want it dripping out of the sides of my lips and down my chin."

"I forgot how filthy that pretty mouth of yours could be."

"Mmmm…but maybe I'll just start at the beginning."

And without further warning, I used one hand on his cock, one on his balls while I took his tip between my lips, stopping at where his foreskin rested and giving it a little lick.

Luke took in a hissing breath and one huge hand clapped onto the top of my head. As I slowly drew him further into my mouth, Luke's fingers curled in my hair and he pulled me deeper until he hit the back of my throat.

He was so close to snapping, the anticipation coiled hot in my gut and I gazed up at him as best I could in this position. He stared down at me, eyes glittering and hot, his jaw clenched tight as he fought to keep control, a beast barely chained. I was hungry for it, to feel him unleash that side he showed no one else onto me.

I edged back until his tip was almost out of my mouth, then I ran my tongue along the edge of his foreskin again. Salty precum hit my tongue and I hummed with pleasure.

"Fuck…Andy…"

His voice had gotten lower, harsh and I grinned around him. I flicked my tongue along the underside of his cock before sliding my mouth along him slowly, relishing the harsh way he was breathing, the muttered half sentences of nonsense.

I didn't even get halfway before he gave another feral growl and tightened his grip on my hair just shy of pain.

"God, you're good at that," he snarled just before snapping his hips and driving his cock to the back of my throat. "That fucking mouth," he pulled out and thrust back into my mouth so fast and deep I gagged. "Almost as good," out and back, harder this time "as your tight pussy."

Both hands were now on the side of my head and he was pulling me onto him even as he thrust into my mouth, bottoming out at the back of my throat each time. It was primal, and rough, this huge Orc snarled and growled above me, using me utterly for his pleasure.

And I was so fucking turned on I couldn't think straight.

When his thrusts started to lose their rhythm and his breaths turned to snorting grunts, I knew he was close. But just as I was about to prepare myself for it, Luke pulled out all the way. Saliva streamed down my chin but before I could ask him what was wrong, he picked me up under my arms and threw me back on the bed.

"I don't have any condoms, but I want inside you, please, Andy?" he panted, huge arms caging me in as he held himself above my body, trembling.

He'd worked my core to the point of pain with his fingers and mouth and yet I ached for more as if he hadn't done anything at all.

"Fuck, yes," I gasped and yanked him down to me.

Luke used his thick thighs to push mine open, the coarse hairs tickling me, until he hooked one arm under my left knee and lifted, spreading me wide open.

"I can't be gentle," he warned as he ran the blunt tip through me.

"Good. I need you fuck me like it's the last time."

The moment I realized what I'd said, something sharp snapped through my chest. It was like my soul had cracked when he'd told me he was dying, and ever since it was leaking out all the things I should've done, should've said.

"Baby," his voice was rough as he kept himself just outside of me, pressing but not entering, "I can't do that. Because if I fuck you here, it's not going to stop as long as we're on this mission, until we're back home. You understand? You're mine until then, this cunt, this body, *you are mine,* Andy."

I didn't realize I was crying until the tears fell hot down my temples and into my hair.

"Say it," Luke pleaded. "I need to hear you say it."

I should've said 'no', should've stopped this before I hurt us both any more than I already had. But I couldn't. I was so fractured, the base parts of my soul so cold since leaving him that I needed his warmth, his steady, open affection.

It was selfish.

It was reckless.

And I couldn't stop myself.

"Yes," I sobbed, "yes, Luke. For the rest of the mission."

One last mission…

And that was all the permission he needed. With a sharp, brutal thrust, Luke speared me to the hilt. We both let out a long, loud moan, the stretch of him was exquisite pleasure edged with pain. He didn't give me time to adjust, and I didn't want it. I needed his savagery, his loss of control and Luke didn't disappoint. There was an almost angry desperation to him as he ruthlessly fucked me and I welcomed it, longing for it to burn away the debris of our marriage, the sharp edges of my guilt.

That need drove me to match him, meeting the collision of his body to mine as he hit my end each time. Sweet pain that was brushed away with each explosion of pleasure that wound me tighter each time.

"So good...no one else, Andy...no one but you, baby," he growled above me.

My nails dug into his skin where I was gripping his perfect upper arms, and I begged for more even though he was giving me everything. My body was a white hot coil, burning and straining for release. Finally, all the jagged pieces of my heart that I'd bundled up so I could pretend to be okay shattered with the release that broke through me like a lightning strike. A moment later, Luke's body shuddered, his hips lost their rhythm and he let out a long, low growl that I felt deep inside of me as he painted my insides with his cum.

Warmth and bliss suffused my body and soul, and I wanted to stay there, hiding from all the responsibilities waiting for me. I just wanted Luke's biting kisses on my skin, the brush of orchid scented air against our sweat dampened bodies. I wanted the simple perfection that we'd started our relationship with before everything became so twisted and burdened with secrets big and small.

I want it all back...I want him back.

Time only went one way though, I knew that, in spite of the time travel artifacts I'd confiscated in my career. There was no going back, no undoing the damage we'd done to one another. We may be repeating old habits to conjure an illusion of going back to simpler times but I knew better as we grasped one another in a desperate need to avoid the reality of our situation. Our history was inescapable, even in these moments. It wrapped around us, it filled our mouths with words we'd otherwise never say, it made our most intimate moments tinged with sadness that was ripping me up inside as the euphoria of my orgasm faded. More tears fell and I let out a shuddering breath.

"What's wrong? Did I hurt you?" he asked, wiping the tears with the back of his fingers.

"No," I choked out, "I just…"

There was too much to say, it clogged my throat and mind and I couldn't get anything out at first.

"I missed you," I whispered, my hands ran in slow exploration up and down his body. "So much."

"I missed you too," he nipped at my jaw. "I've been…hollow without you, Andy."

I closed my eyes and held him close to me.

"Me too."

He didn't approach the elephant in the room, the question of why the hell I'd left him in the first place and I was grateful. I would tell him, I had to now. But admitting it all to him while his cock softened inside of me, the stickiness of cum and sweat on my body, wasn't exactly how I wanted to have that conversation.

Luke pulled back enough to look me in the eyes, his fingers lazily drew circles on my collarbone as I did the same on his hip.

"I know this doesn't change anything," he said, "that afterward we'll go our separate ways but I don't care. Maybe it's the big expiration date above my head or maybe it's just that I never thought I'd hold you again, I don't know and it doesn't matter. I want this, with you, even if it hurts when it's over."

His words were mirror images of my own, the thinly hidden emotions beneath them a twin of the ones that stabbed my heart as I nodded.

"I feel the same way," I whispered.

"So then, no questions about the future, no worrying about after. It's just now."

I nodded.

"Just now."

CHAPTER TWELVE

LUKE

I should be feeling many things.

Fear that I'd just opened myself up to getting my heart broken again.

Elation that I was about to find the final piece of the map.

Nerves at what might lay at the end of the treasure hunt.

And while I was distantly aware of these things lurking, ready to pounce, the only thing that warmed my blood as I strolled through the town square and inhaled the delicious scents of baked breads, roasted meats and sugary pastries was *peace*.

For the first time in so long I didn't feel as if I were bleeding internally, that something essential had been amputated from my soul. I meant what I'd said to Andy; I knew this wouldn't change a damn thing and somehow that didn't bother me as much as it probably should have. I suspected that I was in some pretty deep denial at the moment, that I was doing what I had during my marriage: ignore the problem until it stabbed me through the heart.

Only this time, I also had the strange freedom that came with knowing I was dying and that if I couldn't get this artifact my days were numbered. Would I really deny myself these last days with Andy just because it couldn't last?

No way.

I took a deep steadying breath and checked myself to make sure my glamour was staying in place. A tiny headache was threatening behind my eyes from the strain at having to maintain my Mundane appearance, further proof that the disease was progressing. But it was alright. With any luck, I wouldn't have to hold my glamour for long tonight.

The sun was almost behind the horizon, a brilliantly clear sky was above me, the stars were just beginning to simmer. There were booths of handmade goods, clothes, food and flowers all around the square. Tables and chairs were scattered around and families were eating food and laughing. Above me, garlands were strung, interspersed with hanging lanterns in brilliant colors. Orchids, roses and other flowers I didn't recognize were woven with the greenery above and around many of the booths. There was one flower in particular that seemed to have prominence, but it was odd.

I bent down to examine a bud on one of the food stalls. It was white, the fragrance very much like honeysuckle but not quite. The delicate petals were closed tight, and I examined a few more of the flowers before discovering that none of them were opened.

"Excuse me," I asked the baker nearby, "what's the name of this flower?"

He gave me a gap toothed grin and nodded.

"It's a very special flower, Señor. It blooms once a year, and only for the three nights of the full moon."

My heart jumped and I tried to remain calm.

"Really? I've never seen it before."

He chuckled.

"It only blooms here, to honor our protector and saint. It is a blessing to us."

"How so?"

"It is said that as long as the Flor de Luna blooms in our village, we will be safe from the anger of Dios and the schemes of servants of Diablo. This year we've had more than ever before! It is a very special celebration."

My mouth went dry and I nodded, mind spinning. The baker handed me one of the blooms from the garland and I thanked him as I held it in my hands like the treasure it was.

"What ya got there?" Andy asked.

I looked up to answer her and the words died on my tongue.

I spent some of our limited funds on new clothes since ours were ruined beyond repair. The green and blue linen pants and shirt I wore was cool and simple, if a little tight through the chest. I had been excited to see Andy in what I'd found for her, but I'd never imagined she'd look so stunning in it.

The lights of the hanging lamps and from the shops around the square were pouring a warm glow onto her, brightening her freshly scrubbed skin with a golden hue. Her thick hair was freed from its braids and flowed in chestnut waves around her face and shoulders. The pink and green peasant blouse wasn't form fitting but it clung to her chest just right, the ties loose to give me a mouthwatering view of her cleavage. Tiny flowers, replicas of the Flor de Luna I realized, were dotted all along the neckline and hem, which fell to just above the waist of her low hung green linen pants, the tiniest glimpse of her stomach revealed as she turned to look around the square.

"You look beautiful," I murmured as I slipped the white flower behind her ear.

Her smile widened to reveal that dimple I loved so damn much and a pink flush rose on her cheeks.

"You clean up good too," she said and tugged me down for a kiss. "So what's the plan?"

It took me a second to clue in because all I wanted to do was hold her in my arms, drink in every single thing I could and tuck it away for later. But we had a job to do.

"I figure we wait until the festivities are going a bit and the moon is almost at its zenith then make our way to the chapel."

Andy threaded her fingers through mine as we meandered through the stalls, looking to all the world like a couple of strange tourists who just happened to find this half hidden village.

"What was with the flower? It's everywhere," Andy said as we bought a skewer of roasted chicken.

"I think it's something to do with the priest and the artifact he's buried with. Galahad was always associated with white, and the moon has been a symbol of rebirth and cyclical nature of things. The flower only blooms during this three-day festival every year. And, this year is the biggest crop yet apparently."

Andy's eyes sparkled as she tore off pieces of chicken with her teeth and looked at me.

"What?" I asked, around a mouthful of my own. Then I groaned as the inherited memory of a taste from hundreds of years ago burst onto my tongue. "Oh my God! The spices on this…it's a lot like the seasoning my ancestor used in Henry the Eighths court, of course those were from the spice road but—"

"Luke?"

"Hmm?"

"The flower."

"Oh yeah, anyway, in one of the references I made note of was a farmer who had brought a bag of dead seeds to the tomb of the priest, begging him to bless them with life again so his family wouldn't starve. Legend has it that he had a dream later that night that he was to take soil from the churchyard and bury the seeds in it. When he did, they came back to life."

"So, the flowers are from the priest's tomb?"

"That's what I'm thinking. If we can find them in the chapel, it might lead us to his body."

"Do you know what the inside of the chapel is like? Any kind of layout or anything?"

"Not specifically but if it's like others it will have an entry way that leads into the main area with the knave at the end. There might be a cell of some kind where the priest once lived or even a hidden stair case leading down to a small underground area for holy relics."

"But if this chapel is to commemorate this priest, then it should have iconography having to do with him."

I nodded as I finished off my fourth skewer.

Andy was about to say something else when her eyes widened and she pointed up at the sky. At the same time, everyone in the square started to talk and point.

I turned and gaped at a gorgeous super moon staring us right in the face.

"That…that's big, right? Not normal," Andy asked.

"Yeah. That's…" I turned to her with a wide grin. "This is great. Do you know how rare this is? How many things have to line up for there to be a full super moon on the anniversary of his death? Andy, this could mean the difference between finding it and not."

A dark thorn of worry shook loose in my chest and I could breathe a little clearer. I wasn't one for 'signs' or anything but this felt like a clear one, as if I were meant to find this.

I might have a future after all.

Someone in the crowd began walking around with a large barrel of wine on a rolling cart, handing out cups to anyone who wanted it. He came by us and we took two of them.

"So," Andy held hers up, "here's to finding what we came for."

"We haven't found it yet, but…yeah, it's looking good."

We tapped the cups against one another and I took a sip. It was dry red wine with hints of cherry and rosemary. I could taste the conditions of the soil when the grapes grew, a tang of something bitter and…old. I took another sip and let it sit on my tongue. The flavors opened a bit more, complex and beautiful. But that sharp edge, ancient and powerful, hit me again, warming my muscles and soothing away some of the aches that I'd began to learn to live with.

It was temporary, a moment in time, but it was another confirmation that this was the right time, the right place.

"Come on," Andy said with grin, "I'm still hungry and I know you are too. Let's eat some more before we go find this map."

I let her lead me along to different stalls, loving the way her eyes lit up with delight at the riot of colors and sensations. We ate more skewers and she indulged me in waxing poetic about the taste, which really was quite incredible. We bought sugary buns and drank more wine. Everything was warm and bright, the people so happy, as if nothing bad could touch them. And I thought that was true, tucked away as they were in this idyllic village, their patron watching over them over the years, even from the grave.

When a small group began to play instruments I held my hand out in silent question to Andy.

"Shouldn't we be getting to it?"

I glanced up and while the moon was almost in position, it was still too early so I shook my head.

"Nope. Besides, what better way to convince them that we are on our way back to our room to fuck than to lose ourselves in a dance or two."

She snorted and shook her head.

"You can't dance for shit so I think chances are better of convincing them that you stepped on my foot one too many times instead."

My smile widened and I held up a finger to get Andy to wait for a moment. I ran over to the small band and asked them for a song I could dance the Rumba to. One of the musicians, an older man with thick white hair and a huge mustache glanced behind me at Andy and his smile widened to show two missing front teeth before nodding.

The dancers on the small space parted for me as I made my way back to Andy, and everything narrowed to her; the cool night air, the sensual chords of the guitar floating around us. When I reached my arm around her waist and brought her closer to me, my other hand locked into hers and something electric shot up through my body. The small space between us was warmed and heavy with the past and Andy was no longer smiling. Instead, there was a fire in her eyes as she recognized the chords, she knew what dance we were about to do, and what I was telling her by choosing it. The Rumba was special to her parents, part of their love story, and every one of their children had learned it, along with other dances like the waltz. For Andy, the Rumba was passion that over ruled logic, passion that one would risk the world to hold onto.

"I learned it for you," I whispered. "Before everything fell apart."

"Luke…"

I didn't give her a chance to say anything else before I was leading us through the beginning of a Rumba box step. Someone began to sing, a mournful song about lost love, passion wasted. It wrapped around us like a memory as I spun her away from me, then pulled her back to my front. Her hand snaked up to graze her fingertips against my cheek as I reached down and skimmed my hand along the outside of one thigh. We were surrounded by people watching us, some dancing themselves, but everything in my world had narrowed to where her body was pressed to mine. Andy was trembling, her breath stuttered and eyes half lidded. I'd never seen her so at my mercy as in this moment.

When I reached her waist, our hips began to sway together just before I spun her away from me again, and brought her back. I was in control of her body, leading her through each part of the story of this dance, and she was letting me. This time, her arm wound around my neck, one of my hands settled against her hip and we stared into each other's eyes, completely lost as the music enveloped us. We moved in time with one another, back and forth, pushing and pulling. Our breaths mingled, mouths so close that any movement forward would have us kissing. But I stayed away, my nose skimming hers before denying her anything more.

So close, yet not close enough. Just like our marriage.

Pain exploded in my chest along with the thought but it wasn't the disease, it was the unhealed wound that Andy had left behind.

No, that's not fair. She didn't do it alone, I did too. In my silence, in my fear to push her too far.

The music was reaching a crescendo, and I could tell by looking into Andy's eyes as we danced that she was feeling it too. It was like the song was drawing things to the surface that we'd both hoped to keep buried under the escape of passion. Heartbreak and pain suffused every line the woman sang and there were tears in Andy's eyes as we moved through the final pushes and pulls of the dance, each movement telling our story.

I'd been a fool to think that I could let myself fall back into her arms without having to face the things that had destroyed our marriage; that I could really just have one more mission and then turn my back on her with any kind of peace. There were questions that burned in me now, pain that would not be denied its spotlight. And as the song drew to a close, and the singer lamented holding her slain lover in her arms, I looked into Andy's eyes and knew she was thinking the same thing.

There was a beat of silence, our bodies still and eyes locked onto one another. I closed the distance between our mouths and swept mine against hers. I drank her tears but I didn't absolve her of anything, not yet anyway. And as she clung to me, I could feel the guilt coming off her in waves. When we parted, Andy gazed up at me, eyes wet and shining. She'd broke me when she left, and I still wanted her. If we didn't have a mission, I'd be sweeping her up in my arms, taking her to our room and worshiping her all night. But the responsibilities that weighed heavy on me kept my body still as she collected herself.

"We should talk," she croaked.

"Yeah," I nodded.

And then my eye snagged on the flower I'd put in her hair. Not only had it bloomed, it gave off a faint golden glow too.

I plucked it out of her hair and we both stared at it with wide eyes.

"What does it mean?" she asked.

"That we need to get to the chapel, now."

She nodded and took my hand. There were a few good natured jabs uttered our way from some of the men and women we passed – the show we'd put on sold the love sick image better than I'd hoped.

Probably because it wasn't an act.

The thought made my jaw tightened and for the first time since I started all this, I wished I could just throw it all to the side and get the answers I needed. There was a pressure now, a constant nagging in my mind that told me I had to have this conversation sooner rather later. That waiting until this was over wouldn't do, as much as I'd planned to simply drown myself in passion. Now, that wasn't going to be an option.

We made it up to our room and I grabbed my pack with flashlights, my journals and all the other research I'd done. I wasn't sure exactly what I'd need so we took it all. Andy checked her firearm and slipped it into her boot.

"We should go around the back of the building," she said and paused as she started for the door. "When…why did you learn the Rumba?"

The question catapulted my heart into my throat and back down again. She had no idea how loaded the question was and shockingly, I didn't find myself wishing to avoid it.

"I learned it while you were on missions. I heard you and your mother talking the last time we visited about how I couldn't dance and…I knew how important that dance was to you. I thought if I learned it, if I could show you how I still felt about you, even with all the problems we were having, that you'd stay."

She whipped around and gaped at me.

"You knew I was leaving?" she whispered.

I snorted and shook my head.

"I'm not blind. You'd had one foot out the door for months before you actually left me. It was stupid to think that a dance could fix everything but…I don't know, I thought it would open us both up to talk, but you left before I could take you out so, there ya go. Too little too late."

"Luke—"

"Not right now," I said, my voice forceful and putting distance between us. "We *will* finish this, you can be sure about that, because I've got questions and for once, I'm not going to be too afraid to ask. But not until we get what I need from the chapel."

She opened her mouth in shock, pink tinting her cheeks before snapping her mouth shut. She gave me a quick nod before spinning on her heel and walking out of the room.

CHAPTER THIRTEEN

ANDROMEDA

It wasn't really a surprise that what I had tried to ignore had appeared and slapped me in the face.

What *was* a shock was the fact that a dance that symbolized passion, love and so much more to me was actually the catalyst. In a way, it was a relief. I didn't have to carry the burden of starting this conversation, of destroying our little pocket of ignorant happiness by injecting much needed truth into it. Luke had done that, bravely and directly. Honestly, it was a shock. He'd always avoided arguments with me until there was no other choice, constantly trying to fix what he thought was wrong as if it were solely his fault. He blamed himself a lot during our marriage, assuming that it couldn't be *me*. I hated it, the feeling that I was too perfect to be at fault, the work of trying to reassure him that nothing was wrong, or it wasn't him. And then doing it all over again after we fought.

But this time was different. This time, Luke hadn't tried to sugar coat it, hadn't made it about some flaw of his. He'd met it head on, without trying to protect me. It was a relief as much as it made me a bit afraid. What was I in for, now that Luke didn't feel the need to keep my feelings from being hurt?

As we made our way under the cover of darkness to the chapel, the sounds of celebration getting more distant by the minute, a heaviness settled between us. Gone was the ease we'd carved out on our way here and we were shrouded in tense silence. It wouldn't distract from the mission, I knew that. We'd done much more difficult work in the middle of screaming fights. Still, it was uncomfortable, like a hair shirt on my back.

The chapel was set about a quarter mile from the town itself. If we'd been heading for it directly, we would've traveled along a well-kept gravel path lined with these strange moon blooming flowers on either side. As it was, we approached from the side and came upon a small lean-to like shed on the west side of the structure. There were lights on inside, though dim and flickering, like candles. The space was a long rectangle shape. The belfry was at the front of the church, with a simple cross at its top that shone white in the moonlight.

"I don't want to damage the building if we can help it," Luke said.

I nodded, pushing all of my emotions aside and finding that cool, calm spot in my mind. Focusing on the puzzle in front of us was a relief, and I dove head first into it.

"We could just try the door," I suggested. "They don't seem the type to lock the place."

Luke frowned.

"It can't be that easy…can it?"

"Stay here and let me do a perimeter sweep real quick, make sure we're alone, then we'll try the front door."

Luke nodded and I took off around the back of the church.

There was a simple graveyard back there, the grave markers mostly wooden crosses with carvings on them. I shuddered as I walked by it; I'd been on too many missions with zombies to feel completely at ease around a graveyard anymore. There was no crypt on the small plot of land, no structures at all, so if the priest was buried here, it was likely he was in the church as Luke theorized.

There was a small door at the back that was locked tight, and I peeked in through the small windows, but could only see complete blackness. Whatever light I'd seen around front either couldn't reach this far or I was looking into a different room. I made a mental note of that before going around to the east facing side of the church.

There was another window that was dark, and then milky windows that showed filmy light behind them which I assumed meant they looked into the main room of the chapel itself. There was a sweet little garden nearby, flooded with the same flowers, which were now glowing bright in the moonlight. It was eerie and beautiful and I wondered if we'd find more inside.

When I got to the front, Luke was there looking into the windows and he jumped when I came out of the shadows.

"All clear," I said.

"The door is open."

I gestured for him to lead the way and he pulled open the simple wooden door, that didn't even so much as creak on its hinges. The outside was newly white washed, not a speck of dirt on the walls, no weeds on the path or around the building. The people of this village obviously took great care of this building, and I doubted it was purely out of religious respect.

The entry was small, with a set of narrow stairs off to the right leading to the bell tower, and to the left was a place for coats and such. The floor was simple, unadorned, until we stepped past the entry way and into the church proper. The floor under our feet was a gorgeous, if well-worn, mosaic of blue, tan, red, orange and yellow tiles. There were candles lit in the windows and up front on a small shelf, which was adorned with Flor de Lunas. Simple, thick pews were in neat rows on either side of the center aisle, leading to the front where a light wood pulpit sat off to the side, and a very old crucifix carved from different shades of wood was hanging on the wall. One confessional was off to the side opposite of the pulpit, cloaked in shadow.

A vaulted ceiling was above us, the rafters made of thick beams that were shining with light coming from somewhere that I couldn't identify yet. The place smelled of spicy oils, the flowers, and candle wax, the aroma ever stronger as we moved cautiously toward the middle of the aisle. There was a reverence to this place, holy and pure, that sent unease trickling down my spine. I was sure we weren't supposed to be here.

"Oh my God," I gasped and pointed up at where the walls met the curve of the ceiling.

Luke gazed up, and I could see his mind working behind his eyes. All along the top seven feet or so of the wall, from the back of the chapel around the west wall, to the front wall and then along the east wall, was a detailed glass and stone mosaic. Unlike the one under our feet, which seemed more abstract, this one was depicting scenes, telling us a story. The strange light filtering in, which I realized with some shock was very bright moonlight, illuminated some of the mosaic, but others were in shadow.

"This is it," Luke said, his voice trembling with excitement. "That symbol there," he pointed to an illuminated part of the mosaic above us, "that's a Latin symbol for God or Holiness and then right there, that's the priest and you see the red devil like creatures, there's seven of them, that's the seven Nazis that smuggled the artifacts from Germany…and I think he's holding a cross in his hands…it's white so it could be the cross of Galahad. Then look! Along the bottom of the entire mosaic it looks like the Flor de Luna but…I can't be sure. This is the story of how he came to be in possession of the artifacts. The clue to their whereabouts might be in the mosaic, not with him."

I nodded, straining to see more.

"We need to get closer, there's too much I think we're missing," I said, taking quick stock of our surroundings. "I think there's a small kind of ledge I could climb onto if you can give me a boost."

Luke nodded and climbed up onto one of the pews closest to the wall where the moonlight was shining brightest. He got up on his tip toes and stumbled, blinking his eyes rapidly behind his glasses.

I ran over to him as he fell onto his ass on the floor, his hands shaking.

"Luke, what's wrong?"

He looked around panicked.

"I–I…my eyes, they've been acting up and…Andy, I'm having trouble getting my vision to focus, it just went fuzzy all of a sudden and I got dizzy," his voice cracked and I could see the spiral of fear as it began to drag him down. "It's bad, and I can't see."

I was fighting back a fair bit of terror at seeing him like this, but Luke needed me to be strong, he needed me to be the steady one in the storm, and I couldn't let him down.

I took his face between my hands and turned his face to me. His eyes didn't focus on mine, but instead kept sweeping over my face, over my shoulder. It was awful to see him struggling to simply *look* at me, but I held back that emotion and forced steel into my voice.

"Listen to me," I demanded, "we are close to getting the cure. And I know you're scared, but you gotta hold on for me, alright? You're the brains, I'm the brawn usually, but right now, I need your muscles and your height to get me up there so I can tell you what I see. Okay? This will pass, I promise."

"What if it doesn't?" his whisper broke. "Andy, what if—"

I cut him off with a gentle kiss, trying to take away some of his fear. He clung to me, the kiss becoming desperate, frantic. When I pulled away, Luke had his eyes closed as if he were afraid to open them. And, truth be told, I was afraid to ask him to, but I couldn't do this without him.

"Open your eyes. You can do this."

Luke took in a jagged breath and slowly opened his eyes. It took a few, long seconds before he was able to actually focus on me. Even then he rubbed his eyes vigorously, as if he were still trying to clear them.

"I just need you to boost me," I helped him to his feet, "and then I'll tell you what I see, alright?"

He nodded, still blinking more rapidly than he should, but I could tell that he was starting to be able to see more clearly. Luke took his time getting onto the pew this time, his footing a bit shaky, but he clenched his jaw, a look of stubborn determination in his eyes that made me have to clench my jaw to hold the tears back. He was the bravest male I knew, braver than any agent I'd ever worked with to face this disease the way he was.

I smiled, what I couldn't say shining in my eyes as I stared up at him.

"Don't look at me like that," he said.

"Why not?"

"Because I don't feel brave. I'm terrified."

"Courage isn't the absence of fear. It's the strength to face it all down and doing what's necessary to defeat it, no matter the cost. And that's exactly what you're doing. You're not rolling over and letting this disease defeat you, you're fighting back in the only way you know how."

"I learned from the best," he said, and leaned down and tucked a strand of hair behind my ear.

I wanted to argue with him, to tell him that I'd chosen the coward's way out that day when I walked out of his life. But first thing's first. Save the Orc, then confess that I'd been an asshole.

"Okay," I said. "I'm gonna stand on your shoulders and see if I can reach the ledge."

"This reminds me of something," he said as I climbed up onto his back and then he snapped his fingers. "I think we did this in Marrakesh, that pit with the rats."

"No, you're thinking of Cairo," I said as I got onto his shoulders.

He grunted and steadied my legs as I stood.

"Cairo was hanging *off* the ledge at the citadel. Marrakesh was the pit...or maybe that was Peru."

"Oh yeah," I grunted as I strained to reach the ledge, "that was Peru, Marrakesh was the underground with the ancient fungus that looked like caterpillars."

"That's right!" he let out a long sigh. "Man, there was great food that trip."

The ledge was just out of reach and I needed a little bit more height.

"Let me put my feet in your hands and push up. Ready, one...two...three!"

He grunted as he boosted me and I was able to get enough purchase on the ledge to swing my legs up and over. The area was deeper than I would've thought but it was still narrow enough that Luke would have a hard time fitting up here. It was the one place in the chapel that looked like it hadn't been cleaned in quite some time, with a thick layer of dirt coating the ledge under me and now getting onto my pretty linen outfit.

But that didn't matter in the least as I got my first real good look at the mosaics. The ledge might be filthy, but somehow the mosaic was pristine. Shards of glass and stone, cut and broken then placed in a specific way to create a stunning scene of a lone man standing in the breach between heaven and hell, between the innocent and demons. I ran my fingertips over the rainbow of colors, slightly raised where they were set into the plaster. I'd seen priceless works of art, ancient stone work, other mosaics and sculptures from all over the world. But there was something about *this* one that reached into my chest and squeezed my heart. Tears leapt to my eyes as a sense of the holiness and purity hit me.

"Oh Luke," I breathed. "Oh I wish you were up here. It's beautiful."

"Tell me what you see, starting at the back."

I took a breath and collected myself before I started to step toward the back along the ledge. I was about to tell him about the imagery when I was blinded by a shaft of bright moonlight and I cried out from the shock.

"What's wrong?" he asked.

I blinked and took a good look at where the unnaturally bright light was coming from, then frowned because there was no way that could be right.

"Andy, what are you seeing?" he insisted.

"The light," I started slowly. "You're gonna think I'm nuts but I think the moonlight is getting filtered through something that's amplifying it. Even a super moon isn't that bright on its own."

Luke walked back toward the aisle and examined where the light was shining. There were three bright shafts that were illuminating the inside of the chapel, all three pointed at the aisle almost meeting in the very center where the mosaic tiles converged to form a flower.

"Wasn't the light shining more out when we first got here?" Luke said, pointing at the shafts on the outside. "I mean, those shafts on the right and left were more on the pews, now they're on the aisle."

"I guess, wasn't paying attention."

While Luke was focused on the aisle and the light, I started to examine the mosaic closest to me. The bottom was indeed the strange white flowers, and as I traced them a few feet in front of me, I noticed that they became increasingly open the closer I got to the front.

"Luke? The flowers are blooming as I get closer to the front."

"It's a mirror!" he shouted up.

"What is?" I asked, following the blossoms to the front of the church.

"The way the light is being channeled, it's very powerful mirrors, and as the moon reaches a certain point in the sky, the lights all will meet here in the middle of the aisle. But why? Is he buried here? But why would they do that, why walk on him…?"

I was so focused on following the damn flowers that I almost didn't see it when the ledge ran out. My toes slipped over the edge and I fell back as I lost my balance, half my body falling off the edge.

"Andy!" Luke screamed and started to head toward me.

He'd just gotten to the front of the church when the three points of light converged in the middle of the aisle and flared to life, momentarily blinding us both. When I opened my eyes and was secure on the ledge, I looked up in awe.

The light had bounced up from the center of the aisle to the very front of the church and onto that part of the mosaic. The priest was holding out his hands, one up and one down, and in the down hand was a fully bloomed flower which was glowing like nothing I'd seen before.

I looked down to tell Luke what I was seeing and my eyes snagged on something that definitely hadn't been there before.

Right off the end of the ledge, where I'd thought it was open air, was a hidden stone staircase leading down behind the wall at the back of the pulpit. Only the top portion was illuminated by the bright halo of light the mosaic was casting and I had a feeling it wouldn't be there for long. The rest of the staircase was cloaked in shadow, but I would've bet even money it went down to the priest's tomb, which was probably directly below where he was pointing.

I let out a shriek of laughter and clapped my hands.

"Luke, there's a staircase! Get your ass up here and let's find us a treasure map!"

CHAPTER FOURTEEN

LUKE

After three different attempts, I managed to haul myself up onto the ledge and we descended the stairs, with Andy leading. The stairwell was narrow, so we fell into single file as we trudged down into the dark. My shoulders brushed against the sides of the stone enclosure, and I was grateful that I wasn't claustrophobic because I would have been panicking.

It wasn't long before we'd passed beyond the moonlight that was shining into the chapel and were fully encased in darkness so dense that our flashlights barely pierced through the gloom. The only sounds were the shuffle of our feet on the old stone steps, and our breath. I tried to calm my staccato heart, tell myself that nothing was guaranteed, but every instinct inside of me said this was it, the final piece of the puzzle.

I might not die after all. I may be able to beat this.

I wasn't sure what I expected, maybe a maze, some kind of elaborate booby trap system, but when we got to the end of the stairs, there was a simple wooden door and a cross with those same flowers carved into it.

"Should I open it?" Andy asked, her voice tense, braced for danger.

I ran my flashlight over the seams of the door, the passage so narrow that there was no way for Andy to let me past her.

"I don't see any signs of traps so…yeah?"

Andy drew her gun and handed her flashlight to me. I held it over her shoulder along with mine to give us as much light as possible. Her hand closed on a rough door knob that had decades of dust on it, and I held my breath. There was a terrible squeaking groan as she turned the knob and pushed. The door gave a few inches before it was stuck.

"A little help?" she asked.

I braced my hands on the door above her head and we both put everything we had into forcing the door open. When it finally gave, we stumbled across the threshold into a square room that smelled of mold and dirt.

Cobwebs were stretched over the ceiling, the top of the door and tangled in my hair and glasses. I brushed them away with a disgusted grunt and blew the dust off my lenses. When I could see again, I handed Andy her flashlight and we swept the light around the space.

"Well?" she asked. "What do you think?"

I shone my light around the room. The walls were bare of any adornment with the exception of what looked like torches at each corner of the room. I had expected…well I wasn't sure. Perhaps something a bit more ornate, but as I thought about it, a plain room fit with who the priest was: a humble man who served his God and his people. Then my light landed on something in the middle of the room: a rectangular stone coffin on a dais. On the top was a carving of some kind that I couldn't see from here due to the layers of dirt and cobwebs. There was also writing along the bottom of the coffin that I also couldn't decipher from where I was. I wanted to bolt over to it, to clean off the filth and devour every single clue. But I wasn't a novice at this. I knew better than to launch myself across a floor in a room like this without at least a cursory look for booby traps.

I aimed my light on the floor, and Andy did the same. This felt too easy, and I was waiting for the other shoe to drop on us. But after examining the floor, and finding nothing out of the ordinary, I shrugged.

"I don't think there's anything to be afraid of," I said. "He may have thought that hiding the way he had would mean that only the devout would be able to find him."

"I hope you're right."

I nodded.

"Me too. Just to be safe though, walk in my footsteps."

It wasn't hard to do since my feet were so much bigger than hers, and there was so much dust that I was leaving a very clear trail. When we reached the coffin, Andy helped me clear off the debris, which included old flowers and leaves.

"Does someone come down here and put these on his grave?" she asked as I held up the dead foliage.

"It's possible, which means we don't have a lot of time."

I looked at the writing, which was in Spanish.

"Father Juarez, our protector and the saint of the holy relics," I let out a long breath and held back a sob of relief. "It's him."

There was another carving of a cross with the flowers wound around it. I wondered if there might be anything here that needed diffusing, or perhaps it was a clue. I brushed my fingers over the edges of the carving and an electric sensation ran up my arm. I jumped back from the tomb.

"What is it?" she asked.

"There's power in there…I can feel it. I think they did bury him with the cross of Galahad."

"Is that the trap maybe?"

"It could be. But we aren't here for it so perhaps we'll get a pass."

She snorted.

"When has that ever happened?"

I chuckled.

"Point taken."

We looked over the coffin as completely as possible, but found no evidence of any traps on the outside. We also couldn't find any clues about traps that may be inside the coffin. Sometimes, the absence of information was a good thing. If there weren't any warnings, chances were that there was nothing to worry about. But something about this didn't set well with me. I could feel that there was going to be a catch and I hated not being able to at least have a clue about what it was.

Once we were ready to look inside, Andy produced the small vial of neutralizing spray and had it at the ready as we prepared to lift the lid of the coffin. She lightly sprayed the lid and nothing happened. No sparks, no rumble or tremble of the stone.

"Well, I guess that's that," she said, "no artifact energy on the lid."

"Doesn't mean it's not a trap though."

"Agreed, but if there is one, I have no idea where it would be."

"So we take our chances?" I asked.

Andy shrugged.

"At this point? Yeah, I think we have to."

I licked my lips, and tried to think. Had I read something about this and had forgotten it? Or was it, indeed, safe? I decided to take one more careful look around the lid and the coffin but still didn't see anything suspicious.

"Okay, let's open this. You ready?" I asked.

She nodded and together we lifted and pushed the lid off. It was heavier than it looked and it took a few minutes to shift the lid enough to slide it off the coffin. I was barely able to keep it from crashing to the ground, but managed to set it down on its side, where it still echoed in the small space.

Some might think I would get tired of seeing a corpse. Seen one moldy, decomposed skeleton, seen them all, right? Most of the time, yeah. But there were occasions when an artifact would do things to the body, when I would be able to glimpse the person that had once inhabited this vessel.

And that's exactly what I felt when I looked into that coffin.

If I hadn't seen evidence of decay and the passage of time in the room all around me, I would've thought this was a hoax. That someone must come in and put a new body in here quite often. Because the man in that cobweb covered, moldy, dusty coffin looked as fresh and pristine as the day they laid him in there.

I almost felt like I knew the priest at this point. This man who had risked so much to stand up to evil, who had spent his life in service, was right here before me. A reverence took hold of me as I stared at his weathered face, lined and sagging with age, but there was the hint of a smile still on his lips under a scraggly white beard. He was bald with bushy eyebrows over sunken, closed eyes. His wrinkled, thin hands held the rosary in the picture and mosaic as they rested on his chest, a beautiful white cross at the end, which gave off a faint luminescence. Even his clothes, a simple black robe and priests collar, hadn't deteriorated. Everything, with the exception of his surroundings, was exactly as it must've been when they put him in that coffin.

"It's him," I whispered in awe. "The cross must've preserved him. It had to be. If it can work miracles for people who come and pray, obviously it preserved his body too."

"Okay," Andy breathed out, "what's next?"

"Well, I uh…to be honest, this feels wrong, like I'm desecrating it if I just go digging around in there."

"Yeah, I'm getting the same feeling."

I frowned as I stared at the old man, and wracked my brain for clues from the things I knew.

"Something doesn't feel right about this," I whispered. "Something…I don't think we're supposed to disturb him."

"But the map fragment, we need that last piece," Andy said.

"I know it's just…he looks so…alive."

"We've dealt with this before," Andy said. "We need to get the fragment. You're not a bad guy, you have pure intentions, so the cross should reward us, right?"

"Right…yeah…or it could fry us from the inside out."

"Good to know. I'll have the neutralizer on hand."

"Let me look inside the coffin for clues first," I said. "Maybe there's something in there that will direct us about what to do next."

"Okay, but be careful."

I nodded and took a deep breath.

Please forgive me, Father, for disturbing your rest. I hope you know I mean no disrespect.

I started at the foot of the coffin, gently moving the priests robe out of the way as I let my hand trail along the cold stone. Immediately my fingers glanced across more engraving but I couldn't read it.

"I need more light, come here," I said to Andy.

She came up next to me and shone the light where I pointed.

"Is that writing?" she asked.

"Yeah it's...Latin. 'Veritas est via ad sanctitatem'...Truth is the path to holiness."

"A motto of some kind?"

I shook my head and bent as far over the coffin as I could without falling into it. The writing was actually all around the inside of the coffin, all in Latin, the language of the church.

Holy language...so meant for a holy person...perhaps this is the other shoe I've been waiting for. A test...yeah, that feels right. A test before getting the treasure.

I brushed a bit more of the priest's garb to the side so I could read everything clearly. The carvings ran from about half way down the inside of one side of the coffin, down to his feet and back up the other side.

"It's more Latin with some iconography thrown in for good measure. I think it's warnings about tests...testing a man's heart, a man's mind, a man's...soul. It looks like at least two of those are in reference to the cave itself. There's another cross with a G on it, Galahad was pure of heart, we know that. But it goes on to define what that means. Maybe it's the first test...the test of a man's heart."

"And?"

I continued to read, my mind spinning as I attempted to take all of this in and cross reference it with everything I knew about the priest. He was a man who believed in the purification of the body and soul, who obviously did not trust just anyone to find what he viewed as the treasures of his God.

And that's when it hit me.

I re-read all of it, making sure I was correct with the iconography I was seeing as Andy patiently waited for me to finish.

Son of a bitch.

I stood up straight, my stomach in knots as I looked at Andy.

"I know what we have to do but you're not going to like it. Hell," I ran a hand through my hair, "I don't like it either."

She stared at me warily.

"Okay, what is it?"

I took a deep breath, trying very hard to steady the nerves ricocheting through me at lightning speed.

"There's a part on the inside here," I pointed at the text, "it says, 'If one seeks the treasures of God with deceit in his heart, he will be purified with fire, but never touch what he seeks'. That combined with the other Latin phrase," another deep breath, "I think it's asking us to basically have a confession. Unburden our hearts."

"To the priest?"

"No."

She was waiting for me to elaborate, but the words stuck in my throat. This was both ridiculous and poetic in a kind of messed up way. We'd always said we were more honest on missions than in 'the real world' but this…

"Come on, Luke, spit it out, you're starting to scare me."

I met her gaze, memorizing the way she was looking at me right now before I ruined it all.

"Confess to one another whatever secrets, whatever confessions, are weighing on our hearts."

Andy stared at me for a second before snorting and shaking her head.

"You can't mean that he wants us to…what? Have some belated marriage counseling?"

"It's as good a guess as any. Look, we haven't been truthful with each other about our *marriage*, which Catholics view as a sacrament. Do you really think he cares about that one time we didn't tip well, or the tiny fib we told the lady at the inn about being married?"

"No, but—"

"This isn't the way I wanted to do it but…we were always headed toward this conversation, right?"

Andy turned away from me and paced a few feet while I tried very hard not to feel like a complete asshole for asking her to bare these secrets for the sake of a stupid map fragment.

"Okay," she said, standing at the foot of the coffin. "If it will get what we need, I'll do it."

"I feel like this is wrong somehow. Like I shouldn't ask this of you."

"Maybe not, but I want to help you and I said I'd do whatever it took."

"But Andy—"

"Do you want this or not? You were pushing for this not even five minutes ago!"

"I know," I ran a hand through my hair again, pulling on the ends before I looked her in the eyes and admitted, "I'm scared that I'm pushing you to do something you'll regret."

She took a deep, shaky breath.

"Having this conversation isn't on my top five list of ways I'd like to spend my time, but you're right. We need to have it, and maybe this way it serves a purpose other than just hurting one another more."

I gave her mirthless chuckle and nodded.

"Good point."

"So…I guess you go first." Andy steadied herself. "Ask what you need to know."

I hesitated, my whole body hot and shaky. This would change everything and yet we didn't have a choice.

"Okay," I nodded and blew out a long breath. "Why did you leave me?"

"Boy, pulling out the big guns right away."

"Andy, c'mon."

"What? I'm fucking nervous. You want to have a post mortem about our marriage in a tomb! I mean, as far as metaphors go it's a little on the nose, but besides that, it's also jarring!"

"I know! And I'm sorry!"

"Well then cut me some slack! This isn't the easiest for me."

"And it is for me? You left me, no warning, no conversation, not even a chance to fix whatever was broken. Just a note with your rings on top. Do you have any idea how that made me feel?"

"Oh, you're going to start talking about your feelings now all of a sudden?" she asked, eyes blazing.

"What the hell does that mean? You were the one that always had a wall up. You retreated for months before you left and you wouldn't talk about it. I was always honest about my feelings with you."

"Are you fucking *kidding* me? Yeah, I might've been a little distant toward the end, but I wasn't the only one who had walls up."

I snorted and shook my head.

"Fine," she threw her hands up, "I was a lot distant, but it was a defense mechanism from a lifetime of being used and thrown aside by practically everyone in my life. Friends, boyfriends, girlfriends, they would all act like they cared about me, liked me, but when they got what they wanted out of me, they'd disappear. So yeah, I put up walls, I protect myself because I've had to! But with you I tried to open up, to trust you because I fell so hard for you. I'd never..." she took a rough breath and calmed herself before continuing. "I'd never fallen for someone the way I fell for you It made me feel so damn vulnerable and it terrified me. But I told myself I could trust you, that you loved me too so it was okay to let you in. But you weren't doing the same, you were constantly holding back from me."

I opened my mouth to argue when she barreled right on.

"You would get annoyed with me, frustrated over little things and I'd ask you what was wrong and you'd always tell me it was 'fine', even when it was obviously not. You *lied* about how you felt, you withheld from me like you couldn't trust me. And finally, when it would build up inside of you, it would explode and we'd have these huge fights. Out it would all come, all the shit I asked you about and you said was 'fine' suddenly was a big fucking deal. How the hell was I supposed to trust you when that happened over and over? And so yeah, after a while I didn't feel safe letting all my defenses down completely."

"I wasn't trying to *hide* anything from you I just didn't want to make a deal out of the little shit that's all," I said, my heart hammering in my chest. "I wanted this to work because I was so in love with you I couldn't see straight. So I overcompensated, I tried too hard to make it—"

"Perfect," she said.

"Yeah, you say that like it's bad."

"I never wanted perfect! Do you have any clue what it feels like to live under that kind of pressure?"

"I never asked *you* to be perfect!"

I stared at her in shock. This wasn't at all what I'd expected to hear. I thought I'd hear a litany of all the things I'd always feared would tear us apart, how she realized what a big mistake it was to marry me because were too different. I never thought it was because of how I'd acted due to my own fear of losing her.

The fucking irony.

"Yes, you did," her words came out jagged and it tore apart my heart. "Your need to make the relationship perfect made me feel like I had to be in order to live up to this pedestal you'd put me on. And I felt like I couldn't show you anything flawed because it would shatter that belief you had, that you'd suddenly *see me* and you wouldn't like what you saw."

"How could that ever be true? I loved you, I loved everything about you."

"I kill people, Luke! That's part of my job. I do things that make it hard to look at myself in a mirror sometimes! And I do it because I believe in the job, in what I'm doing, but that doesn't mean that sometimes I don't feel filthy from it."

"That doesn't make you a murderer, it's not like you— ."

"Stop!" she held up her hands, cheeks turning red. "You don't need to make me feel better about it!"

"Then what should I do, Andy? Agree with you? Wallow in it with you?"

"Yes! In some ways, yes! You were always telling me how strong I was, how I was the brave one. You *relied* on me for that, you *loved* me for that and I let that be our dynamic, I get that, but I never thought…I never thought it would be so hard to *live* with."

"I tried to be a better support on missions, and I didn't expect that from you at home."

"Luke, how could what I've done *not* leak out onto every single part of our lives? I carried every mission with me in here." She pressed a fist to her chest. "And when we were home, I never felt like I could be weak and admit how scared I was to you, how wrecked I was about some of the things I've had to do. So you *wallowing*, as you call it, would've been nice. You just letting me fall apart and hold me while I did. You telling me you love me whether I'm okay or not. Or even not saying anything at all, just being by my side."

"I was, Andy, I was right there. Every time you had a nightmare, every time you wanted to get drunk and needed someone to take care of you after. I was there! I saw you, every part, and I loved every single part of you."

"Then why did you work so hard to make it all so damn flawless? Why couldn't you just let us be rough around the edges? Because that's when it was *good*."

For a few moments, the only sound in the cold, gloomy tomb was her sobs. I felt like bees were zooming through my body, a trembling under the skin that was unnerving. Her words had shaken me to my very core and she deserved the truth, an explanation that I found myself loathe to offer because it would expose the deepest fears I'd had about us. Fears that I'd been ashamed to admit even to myself.

But Andy had done the brave thing and bared herself to me. Now it was my turn.

"I always felt like I wasn't enough for you," my voice was raspy, strained. "I'm not the guy that gets a girl like you. I'm not tough, I don't know twenty different ways to kill a man with my bare hands. I fucking puke at the smell of blood and I get excited about things like artisanal crackers and reading ancient manuscripts for fun. I don't go to weapons training classes, I go to Comic-Con and I blow my paycheck on replicas of light sabers, not fancy knives."

I shook my head and chuckled, remembering the day Andy had kissed me in Venice and changed my life forever.

"I couldn't even believe you looked my way, that you found anything about me the least bit alluring when we are so completely opposite. I fell in love with you from the start, and I knew I didn't have a snowballs chance in hell at getting you. But then you were suddenly there, in my life, in my arms, and I thought, 'Don't fuck this up Luke. She's a once in a lifetime woman. You gotta get this right'. So I tried to figure out how to get it right, tried to make sure that you had everything you could ever want, that I was giving you what everyone else couldn't, wouldn't."

"But why? Why did you think that's what I needed to stay with you?"

"Because I was afraid that you'd wake up one day and be so damn *bored* with me and my stupid geek shit and my ancient languages. That you'd resent being tied to me. So I tried to make life good, *perfect*. Yes, I did that. I admit it! Because I needed some way to be *more* than all the guys you saw every day that had everything in common with you, that were so obviously more suited to you."

"You think I was somehow unaware of how different we were?" she asked, tears falling off her chin even as her voice rose in anger. "You think I never worried that you'd get tired of me not being as smart as you and go find a hot smart chick? I knew who you were, Luke, and I wanted *you*! I never wanted you to be anything other than what you were."

"Then why were you gone so much? You always jumped at the chance to leave. I don't resent you for your career, you know that. And you didn't have to do every mission with me either, but you started shutting me out of even that part of your life. The part that I knew we were the best at. And then, towards the end, you were never home at all. So if I was enough, if you loved me, why didn't you want to be around me?"

She closed her eyes and took a deep breath.

"I wasn't having an affair," she said, "that's not why I was gone so much so let's just get that out of the way right now."

"Okay, then why?"

"Because I couldn't take it anymore! I couldn't take feeling like I was a fraud because I wasn't the perfect fucking goddess you thought I was and I hated feeling like I had to live up to it and failing constantly. I hated how much we were fighting, about everything and how you were getting more and more distant."

"I'm not the only one who was distant. You barely wanted to spend any time with me when you *were* home and then you'd leave again! You talk about how you couldn't trust me to be open, well it wasn't exactly easy with you either. You were so damn closed off that even when I was with you, I felt alone. Then I catch you, the night you've come back after being gone for over a month, in a bar with your *fucking partner*!"

"I needed someone to talk to!" Andy screamed.

"Why not me? I was your husband!"

"You weren't home!"

"You could've picked up a phone. I would've come home to you! I would've done *anything* for you!"

"It was too late!"

Those words were a rusty knife in my heart. I'd known it that night, looking at her laughing with that man.

She hadn't laughed in a while with me.

"But you laughed with him," I murmured and began to pace around the room.

"Luke—"

I held up my hand, afraid if she said anything else I'd lash out and make it all so much worse.

A stew of conflicting emotions coursed through me.

Anger.

Guilt.

Frustration.

Grief.

I'd naively thought that it would be simple, or something I'd already worked out in my head. That she would tell me this or that and I'd have a solution for it because I'd been thinking about this conversation for the past year. But I hadn't imagined *this* conversation. And I had no idea where to go from here, how to make this right.

Except to ask.

So, with my heart now a gaping wound, my mind swimming in memories I'd much rather forget, I turned back toward her to ask when Andy spoke first.

"It's not all your fault, you know," she said, and ran a hand over her face. "We have to be honest, right? So here goes. I could've said something. So many times I could've told you what was wrong and I didn't."

"Why not?" I asked, my voice hoarse.

"Because I was afraid that if I pushed you, that it would be a reason to leave me. And I'd been left so many times by so many people that I'd loved that…I just didn't think I could take it if you left me."

"So you left first."

She nodded.

"I hated you for hurting me when you left," I said. "Or at least, I wanted to. But really I hated myself because all I could think of was that I was never really going to get to keep you so why was I so shocked when you left? But it wasn't all me, and it wasn't all you either. It was both of us. I didn't tell you how bad you hurt me when you kept going on missions one after the other, I never said a word about how lonely

I was. Instead I let myself be jealous. It was easier honestly. Easier than begging you to tell me what I'd done wrong so you'd stay."

Our silence hung in the air, giving us a chance to process all of the information we'd both just been bashed over the head with.

"I'm sorry," she said with a shaky breath. "I'm so sorry I hurt you. For what it's worth, I didn't leave because I didn't love you."

"And I didn't try and make everything perfect because you weren't enough. I loved every single piece of you, and I'm so sorry I ever made you feel that I didn't. You were the most extraordinary person to ever come into my life, and I just…I just didn't want to mess it up."

Andy nodded.

"I know that now."

"So I guess," I said, trying to breathe past the way my chest ached, "we both fucked it up."

"Yeah, I guess we did."

The moment the last words were out of her mouth, a faint glow began to emanate from the coffin. We both rushed to it, and saw that the cross had started to shine bright. After a few seconds, it was so bright that it illuminated the entire tomb in warm, pure light.

Just before it became too blinding, the light faded and the sound of stone scraping against stone sounded through the room. I looked down and saw a small drawer-like enclosure had swung out from the base of the coffin to reveal two small scrolls, wrapped in leather and tied closed.

Andy looked up at me, her eyes wet with tears and wide with awe.

Our confessions had done it.

Yet never in my life had I felt a victory was more bittersweet.

CHAPTER FIFTEEN

LUKE

I rushed over to the small drawer and knelt down at the same Andy did. She held the flashlight over me as I reverently removed the two small scrolls.

"Boy, did this guy love his hidden places," Andy said.

I snorted as I stared down at the contents.

"Well? Go on, you found it!" she said.

I swallowed, and my hands shook as I held the two leather bound clues. What if I was wrong? What if it was another goose chase, another clue but not leading where I needed to go?

Andy slipped her hand into mine and squeezed.

"Whatever happens, we solve it together."

I let out a long breath and nodded. My heart might lay in tatters inside my chest, but there was no one I'd rather have beside me as I did this.

With the utmost care, I unrolled the first and was so relieved when I saw the last map fragment that my legs gave out on me and I fell on my butt on the dirty floor.

"It's the piece," I croaked out. "Oh my God, Andy, it's the piece!"

She threw her arms around me and I clung to her, burying my face in her neck. It was instinct, pure and simple to lean on her, find comfort and strength. But after what she told me I wasn't sure it was appropriate. When I tried to pull away, she only held me tighter.

"It's okay," her voice was broken, "let's just hold each other, just for a second."

I let out a ragged breath and nodded against her. She felt so right in my arms, how was I going to let her go after this? Even with everything that had just passed between us, I still wanted to take her home with me and hide from the world while I reacquainted myself with her every curve, with the taste of her.

But we have a mission. And now we can finish it.

I pulled away and looked up into her eyes, longing to press my lips to hers and somehow heal this.

That's not the way, though. A kiss or a fuck isn't going to do it.

So I let her go and she sat back, scrubbing tears from her cheeks.

"What's the other one?" she asked, refocusing us both on what was pressing.

I took a deep breath to steady myself and unrolled the other scroll. Written onto the leather was another map, this one bigger than the fragment. At first, I was unsure what I was looking at. The first part of it was a long rectangle divided into three sections, that ended in a square shape. There were simple symbols on each section and one Latin word in each section.

"*Primum purificate…Mens* and *fidem…Animus* and *gratuiti…Sanctus*," I read out loud.

"Latin again?"

"Yeah…"

My mind began to run through all the clues so far and I sprang to my feet.

"Inside the coffin, were references to tests," I said, finding the phrases etched into the stone. "Here, testing the mind, *mens*…then testing the soul, *animus*."

"Since that was with this final piece of the map," Andy said, "I assume that what you're looking at is a map of the cave, and how to navigate the booby traps the priest must've rigged."

"Yes!" I said, a wide grin splitting my face as excitement raced like a drug through my veins. "This right here, *primum purificate*, means 'first purify' indicating some kind of purification test, and then the last one here, *sanctus*, means 'holy', so he must've put all the artifacts in one room."

"How is that cave still standing? The Archive has a whole, precise system on how to safely store artifacts and this guy just puts them all in a room and leaves?"

"I don't know, that's a great question." I glanced at the Cross of Galahad still faintly glowing on his chest. "He wielded an artifact that very few were ever able to touch without dying. Maybe he had a connection to these artifacts because of his faith. Maybe he was pure enough to understand how to safely store them, even use them."

I looked down at the map of the cave in my hands, another, more frightening thought occurring to me.

"What's wrong?"

"The two sections here in between where the cave begins and where the artifacts likely are. I think…What if he used other artifacts to set the traps?"

"Is that even possible? I mean, most artifacts can't usually be manipulated just any way someone wants."

"Maybe he was special, attuned to the origins of the artifacts in a way most aren't. I don't know but look at this," I pointed at the first of the middle sections, "See this written here, *mens* and *fidem* mean 'mind' and 'faith', so some kind of test of the mind and faith, then the second section, *animus* and *gratuiti* mean 'soul' and 'selflessness', so again a test pertaining to those two. These symbols with them I'm not sure about, but what if they're the artifacts he's used to create these tests or traps?"

"That's elaborate and fucking scary."

I nodded, my mind spinning with both excitement at seeing what this man could've done. And terror at the same thought.

What if the tomb was the easy one? What did he leave there in between us and the Scivias? And will I be able to get us through it?

"Do we need anything else here?" Andy asked, jolting me back to the present.

"No, help me replace the lid though."

I took one last look at the man whose life I'd studied for so long and sent a silent prayer to his God for guidance and grace.

It was a struggle to lift the heavy stone lid but we eventually got it back in place, our efforts echoing ominously through the small space.

"Ready?" Andy asked.

A chill raced down my spine as I stepped up to the doorway of the tomb. This was it, the final leg of my journey. At the end of it, I'd either have what I needed to make a cure for this disease, or I'd have failed and will have to face whatever that future held.

"Hey," Andy gripped my forearm and caught my eye, "I know what we just said…it was a lot. But it doesn't change my decision. I'm with you, to the end. That hasn't changed."

Her words were a warm blanket wrapped around my soul and I pressed a small kiss to her forehead.

"A team to the end," I whispered.

"To the end. Now, let's go see this cave of yours."

I nodded and followed her up the stairs, closing the creaking door behind me and leaving the priest to his rest once again.

We were silent as we navigated the narrow, dark passage which was likely the only reason we heard the voices as early as we did. My heart gave a sharp lurch as we both stopped just shy of the top of the stairs, still hidden by the wall to our left.

"I'm a reasonable man," said a cold voice I knew all too well.

Kristoff! I was hoping that fucker wouldn't leave his comfy tent.

"And I know you feel an obligation to protect your heritage, blah, blah, blah," Kristoff continued. "But I want you to think long and hard about the consequences of such actions. Sure, I just have you right now, but what if I went and got your wife? Your daughter? Your grandchildren?" The tap of footsteps echoed up to us. "What if I went and emptied each house in this village, marched family by family to the back of the chapel and shot them dead? Would it be worth protecting your secrets then?"

Sobs rose up in the chapel and my hands tightened into fists.

"Please," another voice begged, "please do not hurt my family."

"I don't want to," said Kristoff. "In spite of what people believe, I don't relish bloodshed. But I will do it if no other course of action presents itself to me. So, one more time, where is the priest's tomb?"

"I don't know, I swear it! That's a secret long lost to us. Please, you have to believe me!"

"You are descended from the priest's brother's family. You would be the ones to keep such secrets, and you're telling me you don't know anything?"

"I don't, I swear it!"

"Okay, shhhh, okay. You obviously don't know anything, so you're not much use to me."

The man's sobs became louder.

"Oh, thank— "

A gun shot shattered the night and I jumped. A moment later, the wet thump of a body hitting the floor made bile rise to the back of my throat.

Andy looked back at me and I nodded, confirming what she silently asked me with her eyes. Yes, Kristoff was evil enough to make good on his threat. He would go and systematically kill the people in this village to get what he wanted. And we couldn't let that happen.

"Let me go to them," I whispered in her ear. "They want me, you stay back and follow us."

"Are you crazy? They'll kill you."

"No, they need me. I know him, he could've killed me lots of times but he never did. I'm safe. You follow and when the timing is right you can take them out. Let me deal with Kristoff though."

"Why?"

"He's got some kind of medallion, protects him from harm. I don't know the extent of the protection, but I need to get that off him before you can shoot him."

"He's obviously a psychopath! You can't reason with a man like that."

"I know, I was stuck with him in an encampment for weeks. But think about this, it's the best play. If they capture you too, what then? And they have no incentive to keep you alive."

She grit her teeth, mulling over the plan. Finally, she nodded.

"I'll be right behind you," she promised and squeezed behind me so I could go first.

Her hand tightened on my arm just before I turned to climb the rest of the way.

"Wait."

I looked back and she pulled me down for a bruising, desperate kiss. The longing and heat she ignited inside of me didn't make sense after what we'd confessed to one another in the crypt, but I didn't care. I pulled her hips to me and kissed her back with a ferocity that I'd never felt before. If this was the last time I tasted her, felt her in my hands, I wasn't going to hold back. So I ran my hands up her back and into her hair as my tongue plundered her mouth and I devoured her tiny whimpers.

When I finally let her go, Andy's eyes drifted open slowly, the red marks from my tusks scratched anew on her lips. I brushed my thumbs over the marks, willing myself not to think of all the ways this could go horribly wrong.

"Don't take any stupid risks," she breathed.

"You, either," I dug the map of the interior of the cave out of my backpack and handed it to her. "Here, keep this with you so we can navigate the place. I don't want them to have it."

"Okay."

She stepped further back into the shadows but withdrew her gun, preparing for whatever might happen when I popped my head up.

Kristoff was just ordering someone to go get another villager when I stepped up onto the ledge.

"There's no need for that Kristof," I shouted. "I've already been to the crypt."

Three guns swung around and were trained on me. The chapel was illuminated with small lamps they must've brought in with them, and the light glinted off the wet blood pooling in the aisle, bits of bone and brain matter splattered on a few of the pews. I could just barely detect it, but I was still too far away to be affected by the smell. I grit my teeth to hold it together as I made my way off the ledge and toward Kristoff and his men. Kristoff was in a ridiculous white suit that didn't have a speck of blood or dirt on it, his thick white hair wavy from the moisture in the air and his chilly blue eyes sparkled like ice.

"Professor!" he said with absolute glee. "It is so good to see you again and just in time to help me."

I climbed down from the ledge and the moment my feet touched the floor, the two feral Orcs he controlled came over and restrained me.

"Where's your little girlfriend?" he asked.

"She left, probably ran back to the Archive to tell them I went AWOL."

He cocked his head to the side, a grin bloomed on his tan face. I held my breath, my expression hard mostly because I was trying very hard not to throw up as the two Orcs brought me closer to the puddle of blood.

"I don't think so," he finally said in a sing-song voice. "That idiot we tortured said you were in love with her. You're protecting her. Did she get away with your map?"

My stomach turned at the thought of what Trevor had gone through at this psycho's hands. I hadn't liked the guy, but no one deserved that.

"No," I answered him.

"We'll see, won't we," he turned to one of his goons. "Search out back and you," he gestured to another one, "get me his backpack. Time to see what you've discovered in my absence, dear Professor."

As I handed it over, sweat dripped down my spine and my heart was doing a very good job of trying to hammer its way out of my chest. If Andy thought for one second I was in trouble, she'd open fire. And while she was a pretty good shot, I had no idea how many others were outside. She might take these guys down, but there were only so many bullets she had before it didn't matter.

Kristoff pulled the rolled up map fragment out of my backpack and chuckled.

"Very good, thank you Professor Turner," he turned to the man next to him. "Kill him."

"Wait!"

I put my hands up, the panic growing to fever pitch inside of me. I prayed Andy would just stay down but if they kept threatening me, all bets were off.

"You need me. There are booby traps in the cave and I'm the only one that can help you navigate them."

Kristoff's eyes narrowed as he stared at me, his mind trying to suss out if I was lying or not. I held my breath, the tickle of sweat falling down the side of my body. Finally, he nodded.

"Alright then, I suppose you still serve a purpose. But one trick, one moment you don't come through and I'll shoot you myself."

"Yeah, sure that's fine."

Kristoff's face changed from menacing to cheerful in a split second.

"Wonderful! Let's be off then. If this map is correct, we can be there by dawn."

With great self-control, I resisted the urge to look behind me, and followed Kristoff out.

CHAPTER SIXTEEN
ANDROMEDA

I hated Luke putting himself in this situation. He was better than he used to be when it came to lying and acting the part to deceive an adversary, but he wasn't a trained agent. I'd always been protective of him in these situations, always put myself in the line of fire, but this time he was doing it and that didn't sit right with me at all.

It set me on edge, my emotions clouding my instincts and shouting at me to rescue him and get the hell out of here. But I knew better than to give in to my feelings when it came to a pivotal moment in a mission. What was required was logic; a moment to quiet the raging in my mind so that my instincts could rise to the surface.

I took a deep breath as Luke convinced Kristoff not to kill him. It was a good play, and I told myself that it showed that he knew what he was doing, he'd be fine.

I heard them take him out of the building, and waited. Sure enough, a few minutes later I heard the telltale shuffle of feet. They'd left someone behind to make sure I wasn't here. It gave me time to get more centered, and a plan was starting to form.

Finally, the person left, and I heard the chapel door slam. Still, I waited a few minutes more, forcing myself to stay still even as I heard an engine revving outside.

When I peeked my head up, the chapel was dark. The moonlight that filtered through wasn't amplified anymore but I could still make out the dead body they'd just left in the aisle in a puddle of his own blood. I shimmied down without breaking anything and peeked out of the windows. There was movement at the front of the chapel, and I waited some more. This was becoming an extreme test of my patience and I tried very hard not to worry about losing Luke's trail.

I'd seen enough of the map fragment to know the basic markers so even if I did lose them I could still follow the clues to the cave. When the movement outside had stilled and I didn't hear anymore voices, I snuck out of the front entrance of the chapel and ran for the village.

Luke had left the motorcycle there and with any luck it still had enough gas to get me where I needed to go. When I arrived at the back entrance of the small inn, the celebration was over, and the lights from the square had dimmed. All was quiet, the only sound an occasional ruffling or squawk of the birds, which caused me to jump as I ran into our room to grab my pack and some extra clips of ammo. We'd paid someone to launder our clothes earlier in the day and they sat on the bed, freshly folded. I slipped the light colored linen pants and shirt off, and put my dark pants and tank on, then tied my hair into a braid. I slipped my bowie knife into my boot sheath, knowing in my gut that the blade would be wet with blood by the time I was done. There was no need to take the pack though, I needed speed and the only thing in there really at this point was rations. With any luck, we'd be getting a transport after this.

And then straight to being redacted.

I shrugged that off. I knew what I was risking when I'd made the decision to stick with Luke. There was no backing out now.

I ran down to the motorcycle only to have a gun pressed to the back of my head.

"You brought death here," said a deep voice I recognized as the guitar musician from the celebration earlier.

"I did and I'm so very sorry," I admitted. "We didn't mean to and right now, if you don't let me go, they'll get the holy relics."

"How do I know you won't get them?"

"You don't. And in the spirit of truth, we need one of the relics but we passed the priest's test in his crypt, so maybe you could trust us?"

"Prove it."

Damn it.

I swallowed and prayed I remembered enough of the damn Latin to make this man believe me.

"Veritas est...uh, via...um at, no! Ad...um, holiness, it's Latin for holiness. It starts with an 's'. Look, I'm shit, er, um, bad at Latin, that's not my thing, that's my hus-friend's department. So...I mean I got most of it, right?"

The pressure of the gun retreated and I breathed a silent sigh of relief.

"Veritas est via ad sanctitatem. Padre said that only someone who was truly worthy would see those words and live to tell anyone about it. You saw him?" the man asked. "You saw Padre Juarez?"

I turned around slowly to find not only the musician, but several others staring at me.

"Yes," I said, "and I promise you, we do not want to disturb the relics. My friend is sick and he needs help. One of the items in there can heal him. That's all we want."

The man nodded.

"The Tears of Christ."

"What? No...what do you mean?"

He frowned at me.

"There's a vial of the tears that Christ shed on the cross. It can heal anything completely. Isn't that what you were wanting?"

It wasn't but I didn't have time to explain.

"Yes, of course yes, sorry, it's been a long day."

He looked at me with some doubt and I kicked myself for not just playing along from the start. But this new information meant there was a backup in there, something that would at least save Luke even if we couldn't find the book.

"Do you know where the vial might be in the cave?" I asked.

"No," he admitted, "the men and women that helped Padre Juarez with the cave are dead, and they took those secrets with them."

I nodded.

"I need to go, those men took my friend and I have to catch up with them before they get to the cave."

The man nodded and handed over his gun.

"I see you already have one, but I'm guessing you could always use another."

I smirked.

"That's very true."

"We are trusting you," he said with a deep frown. "And believe me when I say that, those who betray the trust of our Padre's flock do not have happy lives."

I swallowed at that and nodded.

"We will only take what we need to heal my friend and his people."

"Then go with the blessing of Padre Juarez and his flock."

It turned out that either Kristoff and his guys were arrogant enough not to care that they left ample evidence of where they'd been, or they were just too stupid to know the difference, but either way I was grateful. I was able to follow them on the motorcycle pretty far until I ran out of gas and had to continue on foot. By then however, I was close enough to the cave that I didn't have to run very   far   to   catch   up   to them.

It was still dark outside, though the barest hint of light from the east was starting to show. I could hear the roar of the ocean nearby, the faintest hint of saltwater tinged the air. Around me, the night was oddly quiet. I made my way through the trees and plants, which became sparse as I neared the small clearing in front of a steep grouping of hills that separated the forest from the white sand beach.

The Protectors were traveling in three different Jeeps. They'd driven right up to the hill which, at this proximity, was practically a small mountain. There were three men at the back, a few in the middle and at the very front was Kristoff, Luke and a couple of other very big men. There was dense foliage growing up one side of the hill and it was there that Luke took them, gesturing to the vines and leaves.

I couldn't take out anyone with my gun. By the time I dropped three of them, they'd have Luke at gun point.

I do have a knife.

It wasn't ideal; I wasn't as good in close range fights as I was from a distance, but I couldn't think of much else. If I could take out enough of them quietly, to get close to Luke, then I could get the rest with my gun. Which would hopefully give him enough time to get that medallion off of Kristoff.

I drew the knife and crept out of the forest, slipping into the mental detachment that had always made me a good soldier, and a good Agent when push came to shove. I compartmentalized the fact that these were living, breathing beings and focused on the mission. I knew that it would hit me later. Sometimes in the middle of the night. Sometimes while I was watching a movie or eating a croissant. I'd end up crying, using the techniques my therapist had recommended. But for right now, I was the soldier I needed to be.

The first man was smoking a cigarette, mumbling about how he hated the forest. I shoved the knife into his lungs before he could exhale his last drag, and he made a low gasping sound and I eased him to the ground.

Next was the man a few feet ahead of him and to the right. I almost managed to get him in the lungs as well but he turned at the last minute.

Instead, I had to clap my hand over his mouth and stab him through the neck. Warm blood coated my hand as I pulled the knife free. I wiped it on the hem of his shirt, needing my hands dry, and not slippery.

The third and final one at the back was far more vigilant than his other comrades. I had to duck next to one of the Jeeps as he turned and ran past me toward the man whose throat I pierced. He examined the scene and noticed the other man. I saw the moment he was going to call for help and ran up to him, tackling him to the ground. It wasn't as quiet as I'd hoped but I'd surprised him. I forced the man onto this stomach and sliced down into his back. I stabbed him once, twice, three times before he stopped struggling. I had no idea why he didn't cry out for help but I was grateful for it nonetheless.

I wiped the knife on his shirt and stowed it in the sheath, drawing one of my firearms this time. From here, the men were too bunched together to be able to take them out any other way except from a distance.

I hid behind the same Jeep and surveyed my options. Kristoff and Luke were still at the front, where two of the larger goons were hacking at the vines and leaves at what must've been the entrance to the cave. There was a group of three men to my left, cutting off the escape to the beach, and four more to the right doing the same to the forest. I tried to think of which would be the best escape route and decided on the forest, which also afforded me the ability to take out more men.

I checked the ammo, had sufficient rounds and took a deep breath. I was an excellent shot and had the medals to prove it, but this time I was more nervous than I'd been since training. This wasn't some artifact that caused mayhem, this was Luke's life and it was in my hands.

I can do this. This is what I trained for.

I opened my eyes and lined up my first shot. They were so close together that I figured that the first two would be relatively easy to drop, but by the time I got to the third, someone would likely be in motion, so I had to get this right.

I took a breath, stilling my mind, closing out everything but the target and squeezed the trigger. I took out the first two with clean head shots.

The third moved back and I had to adjust, hitting him in the face. The fourth managed to get cover so I swung around to the men on the beach side. Those three had started to search for me. I shot the middle one with two rounds to the chest, though I had to stand up a bit more to do it, revealing my location.

The fourth man, the one I'd left alive, decided it was prime time to strike back and I nearly got my head shot off. I ducked down and checked over the hood long enough to shoot at the fourth man on the forest side. Out of the corner of my eye I saw the other two trying to out flank me.

I spun around and got one the moment he went behind me with a sloppy shot to the gut and one to the chest. I was out of ammo at that point and as I went to change the clip a telltale *click* sounded behind me and the hard press of a gun was shoved into the back of my head.

"Enough," said Kristoff, "unless you want Luke to become a mindless beast."

I raised my hands as my heart hammered in my chest. Was he saying what I think we was?

Kristoff took the gun I held, my knife and the other gun in my shoulder holster.

"Stand up."

I did and glanced toward the front. The two that had been clearing away vines weren't Mundane men at all. They were light green Orcs, their eyes red and muscles far too pronounced. Now that I was closer I could see the neural halos on their heads and realized that Kristoff was controlling them. One of the Orcs had his meaty forearm around Luke's throat, the other held a thick syringe to Luke's bicep. If I had to guess, I'd say it was the solution Luke had talked about before, the one that turned Orcs into Kristoff's mindless beasts.

"Okay! Okay, I'm done, just don't do that to him," I said, unable to hide the fear in my voice, "I'll stop I...just don't."

One moment Kristoff was scowling at me, a gun trained to my forehead. The next, he pulled the gun back and burst out laughing.

"Oh my dear! Of course I'm not going to do that to Professor Turner. I need him coherent and able to actually talk, not grunting and foaming at the mouth. Oh, I really had you going, didn't I?"

Was this guy for fucking real?

I must've looked exactly as whiplashed as I felt because he laughed some more before throwing his arm around me as if we were buddies and pulling me up toward the front, the barrel of the gun now resting at my stomach.

"Come, come! This is an exciting moment. I'm sure a seasoned agent such as yourself is very excited to see the biggest artifact cache anyone has laid eyes on in at least a hundred years."

"Yeah…I can barely contain myself," I said, completely dead pan.

"Now, don't be like that. I promise as soon as we're inside you can pick out a nice little souvenir for yourself."

He chuckled some more and the arm around my shoulders tightened until I was pressed to his side, the gun digging into my hip.

"Now, Professor," he said, a hint of menace behind the cheerful tone, "if you would be so kind as to open the cave for us?"

Luke's eyes ran over me, checking for wounds, and I gave him a wobbly smile. We'd tried, we really had, and now we had to figure out how to lose these guys inside the damn cave full of dangerous artifacts and booby traps.

Just another day at the office.

"And if I don't?" Luke asked, shocking me and Kristoff.

He snorted.

"Oh please, do we really have to do this? I know you need what's in there. And I'll make you a deal. You can take one thing, whatever you want, as long as you get us there. Alright? See, I reward my men and you are no different, even though you ran and cost me greatly. I am willing to forgive, dear Professor, unless you give me a reason not to."

Luke glanced at me, a war in those beautiful eyes of his just before turning back to the now uncovered entrance.

"Oh, this is so exciting! Come along, my dear."

Kristoff pulled me with him, my skin crawling where he touched me. It wasn't sexual, it was pure threat. I glanced at him and spotted a silver chain around his neck, the end disappearing below the buttons of his pressed, white shirt.

I bet that's the amulet. I wonder if I can grab it, then disarm him and—

"I know what you're thinking," Kristoff said.

"What do you mean?" I asked.

"You're thinking, how is he so calm right now? Doesn't he know that I could kill him with very little effort?"

I swallowed because I *was* thinking some approximation of that. "Well?" I asked.

He turned a hard smile toward me.

"I have a little secret."

"The amulet?"

"Very good, dear, but no, something else." He leaned toward me until his lips grazed my ear and I cringed. "I know where the book is, and you don't. So if you want *him* to get it, I suggest you stop with the stabby thoughts. Or I'll enslave him anyway, beautiful brain or not."

I'd faced down some of the most scary things on this planet, seen my share of carnage and terrifying supernatural power. But in this moment, all of that paled in comparison to what he'd just threatened.

"Do we have an understanding?" he asked.

"Yeah."

"Splendid! Now, let's see how far the Professor has gotten," he said, as if we were going for ice cream.

Luke was examining the entrance, a stone rectangle with carvings around the edge, while looking at one of his notebooks. I usually loved watching him work, but the longer Kristoff touched me, the longer I had to stand there knowing that we weren't likely to make it out of this alive, the more an oily sensation spread in my stomach and I just wanted to scream.

Finally, Luke pressed on a few places that ended up being more of the hidden depressions in the rock, and a few seconds later a low rumbling sound rolled over us. The stone door moved out of the tight space it had been wedged into, and then slid to the right. A wave of moldy, dusty air hit us, obscuring the first view of the cave inside. By now, the sun had breached the horizon and the gloom of night was fleeing and when the air cleared, there was just enough light to see the first few feet into the cave, which was just a tunnel at this point.

To my great relief, Kristoff let me go so he could gesture to the two men I'd left alive.

"You two will take point," he bellowed.

You son of a bitch. They'll be the first ones to die when something goes wrong.

But with one look at Luke, I knew what he was thinking: We know where the booby traps are. We can set them off and systematically kill everyone.

It was brilliant and incredibly risky. One wrong move, and we'd be the ones to die.

The two men handed out large flashlights to the feral Orcs and Kristoff, and then took point as ordered. The two Orcs went next and then Luke, Kristoff and I brought up the rear.

Stepping over the threshold gave me the chills, but not from fear. It was like stepping into a completely different world, a place that had been frozen in time and we were the lucky idiots who were given the chance to explore it. In spite of the gun at my back, the thrill of seeing something that no one else had in decades was something I'd learned from Luke over the years and now found myself incapable of escaping. One look up at him and I could tell by the small upward curve of his lips that he also couldn't help being excited. I wished we were alone, that both of us could just soak it all in.

The air in the narrow passage was stale, musty, and there was a hint of moisture that reminded me of a room with a leaky roof. The walls on either side were damp, weeping in spots and I was grateful that artifacts seemed to have an incredible capacity for surviving in such conditions.

It would make it easier to discern what was a fake and what was real. But first, we had to get rid of our guards.

We were nearing the end of the passage when the sound of stone scrapping against stone reached my ears just before Luke tackled me to the ground. I heard the unmistakable whisper of projectiles shooting through the air, followed by the crumple of two bodies hitting the ground.

I looked up to see the two front guards on the ground, writhing in agony. At first I wasn't sure what I was looking at. Their torsos were dotted with small wounds, with no more damage than perhaps a thick needle might make. But then their faces started to redden, and they screeched. Before my eyes, the skin on their bodies peeled away like paper curling in a fire, tendrils of smoke rising from their mouths and eyes.

"Oh my God," I gasped.

They were being roasted from the inside out.

Within minutes, their bodies were charred husks, the stench of it hit me like a punch and I gagged.

"Are you alright?" Luke breathed.

I nodded just before one of the feral Orcs yanked him off me and shoved him against one of the walls.

"That was not smart, Professor," Kristoff snarled. "One more like that and I will have to think of a very creative way to motivate you."

"I'm not going to help you destroy the world," Luke snapped.

"Destroy it? Oh, for a smart man you are really stupid, you know that? We don't want to *destroy*, we want to make it better. To take away all the reasons for war, suffering, greed. Can you imagine what the world would be like if no one wanted anything but what was given to them? If everyone was motivated purely by the good of the collective?"

"And you would determine all of that, I assume," I asked as I brushed dirt off my pants.

"Well, of course! Who else? Politicians? The Archive? All corrupted and rotten down to their core. No, the Protectors want what is best for the world."

"By taking free will away?" Luke asked.

"You say that like it's a bad thing," Kristoff chuckled. "What has free will ever gotten anyone, other than suffering? Now, I could talk all day about this but," his expression turned cold in a second, "we need to move on. No more tricks, Professor, especially since you'll be taking point."

I swallowed down a ball of fear in my throat and tried to go up front with Luke when Kristoff's clammy hand pulled me back.

"Oh no, my dear. You will keep me company back here."

"You keep your hands off her!" Luke threatened.

"I'm fine, Luke, just get us through this."

"Yes, listen to your ex-wife and get us through this."

Luke grit his teeth and turned around. We stepped over the bodies of the two men, Luke covering his mouth and nose with his hand.

It didn't take us long to get past the bodies. The corridor we were in was short and soon the passage way opened up from claustrophobic and narrow into a sprawling room. There were torches resting in rusted sconces on the walls and I wracked my brain to try and remember if this was one of the marked places on the map. Kristoff motioned to the Orcs to light the torches and as light spread, I saw that this was merely a small chamber in front of a simple door.

The map was a rectangle split into three. We just past the first division on the map. This is the second. Another test, but what kind? Will Luke really know what it is?

I found Luke in the growing torchlight and stared at him, wishing there was a way to convey what I was thinking. He blinked several times and rubbed his eyes before crouching down for a moment. I was finding it hard to breathe as I watched him get hit with a flare of symptoms. He wouldn't be able to recall the information from the map or concentrate to figure it out and what then? Was I going to have to watch him die?

"Professor, it's time to prove your usefulness," Kristoff demanded.

"He's tired, let him catch his breath," I said.

Kristoff's eyes narrowed as he took Luke in.

"Is he, or is he stalling?"

"I just need…"

Luke stumbled to his feet and then tackled the nearest Orc to the ground. I hoped it was ruse, because if he was having a bout of symptoms then he wasn't going to be able to overpower the Orc at all. I took the opportunity the distraction afforded though, and punched Kristoff hard enough to send him stumbling back. I grappled for the gun, which went off pointed up at the ceiling. Rock and dust rained down on us and I prayed we wouldn't have a cave in.

Kristoff punched me hard across the face and my grip loosened on his gun, just as meaty hands yanked me from behind. I found myself pinned by the throat to the wall by one of the Orcs.

"Enough!" Kristoff snarled. "This is ridiculous. Do what I tell you and find that treasure room!"

Kristoff marched up to Luke, who was being held down on the floor by the Orc he'd tackled. He pressed the barrel of his gun against Luke's temple and my entire body went cold. This man was crazy enough to do it, even though he needed Luke.

"Shooting me isn't going to do anything for you," Luke said.

"Yes, you're absolutely right."

Kristoff jumped up, and stalked over to me.

I saw what was coming and I struggled against the vice like grip around my neck but it was no use, I couldn't move a muscle.

"No! Kristoff, I'll do whatever you want!" Luke screamed in panic.

"Yes Professor, I know you will."

The shot echoed through the cave as white hot pain ripped through my middle.

CHAPTER SEVENTEEN

LUKE

My entire world shattered and narrowed at the same time as I saw the shock and agony on Andy's face. The bloom of red across her stomach poured a foul coppery scent into the air that would normally have me vomiting. But the bile in the back of my throat wasn't from that. It was terror and rage, pouring through my body in a white hot torrent.

Before I knew what I was doing, I'd broken free of the feral Orc's hold and was charging at her.

"Andy!"

I caught her just before he body slumped to the ground.

"You're gonna be okay, just stay with me," I begged.

She cupped the bullet wound, blood seeping from between her fingers, and tears fell in streaks through the dirt on her cheeks.

"Luke, you can't let him get…," her face twisted in pain and she gave a strangled sob. "You have to…be careful. Think of yourself…protect the world from him."

"Shhh, just rest. I'm gonna save you," my words broke as I held her to me.

"That's…my job…to save you."

I kissed her hair and forced back the tears.

"Not this time, baby."

"Do you want to save her, or hold her as she dies a slow death?" Kristoff asked behind me.

I turned slowly, my vision tinting with red around the edges as I caught sight of him. I set Andy gently against the wall and stood up.

"You son of a bitch! I'll tear you apart with my bare hands!"

I lunged for him and it took both of the Orcs to hold me back. I'd never felt this kind of aggression and strength in my life. But then, I'd never had to watch the woman I love slowly bleed out either.

Kristoff, fucking maniac that he was, simply laughed at me.

"You could do that, yeah. Or, you could get your ass into that treasure room, where I know there's something that can save her."

That cut through the rage filled soup my brain was soaking in and I stopped struggling.

"What?"

"A tiny vial of Christ's Tears. It will heal anything."

"No...Luke, you can't," she gasped. "That's...it's for you."

"Or you could take it yourself," he shrugged. "But either way, it's what you're looking for."

"Fine," my voice was rough. "I'll find your fucking room. But the vial of tears is *mine*."

"Sure, sure. You do the job, you get the prize."

I looked over at Andy, her face pale as she held her stomach. The blood was soaking the bottom of her shirt now and I knew if I didn't get some kind of pressure on it, she'd bleed out before I got back.

I had no bandages, so I took my shirt off and knelt beside her. When I lifted her shirt up, the wound wasn't center but more off to the side, close to her left hip. I was relieved because a stomach wound was a whole different kind of bad. I wrapped my shirt tight around her middle and tied it off. Andy grit her teeth and groaned throughout, sweat dripped off her forehead.

"You can't...give me the tears," she gripped my forearms before I stood up. "You can't. It will...cure you."

"It's gonna be okay, I promise," I cupped her face in my hands and planted a soft kiss on her lips.

"Alright, that's enough," Kristoff said. "Tick tock, tick tock. She's bleeding out, lover boy."

My hands itched to rip that son of a bitch limb from limb, but I had something to do first.

Save my girl, and then kill him.

I brushed my lips one last time across hers, memorizing the taste of her and swallowing all the things I wanted to say. She'd live, I would make sure of it, and if we were lucky, maybe I'd get to say them after this was all over.

"I'll be right back," I told her with a grin.

"You better be," she breathed, and pressed the map of the booby traps into my hands.

I stood up, and forced back the rising tide of panic and cloudy thoughts from the Vanquis. I had to push my way through the symptoms long enough to get that vial for her.

I can do this…I can be strong…I am strong.

I stepped toward the door and took a moment to examine it for any triggers. When I found none, I unrolled the map and studied the symbol and the Latin word *mens*.

Okay so, I think that's a St. Peters cross and that's definitely the word for mind. So, a test of the mind that somehow ties in with that symbol. Easy peasy

I swallowed and opened the door. The moment I stepped over the threshold, a wave of vertigo hit me. I teetered to the right and fell, the room spinning around me. When I could open my eyes without feeling like I was going to vomit, I got to my hands and knees and looked behind me but there was nothing.

No door.

No Andy.

It's okay, it's just whatever artifact is in here. Just calm down.

Ahead of me, a strange fog began to creep along the floor. There shouldn't be light in here, it should've been pitch black, but somehow there was the low kind of illumination that reminded me of sunrise. It was becoming ever brighter as the fog thickened around me.

Taking a deep, gulping breath, I pushed myself to my feet and walked forward. Off to my left a pathway opened, everywhere else the cloudy air was so dense that I could barely see the map in my hand. This was where the artifact wanted me to go. I steadied myself and stepped on to the path.

As soon as my foot was down, the entire cave disappeared and I was in a dark room, the blinds drawn tight, not letting in any light. There were dozens of pictures on the wall, of me and Andy, me and my family. Souvenirs from all our missions were scattered around on shelves and a dresser. A tray with half eaten food was sitting on a table by the door. It was sweltering, but a cold trickle of sweat dripped down my spine as I heard the jagged breathing and sobs.

The smell in the room was something I wished I could forget, but would be forever branded onto my mind. It was the scent of death, of someone who was close to the halls of their ancestors. I'd smelled it when my uncle was dying and now…

I don't want to turn around, I can't.

It was in that moment I knew what kind of test of the mind this would be.

I was supposed to face my fears.

And while I was seared with terror at losing Andy, what I was about to see was the dread I'd been carrying around for over a year, it was what had driven me here. And it was what I had to face.

Slowly, I turned and what I saw hit me like a physical blow, my legs going weak from the sight, and I crumpled to the ground.

I was lying on a bed, my eyes white and blind. My cheeks were sunken, and all of the bones on my hands stuck out under skin that had a terrible sickly pallor.

"I need to get out of here!" the me on the bed shouted. "I should be in Cairo! What have you done to my eyes?!"

"Nothing, it's all going to be okay," said a woman sitting by the bed.

No…no Andy you shouldn't be here.

But she was. Sitting there, her hair hanging limp as if it hadn't been washed in days, face drawn and dark circles under eyes that were bright with tears as she filled a syringe with a sedative.

We'd had to keep my uncle sedated for weeks before he died because he would get violent, and before my very eyes, I struck out in my blindness, punching Andy hard across the face.

"You bitch! What did you do to me?!" sick me demanded.

Andy didn't even pull herself off the floor; she just sat there and sobbed while I screamed at her. Then I began to scream at people that weren't even there. On and on it went until I was covering my head with my arms and rocking back and forth.

Make it stop…I can't become this…please help me.

But it didn't stop. It all repeated on a loop. Different people trying to tend to me, on and on until I couldn't take it anymore and jumped to my feet.

This was an artifact showing me living nightmares, but like all artifacts, it could be stopped.

I have to think…I have to push past what I feel and THINK.

It was torture to be forced to stand there, in that tiny, suffocating room, and listen to a potential future version of me dying and insane. But I breathed and thought of the map and the symbols. Then I thought of the priest, of what his reasons for this might've been.

Wait…there was a passage in one of his journals…

It took me a while to remember, between the horror around me and the way the disease was doing a number on my memory these days, but I finally was able to visualize the exact passage.

"No one is truly holy unless they are tested. This has been my test and I shall ensure that no one touches God's treasures unless their lies be purged, their faith brought forth, and their selflessness purified."

"Faith…" I whispered as it all clicked into place. "The opposite of lies at the tomb was the truth which must've been the test of the heart. And this is fear, which lives in the mind. The opposite of fear is faith, which is the absence of what can be logically seen, or known. A true test of my mind, can I believe regardless of what I see before me?"

I glanced back at the dying version of myself, who was now alone. Sweat broke out all over my body and nausea swept over me as I hesitantly approached the bed.

"You're what I'm afraid of, the very thing that's haunted my every waking thought all this time. And I don't feel like it's all going to be okay and I don't know how it will be but…I have faith that if I can't prevent this outcome, I'll be able to go through it. I'm strong enough."

The male on the bed let out a coarse breath, closed his eyes and disappeared. The room faded with him, leaving only the small room. In front of me was another door, and sitting at its base was a small three bar cross with a pair of keys etched into it, overlapping; The Cross of Peter, who denied knowing Christ three times because he was so afraid, but ended up being martyred because he believed so strongly. I took the chance that it was neutralized for the moment; I slipped the artifact into my pocket, and hoped that what I'd done just cleared the way for the others to follow me. As much as I'd rather keep Kristoff as far away as possible, I needed Andy close by if I wanted to heal her quickly.

"You can come through the first room," I shouted back, the mist still obscuring my view a bit.

"Good work, Professor," Kristoff returned.

I didn't stick around to greet him and charged ahead through the next door.

I slammed it shut behind me and was in utter darkness for a split second, until warm light illuminated another simple room. Instead of the fog and darkness of the previous one, this room was bright with a single wooden table in the center. There, in the middle, was a clear vial the length of my forefinger, with liquid shining golden inside. I knew, without a doubt, two things: this was the vial of Christ's tears and that it was also my test.

The map says the words for soul…the purification of selflessness. Well, that's easy, I'm not going to use it for myself.

Still, I wasn't stupid enough to just go charging in. So I stepped toward the table carefully, examining the flagstones for any indication of a trap.

"It's perfectly safe," said a deep voice in a heavy Spanish accent.

I jumped up and stared at a young man in a priest's robe, standing next to the table with a serene smile on his face.

"You…you're the priest."

"I am a projection of what you expected. The priest is enjoying his eternal reward."

"Those are the Tears of Christ."

"They might be."

"And this is a test of soul, of selflessness?"

"The soul is where a man may cultivate love that is truly selfless, and therefore it must be tested by much sacrifice. So in essence, yes, it is. You are much smarter than most, none have ever made it this far."

"Well, I don't want that for me, I never have. So—"

"Are you certain that is the ultimate test of selflessness?"

My hand stopped half way to the vial.

"Consider," the apparition said, "another path. What if you *were* to take the tears?"

"No, that's temptation that I won't give in to."

The priest chuckled and shook his head.

"Do you know what the ultimate act of love was in the entire universe?"

I stopped and thought it through, sensing that I was missing something obvious. I knew this was all Christian ideology, it had to line up with their beliefs, so in that context, what was the answer?

"Jesus dying on the cross for sinners," I answered, though something didn't feel right about it. "An act of complete selflessness."

"True," the priest said, "but that was not the ultimate act. You are willing to die for her, why?"

"Because…" I swallowed, the truth burning up inside of me. "Because I love her."

He nodded.

"And if I told you that letting her die would mean that *you* would live to save many lives, what then?"

"No, no I can't do that."

"Can't *do* that or can't *believe* that?"

Damn, he had me there. I'd always seen my contribution as less than Andy's. She could physically save people in the moment, while all my studying and searching never seemed to do more than bring death.

"Look," the priest encouraged and swept his hand along a far wall.

It transformed into a kind of movie screen, showing me a fast montage of people from all over the world, happy and alive. Families, children, the elderly. Orcs from all across Europe coming together for a massive celebration that I realized I was in the midst of.

"You will save millions," the priest said as I watched. "Your research on Vanquis will result in a cure within five years. And that discovery? Well, it will lead to breakthroughs in supernatural medicine. Within twenty years, you will be directly responsible for eradicating cancer, Alzheimer's and heart disease."

I stared in wonder as all of it washed over me. I felt it in my bones, the warmth of knowing that for once, my drive for knowledge brought life to the world.

"That's…that can't be real."

"It is, I assure you," the priest said. "And that is why you can't give her the tears. You, Luke Turner, must live."

"But the book—"

"Is not a guarantee of anything. Now, I ask you again, what was the most sacrificial act of love in all the universe?"

My heart cracked wide open and I was choked with sobs as the answer exploded inside my mind. The truth hit me so hard that I fell to my knees and began to cry.

From the Priests perspective, it wasn't a son giving himself freely to die. It was a father, giving his beloved child to die alone and frightened in a sea of enemies.

"Please," I begged as my tears fell onto the floor in fat drops, "please don't ask this of me."

"You are in pain at the thought."

I nodded, unable to speak anymore.

"It is tearing you apart inside."

"Is this fun for you?" I roared through the tears. "I love her! More than anything and you're asking me to let her die!"

The priest stood back from me, a smile on his face.

"A lesser man would have used what I showed him to justify saving his own life. You did not."

I stared at the priest, shock and anger heated my blood.

"So, I don't have to…she doesn't have to die?"

"No, she doesn't. But in truth, her fate is not in your hands."

"So making me believe that I had to let her die, you…you weren't serious about that?! What kind of fucked up—?"

"Language…" The apparition actually wagged a finger at me. "You are about to approach a holy place, and with that mouth, you might just burn. But at least your soul is truly selfless."

Just like last time, everything faded, including the vial which I suspected was merely a mirage to tempt me. I found myself kneeling on a cold stone floor, tears drying on my cheeks. I couldn't move, the turmoil of what I'd just experienced was still living in me, and I couldn't shake the feeling that I still wasn't done facing terrible choices in this place.

She's going to be okay…I'm going to make sure of it.

I got up on shaky legs and wiped my eyes behind my glasses, which were getting pretty damn filthy in this place. I scanned the room with my flashlight and almost missed the large coin on the floor at the far end of the room by another door. It was the size of an American silver dollar and was carved with symbols I couldn't see well at this distance with dirty glasses. When I bent to pick it up, I saw saw some Roman symbols on it.

Might be one of the coins that Judas was paid to betray Christ, which would make sense I suppose. An act of selfishness that needs an act of selflessness to overcome.

I slipped it into my other pocket and put my hand on the door handle. There was no indication that another test awaited me, but my skin prickled with apprehension, waiting for something to jump out at me and rip my heart to shreds some more.

But as I opened the door, nothing happened. I walked slowly down a very short corridor which opened up into an enormous cavern. Stalactites hung down from a high ceiling; moisture dripped off them and splatted onto the stone under my feet. About six feet from where I stood was a man-made shed nearly as wide as the ground I stood on. The air was cooler here, and my skin pebbled from the temperature difference. The sound of water rushing by echoed in the space and as I looked around, my flashlight caught on a massive open area that dropped off on both sides into utter darkness.

There was a very old looking bridge to my left that looked like it led off to a possible exit. I walked to the edge and shone my flashlight down to see a rushing river beneath us, and wondered for a moment were it went.

Perhaps it was a way to bring materials in here? If it does lead out, it might be a way to escape from Kristoff.

I swung the flashlight up and caught sight of ropes on some of the thick stalactites. Two were tied off on this side of the chasm and others were hanging loose on the side where the bridge ended. I was pretty sure the bridge would give out with my weight, but if we ran…?

First, get the tears and heal Andy, then plan the escape.

I focused on the shed, which was the size of a large work room with a roof tall enough that I couldn't reach it, even on my tip toes, and nearly as wide as the odd stone platform it was sitting on. I found myself not at all surprised that the wood it was made out of had somehow survived the decades in this damp place. After what I'd just gone through, I imagined that the priest would've come up with a way to make sure the room didn't disintegrate. Upon closer inspection, the walls were coated in something that resembled tar, but I wasn't sure it was exactly that. Whatever it was had kept the wood protected, though. The door didn't have a knob or any way to open it that I could see. The only reason I knew it was a door was that I could see the outline of the wood from the rest of the wall in front of me. There were symbols carved into it and I brushed cobwebs and dirt away so I could take a closer look.

The markings looked familiar, and I knew that I should be able to at least determine its origin but my mind was a terrible blank.

I know this, so the information is there, it's just locked behind this fucking illness!

I closed my eyes and took a breath. There were flashes of recognition, but they tended to slip away the harder I tried to hold onto them. So I stopped trying. I let my thoughts unspool, spin and meander a bit until something hit me. Something random. It wasn't the meaning of the symbols but it was enough for me to follow the memory, until I finally saw what I was looking for.

They're Hebraic, but an ancient version of it…warnings and…

My fingers slipped over the carvings until I came to two shapes in the center of the door that were deeper than the other carvings, and weren't a written language. One shape was a long horizontal carving with just a small vertical line intersecting it. The other was a curved, narrow shape, not quite a crescent.

I wasn't completely sure I was reading the words above it correctly, but if I was…

"These are for keys," I murmured. "But…where are…Oh shit! I've got soup for brains!"

I dug the cross and the coin out of my pocket and looked at them, then at the carvings in the door. Holding my breath, I slipped the cross into the one with horizontal and vertical carvings, and then the coin in the narrower one.

Something clicked inside the door but nothing else happened.

"Okay, what do you do with a key? You insert it and then you…" I turned them both to the right and the door shifted.

As I watched, it popped out of the space it had been set into all those years ago, just enough for me to grab a hold of it and push it the rest of the way open. I pulled the two artifacts out of the door and slipped them back into my pocket. Who knew if I'd need them again?

This was a moment that most, like me, only dreamed of while spending months and years hunched over dusty books and impossible-to-decipher clues. I was about to step into a room full of relics that no one had laid eyes on in decades, or in some cases, hundreds of years. I was frozen on the threshold in spite of the ticking clock. I felt unworthy, worried that nothing had been expunged in those trials, not really.

Voices sounded from behind me. Any second, Kristoff was going to step into this cavern and plunder all of this. I had to stop him and I had to save Andy, but how?

A voice behind me made me jump and turn, even though I wasn't at all surprised to see the priest once again.

"You will know the answer," the priest said. "You are the one I've been waiting for, to protect God's treasures for good."

"How do you know I'll do that? How do you know I won't take them for myself?"

He gave me an utterly serene smile.

"Because you already proved that you wouldn't."

It took a moment to realize what he was saying.

I'd been honest.

I'd been faithful.

And I'd been selfless.

I'd proven, in other words, that I was the kind of person that would sacrifice all of it in order to keep it safe.

Which is exactly what I'm going to have to do. But how…?

"What happens," I took the cross and coin out of my pockets again and stared down at them as an answer bloomed in my mind, "when a dishonest, faithless and selfish man holds these?"

The priest's smile widened.

"How did *you* do it?" I asked. "How did you get these artifacts to obey you?"

"I didn't. I was simply the conduit to use them as God directed."

I didn't believe in the Christian God, but I did believe in the artifacts, in the evidence before me. Somehow, whether directed by God or his own intelligence, this priest had manipulated these artifacts to ensure that only a person who didn't want to use them would discover them. Now, I would use them to protect these treasures too.

I took a breath, and stepped over the threshold.

CHAPTER EIGHTEEN
ANDROMEDA

I'd been shot before, but never in the torso.

That shit hurt.

And not only was I in some serious pain, I was terrified too. The bleeding had slowed thanks to Luke's efforts, but not completely. As near as I could tell, the bullet was still in there and the pain was like burning hot coals shoved into my body any time I moved around or breathed.

Of course, the Orc dragging me along at a fair distance behind Luke wasn't the most gentle either.

Then there was the worry for Luke that gnawed at me worse than the bullet wound. I wanted the tears for him and I knew, because of who he was, that Luke was going to try everything to give it to me.

It has to be his. I know he wants to cure everyone but if nothing else happens here, Luke needs that cure.

We followed behind Luke, only being allowed to go into the next room when Luke had overcome whatever challenge was in there. Then, as soon as we passed through the room or passageway, a wall suddenly appeared behind us, cutting off the exit. It was times like this that I truly hated artifacts, because there was no other explanation for weird shit like this. What I couldn't figure out was how the damn priest had been able to use them like his own personal security system.

Maybe because he was a priest and they're religious artifacts?

It was impossible to think that through as the Orc dragged me along. I was in too much pain and when that wasn't clouding my mind, all I could think about was Luke and worry about what he must have been facing. He'd never done anything like this on his own, I was always with him. But this time, I couldn't be, and I hated not being there to protect him.

Every time we had to wait for Luke to figure it out, Kristoff would mumble to himself and fidget with his amulet. He ignored me, so I managed to get a decent look at it. The chain didn't appear to be all that strong, and I wondered if all it would take is one good yank for it to come off. But he never got close enough for me to try.

I had no idea what all was in this treasure room but it was a collection of items powerful enough that Kristoff was getting more and more excited as we got closer to it. That was reason enough to try and figure out how to keep it from him. But as hard as I tried to recall the information on the map I'd handed Luke, the pain and the blood loss were doing funny things to my head. It was getting harder to concentrate the longer it took to get through this damn cave.

When we finally walked out from the final passage way and on to a huge stone platform with a large shed on it, I was seeing double. Without any warning, I puked all over the poor Orc who was holding me upright. The guy didn't even react, but Kristoff did.

"Ew, seriously? We are on the threshold of one of the greatest discoveries of our lifetime and you throw up?"

"Well maybe *someone* shouldn't have shot me…asshole," my words were a bit slurred and I was sure unconsciousness was imminent.

"You," Kristoff motioned to the Orc that now had my stomach contents all over his pants, "look around, see if there's any more booby traps and find our escape route. You," he waved over the remaining Orc, "pick her up and let's go. The door is open and I bet our Professor is in there as we speak."

The sick excitement in his voice while I slowly bled to death didn't help my nausea, but I managed not to vomit all over this Orc. He wasn't gentle as he picked me up bridal style and carried me with clomping steps that jostled the wound painfully. When we got to the doorway, a low buzzing sound hit my ears and I flinched. The air was thick, like an invisible piece of fabric was over the doorway making it difficult to actually step into the shed. The more the Orc and Kristoff tried, the more uncomfortable the buzzing became until I let out a long whimper as the pressure built around my mind.

Just before it became so intense that I knew I would pass out from it, everything eased and I could breathe again. As I opened my eyes slowly, I took in the square room.

It was warm, pleasantly so, and I swear I smelled my *abuela's* tamales somewhere, the scent comforting me even as I trembled from the shock starting to set in. The walls were covered in crimson cloth that looked as fresh and beautiful as the first day it was hung. The place was big but felt small inside due to the fact that it was crammed full of shit like some hoarders treasure trove.

To my left was a collection of gold and silver cups, plates, knives, even a damn sword. Next to that was a huge bookshelf overflowing with manuscripts, a few of which were scattered onto several low tables. Then to my right were a half dozen chests of various sizes, symbols etched onto them all in. Some covered in jewels, some just plain wood or metal. In the very center was a large round table with various necklaces, rings, and a small cabinet with a dozen or so vials on display.

I swallowed down the nausea ripping me up inside, and forced my eyes to focus. Where was Luke? Where had he gone off to? The room wasn't that fucking big.

Then he stood up and turned to face us. Relief washed over me when I saw that he was unharmed.

"Luke," I breathed, my head lolled against the Orc's shoulder.

"Oh my God, Andy," he took a step toward us, a clear little bottle in his hand.

Kristoff stopped him with the gun pointed right at him, a wide grin on his manic face.

"Not so fast, Professor. I need to be sure you've actually completed your task."

"She needs it now, this isn't what you promised."

"I promised you could have it, not that you could give it to her. But if you do one more tiny favor, I will allow it. Now hand the vial over."

Luke's face darkened, lips set into a dark line.

"Don't be stupid," Kristoff chided. "I could easily shoot you and leave you both here to die. You want to waste more time she doesn't have?"

Luke bared his teeth in a snarl and handed the vial over.

"Good, now I need you to find something for me."

"What?" Luke snapped.

"The Scivias of Hildegard."

That name sounded familiar, but my mind was growing foggy. My head felt like someone had wrapped my brain in cotton, and I groaned as pain burned through my middle.

"Andy," Luke rushed to me and took me out of the Orc's arms. "Hey, look at me, don't close your eyes."

I gave him a weak grin and coughed, copper coating my tongue.

"I'm so tired," I whispered.

"I know baby, but you have to hold on, just another few minutes. Please."

"I'll...try."

He kissed my forehead and sat me down on the floor next to a large bowl. I glanced into it and saw myself emaciated, skin rotting and my eyes dead. I gasped and jerked back, wondering what the hell that was and how fast we could get out of here. Suddenly I didn't trust the smell of comfort food from my childhood, or the beauty around me. I knew first-hand how artifacts could look pretty and yet be more deadly than anyone could imagine.

I scooted away from the bowl and hoped like hell that Kristoff would just be happy with a damn book and...

No...the book! That's the one Luke needs!

"Luke," I gasped as he began examining the bookshelf to my left, just out of reach. "No…you can't."

"Andy, I need to concentrate."

"But—"

"My dear, do not make me put a bullet in that pretty head of yours," Kristoff warned.

"Threaten her again and I'll burn this place to the ground," Luke growled.

Kristoff's smile melted the second he saw Luke's face. He was dead serious and the asshole knew it.

Luke turned back and began pulling different books off the shelves. He angled his body to block my view at one point and then turned back. He did this several times and Kristoff was becoming increasingly antsy, pacing and mumbling to himself.

"Why do you want the Scivias?" Luke asked.

"It is a relic of the greatest power. Did you know that if Hildegard had wanted, she could've ruled this world from her little abbey? Her visions and art, the language she created, all of it held the keys to rewrite this world at it's very base. And instead of taking the gift God gave her, the idiot hid it away in symbols and cryptic messages scattered across her writings. This is the only version of the Scivias that has the secret words and images in it."

"And this is all you want?" Luke asked.

Kristoff grinned.

"Now that we know where this is and how to access it, I have people on standby to come collect the rest. But for now? That book is everything."

Luke turned to us, a beautiful crimson and gold book in his hands. He swallowed, glanced down at it and then at me.

"No…" I shook my head and tried to stand up, but my legs were too weak.

Luke walked over to us and I swore there was a much smaller book under the larger one, but I couldn't be sure that wasn't a trick of my vision going in and out. It didn't matter anyway, because suddenly there was a flash of something in Luke's hands a second before he feigned a trip and fell into the Orc. Something like gold powder erupted over the beast and he started to scream as smoke rose across his flesh. Luke dove down and cradled me against him when the Orc went up in flames. As the Orc screamed and smoke filled the small room, I felt something shoved into my back pocket by Luke. He met my eyes and gave me the ghost of a smile.

What the…?

I was sure if I wasn't dying, I'd know exactly what he'd just done, but right now all I could concentrate on was trying to stay awake.

"That was not smart," Kristoff hissed, the gun in Luke's face. "Hand over the book."

Luke stood up and shook his head, the large crimson book still in his hands.

"Not until you give me the tears."

"You killed my associate. That's not following the rules, dear Professor. But perhaps I should punish you by destroying it?"

Kristoff held the vial up high, threatening to dash it to the ground.

"Okay," Luke held out his hand to stop Kristoff and then extended the book to him. "Here it is, no reason to do that."

The maniac plucked the book from Luke's fingers and cackled.

"Now give me the vial," Luke demanded.

"You forgot to say…" Kristoff coughed and looked a little confused. "You…you forgot to say…"

He gasped and heaved, as if he couldn't breathe, and dropped the vial to clutched at his throat as his face turned red. Luke dove down and caught the vial just before it hit the stone floor. I had a second of relief before Kristoff began to thrash around, knocking over objects as he panicked.

"Wh-what have you…done!"

I stared up in shock as Kristoff's face began to age rapidly. His eyes widened and blood poured from his lips a moment before he fell to his knees. The book slipped from hands that had turned bone thin and two metal objects fell from between the pages. One was an odd looking cross and the other was a large coin. The ground beneath us trembled and I heard rocks falling outside.

"Shit, I didn't think…" Luke said.

"What did you do?" Kristoff shrieked, as he fell backwards and disintegrated before my eyes. The chain with the amulet that had been around his neck fell into the pile of dust he'd turned into, along with my bowie knife. Just before Luke picked me up, I snatched both from his remains and stuffed the medallion into my front pants pocket while I clutched the knife.

We were barely out of the room when the ground under it gave a loud rumble. Right in front of us, an enormous crack appeared and a second later, the room and all its contents fell into the cavern below.

"It's okay," Luke said, "there's a—"

The only remaining feral Orc, the one I'd puked on, screamed in confusion. The link he'd had to Kristoff was now severed and the world around him was shaking and crashing. He panicked and ran to the bridge, which collapsed under his weight when he was half way across.

"That was…our only way out, wasn't it?" I asked and let out a grunt of pain.

It must've been adrenaline that had kept me conscious and able to function even this well because suddenly my entire body was going cold, and I started to shake uncontrollably.

"Stay with me baby, I'm gonna fix this."

"No," I screamed through gritted teeth. "D-don't you…d-dare! You need to live!"

"So do you!"

"The world…it doesn't need me…like it d-does you. Please…" I started to sob, the cave shook around me, but all I could think of was surviving and losing Luke. "I can't…I can't lose you."

"Just shut up and let me—"

"No!"

"God damn it, Andy, for once, let me be the strong one and save you!"

He stopped any further protests with a hard kiss that would've set my toes curling if I hadn't been dying.

I let myself sink into the firm press of his mouth on mine, the gentle scrape of his tusks. If I was going to die, I was going to savor this last time Luke kissed me. But the moment was shattered as white hot fire replaced the chill in my bones.

I let out a screeching yell against his lips and arched my back as the sensation grew. Black spots dotted my vision and I was on the brink of passing out when the torture began to ease. As it did, the fire became ice and I hissed.

Luke sat back and we both stared at where the bullet wound had been. The skin was closing and the feeling of my body knitting itself back together was beyond odd. Just before the wound closed itself completely, my body pushed out the bullet, it fell with a clink to the stone floor. Red skin faded to pink and then to nothing, as if I'd never been shot at all.

I shuddered as the ice cold sensation began to fade and left me feeling tired but very much alive.

"It worked, oh thank Gods that was the right vial!" Luke breathed.

The rebuke I had at the ready died on my tongue as I realized that he hadn't been entirely sure *what* he was pouring on my wound. Considering what I'd just seen when someone touched the wrong thing, much less had it poured into a hole in their body, I was more than a little testy about it.

"You weren't sure?" I gaped at him.

He opened his mouth to say something when the cave gave a loud rumble and larger portions of the ceiling started to fall.

"You can yell at me after we survive the cave in," Luke said, pulling me to my feet.

"Good plan."

I swayed a little, still dizzy, my legs a bit wobbly but whether that was from my still healing body or the ground under me shaking, I wasn't quite sure. Though with each passing second, I could feel the strength returning to me, and my mind was starting to clear. I glanced around, realizing we were standing on what had become a large stone platform surrounded by chasms on three sides and completely blocked off on the fourth. We were trapped.

"The bridge is gone, how are we gonna get out of here?" I asked as I shoved the sheathed bowie knife into my boot for safe keeping.

Luke narrowly dodged a huge rock that fell from the ceiling as he ran over to where the bridge had been. The wooden posts that had secured the bridge were still there and attached to one was a rope that was secured overhead to a large stalactite. I knew what he was thinking even before Luke gave it a strong yank.

"Climb on my back and hold on!" he shouted above the chaos erupting around us.

I would've said he was crazy, that this wasn't the time to re-enact his favorite moment from *Star Wars: A New Hope*, but it really was our only option.

So I gave him a kiss on the mouth and said, "Good luck."

He smirked at me, loving the fact that I had referenced that movie moment even as death was raining down on us.

I climbed onto his back, my body pressed against his bare skin and prayed the part of the ceiling that the rope was attached to would remain stable just long enough for us to escape.

I closed my eyes and hung on for dear life as Luke got a running start, hung on to the rope and then leapt off the edge. My stomach dropped as we swung, both of us screaming with as much glee as terror. It helped that the place we needed to get to, a wide stone ledge, was downhill.

Luke let go as we got over the ledge and we fell hard to the stone ground. The wind was knocked out of me for a moment and I laid there, coughing. My side ached, still healing from the gun shot apparently, and I managed to scrape the hell out of my arms when I fell onto the ledge. But, it was better than falling to my death like the feral Orc had done, so I'd call it a win.

"Are you alright?" Luke asked as he crawled over to me.

"Yeah," I turned over onto my hands and knees as well and gave him a shaky smile.

That's when I felt a strange kind of weight in my back pocket. I reached back and dug out a small book covered in a thick plastic bag. My eyes widened when I realized that I hadn't hallucinated that smaller book Luke had been carrying under the one he'd booby trapped for Kristoff.

"Is this…?" I asked.

"Yeah," he whispered and took it from me. "I found it, Andy."

The cave gave a deep, ominous rumble right before another huge quake ripped through the cavern. Three huge stalactites fell right where we were standing across the chasm, including the one with the rope. Thick dust flew up into the air and I saw someone in a priest's robe standing there, in the midst of it, waving at us.

"Is that…am I still seeing things?" I asked.

Luke swallowed and waved back.

"I'll explain later," he stood up and shoved the book into his back pocket before helping me up. "We gotta get out of here, before we get buried too."

We bolted through the narrow tunnel in front of us which led us to another narrow passage that curved downward. We were running full speed, no flashlights, which was probably why we didn't see the drop off until it was too late.

The next thing I knew, I was falling through the air screaming, right before I fell into cold, dark waters.

CHAPTER NINETEEN

LUKE

I saw Andy fall a half second before I lost my balance, unable to stop myself in time and fell off the same damn drop off. If there had been a different way out of this cave, I hadn't seen it in time.

I hit the water hard, the air pushed out of my lungs. I was dazed at first, and just let myself fall, before realizing that I was going to drown and swam fast to the surface. Somewhere in the dark waters, my glasses had fallen off and the part of the cave we were in now was not only dark, but it was also fuzzy.

But it's not completely dark, which means there's light coming from somewhere, if we can only find it.

"Andy?" I shouted, my voice echoed in the space.

Nothing.

No response and my heart gave a frightened lurch. I couldn't see for shit, but I still dove down and searched the cold water for her. I swam as deep as I could before the demand for oxygen made it necessary to breach the water. When I did I, saw her several feet away screaming my name.

"I'm here!" I yelled and swam closer.

She flung her arms around me, trembling.

"I thought you'd drowned or something!"

"I couldn't find you so I dove down. Are you okay?"

She didn't answer at first, just clung to me, and that's when I saw the tiny flicker of something in the water.

Shit. There's fish here. Maybe she hasn't noticed.

"Andy?"

"There's fish," she whispered, her voice laced with terror. "I know it's stupid but I…Luke, I'm so scared."

"I know, baby, and it's not stupid. Fears like this aren't logical."

Her arms tightened around me and she shook her head. I remembered what she'd said to me in the tomb, how she sometimes needed me to let her be afraid, for me to be the strong one. So instead of telling her that she was brave, which she was, I held her tighter as I tread water.

"I'm here," I said, "you don't have to face this alone, okay? You can be afraid and I'll be brave for both of us."

She relaxed a little against me and nodded.

"The one thing I can't do for you though," I continued, "is swim. I need you to do that for me, okay?"

"I'll try."

I pressed a light kiss to her wet hair and she let me go.

"Now, there's light coming from somewhere, we just need to find it and get out of here. Are you wearing your boots?"

She made a choking sound when she realized what I was going to ask.

"Andy, you need to swim and those damn boots are going to weigh you down, you understand?"

She nodded, eyes closed as she took deep, shaky breaths.

"Okay…okay, I can do this…I can—" she whimpered.

"You still have your knife?"

"Yeah, in my boot."

"I'm gonna cut your laces, okay? Hold on."

I dove down and retrieved the knife with its sheath. I carved her laces away as quick as I could and helped her strip off the boots. Then I did mine and toed them off under the water before coming back to the surface.

"Here," I handed her the now sheathed knife and took in a huge gulp of air.

She tucked it into her waistband and we both started looking around for a way out. Andy gave a whimper a few seconds later and then screamed.

"I'm sorry, I'm sorry! It touched me and I…"

"It's okay, I've got you baby and I swear we're safe."

She whimpered again and nodded.

The cave was filled completely with water; there wasn't any stone exposed except for the walls. But the water was definitely from the ocean, outside the cave, judging by the saltiness of it.

The more my eyes adjusted, the more I realized that the light was coming from under the water to our left.

"Andy, I'm going to swim over there, I think there's an underwater tunnel letting in salt water and light."

"Don't leave me!"

She clung to my arm, making it difficult to stay above water.

"Come with me," I sputtered.

She nodded fast and we swam over to where the light was filtering in.

"I'm gonna dive down, check it out."

She gave a tiny sob but nodded.

I wanted to take this away from her, to kiss her silly and make her forget all about it. But we had to get out of this place. If this was some kind of inlet for the sea, we might be screwed when high tide came.

I took a deep breath and dove down. There had been a lake where I'd grown up; the middle was incredibly deep and no one in my entire town could touch the bottom. I'd come close, almost drowning myself to do it. That challenge, though, had cultivated a lifelong love of swimming so I knew I wasn't in any danger.

I worried about Andy though. She could swim in pools, I'd even seen her swim in man-made lakes, which I realized was probably because she believed there weren't any fish in them. But this? I was worried that her fear of the fish, along with the small pull of the tides, would make it extremely difficult for her.

Diving under, however, I found the opening not that far down. It was a pretty good sized little tunnel, and bright light filtered through, but not a lot of it. The only question was how far we'd have to swim before getting out into the open.

I breached the surface of the water again and took in a gulp of air.

"It's there," I said, "a long tunnel that has light at the end of it."

Andy took a breath and nodded.

"Okay…okay, I can do this."

"Yeah, you can, baby. You just gotta take a really big breath, okay? You go first."

"You're the faster swimmer, I'll just slow us down."

"I can hold my breath longer, it's fine. I can push you if you start to slow down."

She closed her eyes and tipped her head back.

"This is one helluva last mission."

My heart squeezed painfully at those words. I knew we had a lot of shit to work out, that there were things we'd only just begun to really unpack and understand about one another. But I didn't want this to be the last of anything. I wanted this to be a new beginning.

Not the time. We're gonna drown if we wait too long and the tide comes in. Survive, then try to win her back.

So I pressed one palm to her cheek, loving the way she nuzzled into my touch.

"We've got this, Andy. We always do, right? Every time, no matter what, we survive. And this time isn't going to be any different."

"Yeah…yeah, you're right."

"Damn straight. Now, get your ass down there and let's get out of these fucking caves."

She let out a shocked laugh.

"Damn, you're sexy, when you're bossy."

I chuckled.

"I'll remember that."

Andy took a deep breath and dove under. I did the same and followed her. She made it to the tunnel fast and we both darted into it. I hadn't been able to see how low the ceiling of it was, but once we were both inside, it was cramped and there was a moment of true fear as Andy began to slow down.

I put my hand on her rear and pushed her forward as I put more work into kicking and paddling with my other hand. The light got closer, but my lungs started to burn. I knew Andy had to be hurting for air too because her movements were getting sluggish.

But just as I started to worry that I'd have to drag her out of here, the stone disappeared and there was nothing but light above us. We frantically made for the surface and I had to yank Andy up at the last minute when she started to panic.

We both gasped and coughed when we broke through. Breathing had never felt so damn good before.

"We…made it!" Andy sputtered.

I nodded, turning until I found the shore. To my great relief, we weren't all that far from it.

By the time we were close enough to shore to put our feet down, my limbs felt rubbery and weak. The waves pushed us hard, and we both lost our balance, falling into the water once more. Andy and I both floundered a bit before crawling on the wet sand and collapsing just outside of where the waves touched the land.

We fell onto our backs and just relished breathing for a few minutes. The sunlight was warm and welcoming on my chilled skin, but it didn't feel half as good as when Andy's fingers found mine and twined around them. My head lolled to the side and I took in every little detail of this magnificent woman. Her dark, wavy hair and light brown skin was crusted with sand. Water droplets reflected the sunlight, making her look like someone had dipped her in gold and diamonds. She'd been on the brink of death less than an hour ago, she'd swung across a chasm with me, faced her greatest fear and nearly drowned. And now here she was, holding my hand while the waves crashed on a white sand beach.

We were breathing, and she was by my side.

Andy let out a breathy giggle that bloomed into a full blown laugh.

"What?" I asked.

"We're fucking *alive!*"

I chuckled as the same wave of emotion hit me. Then I was full on belly laughing too.

The two of us must've laid there, exhausted and sore, laughing our asses off for a good fifteen minutes, just so damn grateful.

When I looked over at her gorgeous, smiling face, everything else faded. Every worry, every ache in my joints, everything but *her*.

I love you…I love you…I love you…

The words beat with the drum of my heart, but I didn't speak them. Instead, I reached out and brushed my fingers against her cheek, and the wedding band glinted against the sun and caught my eye. I hadn't been able to let her go since the day she walked out on me, and it had frozen us both in place for the past year. But neither of us could go forward like that. We had to move on, whether together or apart I didn't know. But I knew we couldn't stay like this.

"What's wrong?" she asked.

"Nothing," I said, focusing on her.

We'd survived this, we were breathing side by side on a beautiful beach, all alone. There was this one last moment, a last few minutes, an hour maybe, to just *be* with her before everything else barged in and made us face the wreckage we'd brought into one another's lives.

I rolled over onto her, one of my big thighs between hers. Andy's fingers brushed sand from my shoulders as she ran her hand along my skin and I shivered but not with cold. We'd be reporting back to the Archive after this, facing whatever consequences the director had for disobeying her orders. This could possibly be the last time we were alone and I wasn't going to waste it.

When I brushed my lips over hers, my soul was desperate to hold on for one more moment, one more slide of our bodies against each other. I could face whatever came, the disease eating away at my mind and body, the loss of my career, all of it, if I had this memory to cling to.

Andy tasted of salt and something else that made my tongue tingle a little. I suspected it was from the tears that I'd poured onto her wound. It wasn't long at all before my gentle whispers against her mouth became harder, more demanding. I found myself ravenous for her the way I'd been for oxygen under the water. She clawed at my hair, pulling me down harder, and her wicked tongue slid and twined with mine, and I groaned into her mouth.

When I pressed my body harder into hers, Andy let out a grunt that was not from pleasure.

I pulled back, eyes running along her body. Had I hurt her? Was she wounded and I hadn't noticed?

Andy dug into her front pocket and pulled out a thick golden medallion on a long silver chain.

"I took it from the asshole when he turned to dust," she said, holding it up for me to see. "I thought…I don't know, maybe you could have it. Maybe it would help keep the illness at bay. But then he died like he did, so maybe it doesn't work all that well."

I plucked the medallion from her hands and examined the markings, which were Egyptian hieroglyphs.

"Kristoff was overcome by two incredibly powerful artifacts. I took a chance that his medallion would be no match for them, and I was right. But Vanquis isn't the same. This might help to keep the symptoms at back at least."

"Good, since you gave me the tears, even though I told you—"

"Andy?"

"Yeah?"

"Shut up and kiss me."

She gave me a broad grin and wiggled under me.

"You really are sexy when you're bossy."

"I'm always sexy baby," I said against her mouth.

"Mmm…yeah you—Oh!"

I bent down and took one of her nipples in my mouth, working it through the soaked fabric of her tank top while I rolled her other stiff peak between my fingers.

"I almost lost you," I breathed on her skin as I kissed my way up her throat.

Andy's only response was to thread her fingers through my hair and pull until she could capture my lips with hers. She stirred inside me a deep, hungry need to see her come apart, to suck her release off my fingers. I wanted her taste, her smell, every single part of her imprinted on me forever.

I yanked on the buttons of her pants as she did the same to mine, her mouth biting my salt encrusted skin.

"I need you," she breathed. "I want to…make you…oh, fuck, Luke!"

She clutched my shoulder with one hand and bit her bottom lip as my fingers found her wet and slick to the touch. I stared into her eyes as I pressed tight circles on her little pearl.

"You gonna come for me?"

She could only whimper as I plunged two fingers deep into her. My palm pressed against that sensitive part and I let her ride my hand with hard, rolling thrusts that made my cock ache. I would give her this but it wasn't unselfish. No, watching her take pleasure from my hand, consuming the moans breathed into the air between us, I was greedy for all of it. If I had my way I'd find another cave and spend weeks making Andy come on my tongue, my cock, my hand.

"I can't lose you," she breathed. "Luke, a world with you…"

"Shhh, baby, I'm here," I claimed her mouth in a savage kiss, reveling in the bright red marks I was leaving on her skin. "There's nothing but right now, right here, just us."

"Yes, right now," she breathed against my throat as she pushed me onto my back.

As I watched in breathless awe, Andy stood up and shimmied out of her pants and underwear. She was naked from the waist down, the scent of her release carried on a salty breeze and I inhaled deeply.

"I need you inside of me," her voice was hoarse with desperation as she straddled me and took my cock out of my pants.

I sucked in a breath when she dragged my weeping head through her slick folds. She was so fucking wet and ready, and I was panting as I tried to hold back, letting her lead.

"Please, baby," I croaked, my hands squeezing her hips.

"Tell me. I want to hear you say it."

"I want to fuck you, want to feel you come around me right before I fill you up."

She threw her head back, and the sunlight illuminated her hair, casting a sacrilegious halo around her head. I was longing to defile her, to fuck her so deep, to fill her so much that Andy would feel me for weeks after.

"You want that," I said, sitting up half way and clutching the back of her neck. "You want me to fuck you deep, don't you?"

"Yes," she breathed as she slipped herself onto the tip of my dick.

We both let out an obscene groan as she worked herself slowly down onto me. The roll of her hips, the tight fit of her cunt around me, had me wild by the time she was impaled completely on me. I let go of her neck and held her hips firmly, not letting her up as I now tortured her with tiny swirls of my hips, hitting that perfect spot deep inside of her.

"Fuck me, Luke," she pleaded, "please…I need you."

I let her up then, the edge of her pussy just barely on the head of cock before I slammed her back down onto me at the same time I surged up. Slowly, I dragged her up, only to do the same thing again.

Over and over, I fucked her hard and deep. A savage instinct took over as her cries punctuated the pounding of the waves on the shore. All those questions from before, the soul crushing ache of believing that the reason she left me was because I wasn't enough, that was gone. Swept away by the fire of our confessions and the sight of Andy teetering far too close to death. This was rebirth, this was *life* celebrated, reveled in. And this was love, pure and complicated, messy and beautiful.

Just when I saw the moment before she was about to come, I unleashed on her. Rushing up, I seized the back of her neck again and pulled her in for a searing kiss as she came apart around me. I hungrily delighted in the screaming moan that flew from her lips.

The feral part of me, the one that wanted to scrape my tusks over every inch of her body and brand her with my cum took over. Before I could stop myself, I'd pulled her off of me and planted her on hands and knees in the coarse sand. She was flushed, glassy eyed and the aroma coming from her pussy was irresistible.

I gave her one, long, deep lick from clit to taint before grasping her hips and brutally spearing her. The slap of our sweat soaked bodies, my grunting roars and her screams, all blended into a profane symphony of our own making. I didn't care if anyone heard us, I didn't care if we were caught. Let someone see me fucking this woman; she was mine and I was hers and I would not be denied one last time with her.

The inferno of my release snuck up on me; my balls tightened and suddenly I let out a triumphant roar as it all came crashing down on me. My movements became erratic, and then I could only hold myself deep inside of her as I filled Andy with my cum.

I was faintly aware of a gentle breeze cooling the sweat on me, of seagulls flying overhead and the brush of the sea against my toes. But all that paled in comparison to her. The feel of her body around mine, the taste of salt on her skin as I kissed and bit my way from her shoulders her perfect peach of an ass. I didn't want to leave her because the moment I did, this would be over. We'd have to find a way home, and the glass bubble we'd built around us during this mission would break irrevocably.

So I kissed my way up and down her body, loving the tracks my tusks left on her beautiful skin. She reached back and seized a handful of my hair to hold me in place at the crook of her neck as I nibbled her there.

She was crying, her tears wet my cheek when she kissed me, soft, slow, like she was saying…

"No," she whispered against my mouth as I pulled her against me and sat back on my heels.

"I know," I said, her thighs on either side of mine.

We were both breaking, and neither of us knew how to put each other back together. Sex was a poor glue; it couldn't hold us together after the ecstasy wore off. And after the truths we'd laid bare in that tomb, it would take so much more than a good fuck on a beach, celebrating being alive, to fix it all.

Was that just last night?

It felt like we'd lived weeks since then, and yet the pain our words had conjured was so acute, I felt it even in the afterglow of being inside of her. It was tempting to simply ignore it all, say it was okay and stay together after this. But I knew that we'd just be headed for another heart break, and this time it would be even worse than before. I couldn't survive that. We couldn't make the same mistakes as before and expect different outcomes. And while I was more than willing to face all the problems that broke us up in the first place, I wasn't sure about Andy. She'd had a lifetime of practice, running from all her fears, including the ones that had caused her to leave me like she had.

We need to fix what broke us, and we can't do that by going home and picking up where we ended things like nothing happened. Which means…

My eyes snagged on the ring on my finger once more and my heart cracked in two. I'd been holding on so tight to her, even when she wasn't with me. And if I wanted any chance of ever making this right, of ever having a real shot with her, I had to let her go. *Really* let her go.

"Andy," I murmured, my arms wound around her body as my heart shattered. "Andy…"

She was clinging to me too, her hand tangled in my hair as I rested my head against her shoulder. We sat like that in silence until I softened and our mingled cum was cooling uncomfortably on us.

I released her with a soft kiss, memorizing every little thing about her mouth on mine. We both stripped out of our remaining clothes and rinsed off in the ocean. I couldn't stop staring at Andy as she dove under the water and came back up, the sun setting her skin on fire. If I'd had my way, she would be walking around with my dried cum on her thighs, the scent telling everyone who she belonged to. But she didn't belong to me right now, or if she did, Andy hadn't said it and I would not make demands like that right now. Not when everything was mixed up in the emotions of our confessions and the rush of the mission. If we were going to have any kind of future, we both needed to cool off, give it space to be sure.

She caught me staring at her but instead of making a joke, or staring back, she looked away with a grimace of pain. I was a jerk to feel a little better that this wasn't easy on her either, but I couldn't help it. If she was hurting at the thought of us parting, maybe, just maybe there was hope.

When I went back to shore, I didn't want to put my pants back on. They were crusted with salt and sand, even after I tried to shake them out, and slipping them back on was uncomfortable but what else was I going to do? I could tell from the face she made that Andy was feeling the same way.

"What now?" I asked.

"Now," she handed me the medallion, "you put this on and we find a way home."

I hesitated, examining the writing on the round, flat surface to try and see if there would be any adverse side effects from wearing it. When I didn't see anything the ancient script, I slipped it over my head.

"Do you feel anything?" she asked.

"Not really, but—" I took in a sharp breath as a cool sensation ripped through me.

"What's wrong? Does it hurt?" Andy reached for me but I stepped back.

"I-I think it just started working."

"And?"

I took internal inventory, checked to make sure nothing hurt, that I wasn't changing in unexpected ways. That's when I realized that my mind felt clearer than it had in months, that my eyes were aching less and my body was starting to feel renewed.

I grinned down at her.

"I feel better…stronger."

Andy's eyes filled with tears as she flung her arms around me.

"We're going to beat this yet, just you wait," she said.

And, for the first time in a long time, I thought she might be right.

CHAPTER TWENTY
ANDROMEDA

We decided that since both of us were sans shoes, traipsing through the rainforest might not be the best option. So instead we walked along the gorgeous beach where Luke had just fucked me so thoroughly I knew I'd be feeling this for days. My damp, salty clothes rubbed uncomfortably on my skin, the salt stung some of the scratches Luke had left on my body but I didn't mind. I liked having his marks on me, I'd forgotten how good it felt to have that physical proof that I was his.

But I'm not and I have no idea how to fix it.

We hadn't been walking long when I spotted a group ahead of us, all dressed in dark clothes and holding something in their hands. It was too far away to see what, but I'd bet it was guns.

"I see them," Luke said when I stopped him. "But we don't have any good hiding options."

I looked around the shoreline and agreed. The water was to our left, and to our right was a mix of sloping sand hills and rocky outcrops. We could try and flee into the forest, but on bare feet we'd be at a disadvantage to escape fast. And if we'd already seen them, chances were good that they also had seen us.

I gripped his hand tightly.

"We could get into the water, swim further down the shoreline," I suggested. "I doubt they're equipped for water."

Luke squinted, his vision at a distance not great without his glasses.

"Am I seeing things or is that one waving at us?" he asked.

I frowned and looked at the group. They'd gotten much closer by now and one of them was indeed waving. He shouted something that was lost in the sea air and the roar of the waves but it didn't appear to be menacing.

"If they were planning on capturing us I doubt they'd be waving at us," Luke said.

"Good point. It could be the Archive but how the hell would they know where we were?"

"Did Sprite give you any equipment or have anything of yours for any length of time?"

I thought back and at first I couldn't remember them having anything that I still had on me to slip a tracker into. Then the knife in my back waistband pinched my skin and I let loose a string of swear words.

"They fucking bugged my knife! Damn them!"

By now the group was close enough for me to recognize some of the equipment the front two men were carrying and it was, indeed, the Archive. Sudden panic sank its teeth into my gut and I stepped in front of Luke.

"You let me do the talking, okay? I'm going to fix all of this and take complete responsibility."

His face scrunched up in a shocked frown and he shook his head.

"No way! Andy, we are in this together or not at all, just like always."

"This is different. This isn't joining a rebellion for the good of the world or making sure we don't get in trouble for sinking a Medieval Venetian villa. This is…Luke, this is basically treason and destruction of Artifacts. It's serious."

He cupped my face between his massive hands and planted a soft kiss on my forehead.

"I know. And I'm not letting you take the fall. Together or not at all."

I let out a long breath.

"You really are a stubborn Orc."

"Right back at ya, but you know, Mundane instead of Orc."

He chuckled and I bumped my shoulder against him.

"Agent Kane?" came the faint shout from the leader of the group.

I waved my arms and Luke and I met the group half way.

"We've been looking for you two."

The leader was a tall woman with red hair and freckles who looked like she would fit right in at a Kindergarten art fair as well as an Archive dig site. She extended her hand and gave me a smile.

"Agent Summers, it's nice to finally meet you."

Unease skated its way down my spine as I shook her hand. I'd heard some variation of that my whole life, and it was rarely said by someone who was simply happy to meet me.

"And this must be Professor Turner, pleasure," she said, her eyes skating up his bare, muscular torso.

A hot spike of jealousy hit me square in the chest and I just barely resisted the urge to grab Luke's hand to stake my claim.

"What's the situation?" I asked instead, my voice clipped, all business.

"We have a ship about an hour out that will extract you and the professor, take you back to the air strip and then on to London. Director Dearborne is very anxious to hear news of your mission."

I'll bet.

"We need to get a quick debrief from you two," Agent Summers continued, and turned to a broad shouldered man to her left. "Agent Olsen, will you please debrief Professor Turner?"

I knew they would separate us; it was standard procedure to ensure that a team's story all checked out and root out any potential lies. Luke and I had been through it dozens of times before. But this was the first time that it really, truly meant good-bye.

"Can you give us a minute?" I asked, my voice hoarse.

"Yes, of course."

Agent Summers and Olsen stood off the side, just far enough to give us the veneer of privacy but close enough to potentially over hear anything suspicious.

Luke's hands settled on my waist as I pulled him close, my arms around his shoulders. He buried his face in the crook of my neck and I closed my eyes, committing this moment to memory.

"Thank you," he whispered, his little tusks scratching along my skin as he spoke.

"Any time," I said, trying to make it come out light hearted but my throat was so tight.

There was too much to say to get it all out in the five minutes Agent Summers was giving us. It spilled out of my heart and choked me and all I could get out were tiny whimpers as I clung to him.

"We'll see each other again," Luke finally said, pulling back to look at me. "I promise."

I nodded as tears cascaded down my face.

He was about to let me go when I yanked him down to me, crushed my mouth to his and tried to pour all of what I wanted to say into that one kiss. When I finally pulled back, I tasted salt on my lips, our tears mingled in a shared heartbreak.

"Until next time," I whispered.

He nodded, eyes devouring me, committing me to memory the same way I was him. When he finally let me go, there was a war in Luke's eyes and I knew this was as hard for him as it was for me. I watched him walk away, knowing he wouldn't look back, but hoping nonetheless.

Agent Olsen took him down the beach, far enough that I could still see him, but not hear.

"Agent Kane?" Summers asked, forcing me back to the job in front of me.

"Yeah, sorry."

There were two camp chairs set up, and she gestured to the one facing away from where Luke was. Usually, we were placed in a mandatory twenty-four-hour isolation to both check our stories and our physical wellbeing. I'd never been debriefed at the actual site of the mission before so this told me that there was a time factor, though what that might be since the cave was gone, I couldn't tell.

Someone handed me a bottle of water and a protein bar. I downed half the water in one go and then tore into the bar. It was hard and tasted like cardboard but I was hungry enough that it didn't really matter.

I knew that what I said in the next few minutes was going to determine how the Archive treated both Luke and me. If they thought for a second that we were compromised, it would end in our redaction. I had to put aside the way my heart was bleeding in my chest, the gaping hole Luke had left when he walked away, and focus on this completely.

So I took a breath and forced my mind away from Luke and worrying about him. I had a job to finish, that was the only thing that was important right now. Luke was right, we'd see each other again. I'd make sure of that.

"I know you have questions," I said, "so fire away."

"Very well. Tell me about the Protectors you encountered," Agent Summers began, clicking on a small recording device at her wrist.

"I didn't interact with them much," I said around a mouthful of protein bar. "Luke was in their encampment for a while."

Summers nodded.

"But you did interact with them when they captured you? And then in the cave?"

I collected my thoughts as I chewed the last of the protein bar.

She asked it assuming we'd actually been there and I spotted the shrewd gleam in her eye under the pleasant exterior. It was very smart of the director to send an agent skilled in interrogation. I'm sure Dearborne thought we'd either be too tired to pick up on it or that I wouldn't know what to look for. But a lifetime of needing to read to between every line, see behind every mask of dozens of socialites that had trained to hide everything from birth, and I was very, *very* good at seeing it.

"You assume we found it," I said.

She paused, her smile frozen, her posture straightened.

"I've read your file," Agent Summers said. "I know why you may not trust me. Hell, I'm surprised either of you stayed after what you went through with *that* woman. But I assure you, I am not here to get you in trouble. Dearborne isn't Francesca."

"She's not, but she also sent me here telling me the mission was one thing when it was actually another," I said.

Summers' eyebrow arched, obviously surprised that I'd known that, before she smiled and nodded.

"That's true. We needed to know whether Professor Turner had been turned to the side of the Protectors. We knew you may have residual feelings for the professor, but that you'd do what needed in the case that he was a traitor."

I choked on a swallow of water and hated the fact that I hadn't seen *that* coming.

"You sent me here to kill him?"

"If he had betrayed the Archive, yes."

She said it so nonchalantly, without so much as a blink.

Fury ran through me like molten steel and I glared at her.

"I'm not a fucking assassin!"

"No, but you are the only one that Luke would be honest with if he had been turned. If you hadn't been able to finish the mission, we would've done so."

At that point, several things happened in my brain at once.

I surmised the distance between us and the rest of the team, how many weapons everyone had, who was actually paying attention to us, if there was anything around us I could use as a weapon and how fast I could get access to it.

We were outnumbered; we'd be gunned down before we were able to get away. But I had a very good chance of taking out Summers and at least three others before then.

If they thought for one second that Luke was a traitor and tried to kill him, I'd make them pay for it, dearly.

"Stand down, Agent," Summers said, her hand drifted to her side arm. "We do not think Professor Turner has turned traitor. This isn't a wet op, so relax."

"This is bullshit," I said, the venom oozed from my voice. "I thought the Archive was different now and you're telling me the director is running back door ops—!"

"It's different," Summers leaned forward, the frown wrinkled the space between her eyebrows, "but we are beset with leaks and traitors that are defecting every day to the Protectors. We need to get serious about those leaks or what you two did, what so many sacrificed to bring Francesca down, will all be for nothing."

Her voice caught just a little at the end and I wondered who she'd lost in all that mess.

I looked behind me, just to make sure Luke was okay. He was sitting with his back to me, tipping back a water bottle and two agents were laughing, presumably at something he said.

He's alright…he's okay.

I wanted to rage and scream at Summers. I wanted to march right into Dearborne's office and let her have it. But my training was slowly dampening that instinct. You didn't speak ill of a commanding officer, ever. You didn't disobey orders. You didn't attack your fellow soldiers or agents.

Except I have disobeyed orders, haven't I? And the world didn't end.

I wasn't entirely sure what to do with that knowledge, but it stunned me into a moment of silence as my brain tried to process it.

Someone leaned down and whispered into Summers' ear and she nodded.

"The transport has sent a boat for the two of you, should be here in about five minutes," Summers said. "Before they get there, anything else you want to report?"

I thought of the medallion around Luke's neck, how they might think it was an artifact. If they did, they'd take it and I couldn't allow that.

"The necklace Professor Turner is wearing, it's a medallion that helps keep his Vanquis symptoms at bay. It's his, not an artifact."

Summers' face softened at the mention of the deadly disease.

"I'm sorry, that must be very difficult for him to manage. I'll be sure no one takes it from him."

"Thank you. We did find the cave," I said, knowing that I had to be as honest as possible. "But there was a cave in, and all of the artifacts became buried."

"It collapsed?" she asked, eyes wide.

"Yes, whether due to the Protectors that had captured us tripping a booby trap or some other reason. We barely made it out with our lives."

"We'll need the location of the cave nonetheless."

"It's completely collapsed, what do you expect to find?" I asked.

"C'mon, Agent Kane, you know as well as I do that there's no way the director is going to just let this go without a fight. If there's even the smallest chance of excavating one artifact from a cache like that, she's going to take it."

"You don't want to do that," I said. "I've never seen artifacts used like they were there. The priest who carved out that cave and protected those artifacts, he was able to wield them in tandem with each other. It was…it was *otherworldly* in a way even we don't see every day. I can't explain it but I know that the artifacts wanted to be buried. It would be a suicide mission to excavate that cave."

"Again, that decision is above my pay grade. The location please?"

Well, I did try to warn them.

"Luke would likely be better at that, he's studied the maps more extensively than I have."

Summers nodded as two small boats arrived at the shore. They were the kind that black ops used to land on a beach - light and fast. Three agents climbed out of each and I watched the group that went to Luke. I still wasn't comfortable being separated from him after learning that they'd had even a moment of doubt about him. But the agents weren't rough with him, they didn't handcuff him or look threatening.

He caught my eye and I longed to run to him, to not let him out of my sight. But I knew the drill and so did he. If we wanted to get out of this without punishment and have even the slightest chance at getting Luke what he needed from that book, then we had to play by their rules.

He raised a hand and waved at me. I did the same and ignored the agents that walked up to me as I watched Luke get into his boat.

"Agent Kane?" Summers asked in a gentle tone. "He's going to be alright."

I nodded and turned away.

"Your escort is here," she extended a hand and I shook it. "It was nice meeting you. Good luck."

CHAPTER TWENTY-ONE
ANDROMEDA-ONE
WEEK LATER

I sat up straight in the same chair I'd used when Director Dearborne had briefed me for the mission. Except this time, my stomach was in tight knots and my hands were clammy with nerves.

This wasn't the same trauma response that I'd had before, I wasn't having flashbacks of Francesca. No, this was about what was right, what I was about to ask of the director. This was about making sure Luke was safe and able to create that cure. I had my work cut out for me, I knew that. He'd gone off book, done what he'd been instructed not to do. He'd caused the destruction of a cave full of artifacts that the Archive was salivating over. And I had helped him.

I'd just spent a week quarantined in one of the Archives special medical facilities that helped Agents affected by artifacts, or who were injured on missions. It was also where most of our checkups occurred. It was normal to want to make sure an Agent was healthy when they returned from a mission, but it was not normal to force them to be under observation in a gray room for five days with mandatory psych evals twice a day.

Apparently being healed by such a powerful artifact as Christ's Tears came with a mandatory thorough, and I do mean *thorough*, medical exam and stay in the observation wing of the Archive hospital.

If I hadn't been going crazy with worry for Luke it would've been okay. The food was pretty good, not usual hospital fare. I had all the satellite and streaming channels I wanted, books, and the very best sleeping pills on the planet.

Some would consider it a vacation. But I was crawling the walls by the time it was over.

I was discharged with a clean bill of health, and an order to report to the director's office in two days. Then they sent me off to my Archive-provided furnished flat, and that was that.

Now here I was once again, at eight in the morning, and feeling like I was awaiting a court martial. Though getting fired from the Archive came with far more unpleasant consequences than a dishonorable discharge.

I was certain that the report Director Dearborne was currently frowning at was the one from my debrief on the plane ride back to London. That had been not fun at all. Where Agent Summers had been pleasant, the Ephemeral on the plane was borderline hostile. It was a good tactic honestly, one I would've recommended for someone with my background, especially after the display of emotion I'd shown on the beach. But I'd had an eight-hour ride, on what amounted to a military grade yacht, to calm myself down and think things through. So by the time the Ephemeral got to me, my mind was pretty shored up.

Ephemerals are meant to be intimidating with their ram's horns, red skin, sharp incisors and tails. They look like the stereotypical demons, though they aren't. At least as far as anyone knows. This one had salt and pepper hair and a gravelly voice that, under other circumstances, I may have found sexy.

He'd tried his best to break my hard outer shell, but to no avail. I told him exactly what I wanted to, nothing more and nothing less and he knew it. So the fact that the director had been staring at that report for almost fifteen minutes now, her frown getting deeper and deeper, meant that she was no more pleased than he had been with my account of the events.

Director Dearborne ignoring me as she was, letting me see her displeasure rather than hear it, was also an intimidation tactic, one that I hated. I would much rather have the threat thrown in my face than be forced to sit here and sweat it out. She was waiting for me to break, or at least show some cracks, so when she came in all calm and collected, I'd trip myself up with little effort from her.

Well screw that, there's too much riding on this to fuck it up.

I didn't need to talk to Luke to know that reopening the Archive Medical Research Department was going to be a near impossible sell. Francesca had done some truly heinous things there, and it had become a place synonymous with torture and horrifying experiments. Luke wanted to take it back to its roots, to return the department to what it had been originally. But most could only see the horror show it had become, not what it could be.

If I could put my weight behind him and what he had told me he wanted to do, maybe it would help.

Finally, Dearborne looked up at me and set the file down. She leaned back from her desk, arms crossed, and frowned at me.

"Well?" she asked.

"Well what, Madame Director?"

"You blatantly disregarded the purpose and parameters of your mission by assisting Professor Turner in not only finding the cave, but going inside and then destroying it."

"I believe going inside was not an option considering we'd been captured by the Protectors."

"Which is exactly why you were to stop Professor Turner from even getting to the cave! Do you have any idea what could've happened if the Protectors had gotten their hands on even one of those artifacts?"

"Yes, ma'am, I do."

"And yet you led them straight to it! Why, Agent Kane? Why would an Agent with a sterling record like yours risk your entire career, not to mention the safety of the entire world, in this way?"

I took a deep breath, my very bones trembling, as I readied myself for a course of action that was in direct contradiction to the safe identity I'd created for myself in my career. When I did this, I would no longer be the reliable little soldier, the decorated agent that could be expected to follow orders, even if it meant hurting someone she loved.

I would be casting that aside and taking the first step into someone new. Someone who I could look at in the mirror and be proud of.

Didn't mean it wasn't terrifying though.

I raised my eyes to hers, held them as I straightened my spine even more, and said, "Because it was the right thing to do."

Her eyebrows raised.

"Oh, really? Do enlighten me. How was it the right thing, in your opinion?"

"Do you know what Luke Turner sacrificed during Francesca's tenure here?"

I didn't miss the way Dearborne's mouth twisted a bit at the mention of that bitch's name and it gave me courage. Maybe her deep hatred for the woman would give me the edge I needed to make my case.

I continued, "His family had to go into hiding, even though his uncle was dying of Vanquis. Do you know what that is?"

"I'm familiar with the disease, yes."

"Have you ever seen anyone die from it?" I asked.

The director shook her head.

"I have. It's horrible. They're blind, their mind is twisted and confused, their body is weak and ravaged. It decimates the Orc that has it. And Francesca drove his family from their home, away from any comforts his uncle might've had in his last days. He died in exile while his family cowered in fear of being discovered."

The narrow column of the director's throat worked as she nervously swallowed.

"What's your point, Agent Kane?"

"Luke has Vanquis," my voice hitched at the end, but I charged through it. "And there was a book in that cave that could assist in making a cure, for *everyone*. He hoped that finding it would help not only him, but every single Orc that would ever contract Vanquis. He didn't do it for selfish reasons, that's not him."

"We don't use artifacts for personal reasons, you know that."

"Bullshit," I shot to my feet, my face hot with anger.

"Excuse me? You forget yourself."

"No, I do not. I've served here faithfully through some of the most hellish years the Archive has known. I have buried friends, colleagues, their families, their friends. I have bled and killed and almost died countless times for this agency and every single time I did it believing that it was for a greater good. I stayed after Francesca because I believed that *you* would be different."

"I *am* different," she snapped, eyes blazing as she glared at me.

"Then prove it! Before Francesca got a hold of it, the Medical Research Department was making breakthroughs that helped cure diseases all over the world, that helped save the lives of agents. It can do that again."

Director Dearborne crossed her arms again, eyes narrowed.

"So that's your play."

"What? My *play*? No, it's my *plea*. It's what's right."

"That department—"

"Can be different under your leadership."

"— is triggering to many people. You would be asking your colleagues to reopen the horrors they experienced in that place. For what? Your ex-husband's illness?"

I had to bite my tongue to keep from leveling a truly massive amount of swear words at the woman. As it was, my furious stare seemed to convey enough because she sighed and shook her head.

"My apologies," she said. "I have read your file actually. Yours and Professor Turner's. I know what you both sacrificed during the rebellion and I thank you very much for it."

I snorted.

"I'm aware that's not enough," the director continued, her tone sharp. "But what you're asking…Agent Kane, I don't think you understand just how difficult that request is. The board is understandably cautious about anything that could be even tangentially connected with Francesca. And that department in particular was corrupted more than most."

"That's no reason to abandon the good work it could do. And if that book does have a cure for a terrible disease like this, don't we have a duty to find out? To help?"

The director sighed and briefly let her tough exterior slip. "The ethical snowball you're wanting me to start is another problem. If we do this, why can't we use an artifact to create peace between warring nations, or convince religious fanatics that destroying the earth isn't going to bring about the second coming of Christ?"

"Those are man-made issues, which the Archive has always had a policy against interfering with. But cancer, heart disease, Alzheimer's? These are diseases that kill indiscriminately. These are things in the gray area where we can make a difference."

She let out a long exhale through her nose and rubbed her forehead with her fingers, her elbows on her desk, while I held my breath. This would likely be my only chance to convince the Archive to restart this department. If it didn't work, if she was too scared to try, and if she was too angry at my disobedience, Luke and all the other Orcs suffering from Vanquis would be screwed.

Finally, she replied, "If, and it is a very big *if* right now, but if I chose to push this and bring back the department, it would need some very strict rules. There's no guarantee that we'd even be able to create such a cure if it went against any other rules the Archive has in place regarding the use of artifacts. The department would need constant and strict supervision, it would require regular inspection and complete transparency, and that could lead to delays and scuttling of programs, including the cure for Vanquis. I suppose what I'm trying to say is, just because we bring the department back, doesn't mean that it will lead to a cure."

My heart was slamming against my ribs and I felt like I was about to faint, but I somehow managed a nod that was convincing.

"Not to mention that it will take time to just approve the re-creation of the department, and then staff it."

I nodded again, my mouth too dry to speak.

She narrowed her gaze at me, and I braced myself.

"Alright then, I will approach the board with it this next week."

I let out a long breath and let my shoulders relax. I felt like I'd just run uphill for a mile in the freezing cold; my muscles burned from the tension and my knees wobbled. But I was elated, relieved and so incredibly hopeful for the first time since we landed in London.

"Thank you," I breathed, not at all surprised by the tears in my eyes.

"Don't thank me yet. This is not going to be an easy sell."

"I know, but I also know that having your backing is no small thing. So, thank you, Director Dearborne."

She gave me the barest hint of a smile, and nodded.

"However, there is the matter of disciplinary action for disobeying your mission parameters."

"Yes, ma'am."

"You are on leave for the next month and demoted from West Coast Head of Security."

I would have expected to feel devastated by such a punishment, but instead there was a creeping sense of peace. That job had been an escape, if I was at all honest with myself. It had never been a dream.

Luke…Luke was always the dream.

I swallowed back that pain and nodded.

"Yes ma'am, I understand."

"You're dismissed, but stay in London until I know where to reassign you."

I turned to leave and stopped. She was right, this was going to be a near impossible sell. There was no reason for the council to side with Luke and me, even if the director did put her weight behind it.

But there was one way to sway them. One tactic that I'd never used for anyone else, that Luke would never ask me to do, and yet, he was the only one I'd do it for.

"Ma'am?"

"I really wish you'd just say Director Dearborne," she said with a more relaxed smile. "What is it, Agent Kane?"

"I have a request."

"Another one?"

CHAPTER TWENTY-TWO

LUKE

I stared at the director, sure I'd misheard her.

"Professor? Are you alright?" she asked.

"Um…yes, I just…I had a whole speech prepared and now I don't need it."

She chuckled.

"No, I suppose you don't. Agent Kane was very…persuasive."

I nodded and licked my lips, trying to work some moisture into my mouth.

I'd spent a week in a medical facility being poked, prodded and observed for any kind of anomalies that using class five artifacts could've produced. Other than Vanquis, which was being controlled very well by the medallion, I was in perfect health.

When they released me, I'd asked everyone I knew to try and help me find out what had happened to Andy. I finally heard that she had also spent a week in a facility and was now out, living under observation in a flat in London that the Archive had given her. I would've gone to see her, but the Archive had sent me from one facility to another as part of my debriefing.

They allowed me to work in the Archive Library in my spare time, but supervised. I knew they were looking for any signs that I'd turned, anything that might indicate that this disobedience was indicative of a larger issue.

It was frustrating to be kept somewhat like a prisoner with no indication of when or if I'd be released. But it did afford me plenty of time to think about how to start mending things with Andy.

There were lots of options, lots of things I'd considered but it eventually came down to something simple that would show her that I was serious about a fresh start between us. It wasn't going to be easy to be the transparent person she needed. I'd trained myself to hide, thinking it would keep her with me. Now, I had to toss all that aside and trust that I was enough, imperfections and all.

I was working out the last details of my plan when I got the word to go to the director's office.

With my heart in my throat, I'd walked in there, fully expecting to have to defend myself and my actions once again. I was ready to do that, and more, to ensure that I was released and Andy didn't face any lasting consequences for her actions.

But then the director had turned all of that on its head with one simple statement: They were reopening the Medical Research Department and I was going to be the head artifact researcher.

"Do you need a minute?" the director asked.

"Um. No I just…how did this happen? I assumed after all these weeks that you were going to fire me."

"Well, that was a possibility, I won't lie. But these three weeks weren't just about making sure you were still loyal. It was myself and Agent Kane working tirelessly to get this department back up and running."

My throat tightened and I gave Dearborne a little smile.

"Andy was working on this?"

"She was the driving force. If not for her, the whole thing would've languished in red tape."

"How? What did she do?"

Director Dearborne's lips twisted into a sardonic grin.

"Let's just say that the Kane name has a far reach. Even in the Archive."

I ran a hand over my face as it hit me full force what Andy had done for me and my entire species.

She had never, ever wanted to use the influence her name gave her. She hated it, and had jumped at the chance to take my name to hide the fact that she was a Kane. I hadn't really understood it fully when we were married, but after her confessions in the cave I finally did. People wanted to use her all the time, never wanting *her*, only what they could get from her. I couldn't blame her for hating her last name in some ways, for never wanting to use it. Yet here she was, doing for me what she refused to do even for herself.

"Professor, are you sure you're alright?" Dearborne asked.

"Yes, sorry this is just a shock."

"I can understand that, but time is of the essence. I'm afraid that you'll need to hit the ground running. The medical specialist team has already been assembled, but you will need to pick your research team, including at least three agents for acquisition missions."

I nodded, mind reeling. Not only was I getting exactly what I'd hoped for, but also a promotion; influence into the department to make sure it was used appropriately.

My mind flashed to the things I'd seen in that cave, and I wondered if I could create those cures after all.

"I will begin immediately," I said. "I already have some ideas."

"I'm sure you do," Dearborne said with a chuckle. "You'll need to report to the department's new home here at headquarters on Monday morning to oversee the handling of the Scivias."

My eyes widened and I almost couldn't breathe.

"Vanquis is your first assignment," she continued, "and I'm counting on you to guide the team with this artifact. No one knows it better than you. You'll have full access to all library materials, as well as expedited requisitions for additional artifacts. Although, class fives must still go through the appropriate channels."

I nodded as I tried to stop my mind from spinning. This was a lot, almost too much. I was buzzing with excitement at the possibilities in front of me. Not only for the cure for Vanquis, but all the other things I'd be able to explore and discover. This was more power and access than I'd ever been given.

Even with all of that, there was one thing that was top of my mind, that was burning in me more than all of this.

Andy. I need to see her, to tell her thank you. To tell her…that I love her, that I want her, I need her.

I checked my watch and grimaced. I hoped my guy in acquisitions waited for me because if he didn't, I'd have to rethink my plan.

"You have somewhere to be?" Dearborne asked.

"Yes, actually. I'm sorry, Director."

She waved it away and plucked a manila envelope off her desk.

"It's alright, I understand. You are free to leave the facility. Here is your new ID, key card and all the particulars of your department. I'll need your short list for your research team by the weekend."

I nodded and took the envelope from her as I got to my feet.

"Congratulations," she said. "I look forward to seeing what you and the rest of the department will do."

"Thank you." I felt like I should say something else. But in the end, just gave her a smile and walked out.

For the first time since my diagnosis, I felt light, hopeful. This wasn't just a promotion the director had given me just now. It was a new beginning.

And I intended not to waste another minute of it without Andy by my side.

It had taken several hours to wrap everything up and get the two boxes I now held in my hands. I'd been impatient as I made the deal with my friend from acquisitions. But now, as I stood in front of her flat, I was rooted to the spot. My heart hammered in my chest, and my palms were sweaty, just like when I first asked her out in Venice. Only this time, I knew so much more. I was ready for her in a way I hadn't been then.

So I took a deep breath and went to the front stoop. My finger shook when I pushed the button and I had to hold the two boxes close to my body to make sure I didn't break the cookies inside.

"You finally got to the front door," said Andy through the speaker. I chuckled.

Of course she saw me.

"Come on up."

The door buzzed and my long legs made short work of the stairs to her third story flat. I didn't even get the chance to knock before the door flew open and there she stood.

Her hair was pulled back in a high pony tail, a crop top and green yoga pants showed off her figure with a tantalizing tease of skin. A flush brightened her face and she gave me a wide smile.

"Hi," she breathed.

"Hi."

Her eyes snaked down me and stopped at the two boxes I held against my chest.

"Um…what are those?" she asked.

I gave her a playful smile as I stepped over her threshold.

"An apology, and an offering."

She took them almost reverently from my hands and bit her bottom lip.

"Where, in the world, did you find not one but two boxes of Thin Mints? It's definitely not cookie season."

"I bribed someone in acquisitions to get them for me."

"With what?"

I ran a hand down the back of my hair, oddly shy to confess it.

"Well you'd be surprised how much Han Solo's blaster from *Return of the Jedi* is worth to someone with a stockpile of Thin Mints," I said with a nervous laugh.

She stared at me, lips parted.

"You…you traded your original, 1983 prop Han Solo blaster for…for my favorite Girl Scout cookies?"

It was a loaded question and I think she knew that, which was why she'd stumbled over it.

"I traded my original, 1983 prop Han Solo blaster for *you* Andy. Because I love you and I…I have a lot to make up for. A lot of tears, a lot of stupid things. But I thought I'd start with making up for eating your Thin Mints and we could go from there."

Her laugh was light and she shook her head as tears fell down her face.

"You are such a foodie."

"Says the woman who was livid that I'd eaten her cookies."

"Touché," she wiped her eyes and went to set the cookies down on a nearby table.

I followed her, willingly caught in her gravity. I'd been so lonely for her these past weeks and yet here I was, standing behind her and I couldn't remember any of the things I'd wanted to say. Only that I ached to hold her, kiss her.

"Director Dearborne called just before you got here," she said, her back still to me. "Told me that you accepted the position."

"I don't know how to ever thank you for what you did."

"You don't have to, ever. I did it because…"

Unable to stop myself, I crowded behind her, my hands skimmed her outer thighs until they settled on her hips. Her breathing became rushed, the warmth of her body wrapped around me. I couldn't hold back any longer and ran my nose along her neck, becoming lost in the vanilla and campfire scent of her.

"Because?" I breathed against her.

"I love you," she whispered and wound her arm around my neck. "I love you, Luke."

I turned her around until I could see her face, flushed with tears, her plump bottom lip caught between her teeth. My fingers trembled as I brushed them against her chin and tilted it up so she looked at me. The sight of her, open and so near, took my breath away.

"I love you too," I said. "And I know that a box or two of cookies doesn't fix what I broke. But I've been thinking of us these past weeks, all the things that went wrong and I realized something."

"What?"

My heart hammered hard behind my ribs, and my mouth became dry as the words I'd rehearsed pounded through my brain. I took a deep breath, willing courage into the action and said, "I know that I'm going to be annoyed by your habit of stashing your socks all over the place. That you're going to hate my singing. That I'll never understand the appeal of a slasher movie. And you'll never read Aristotle for fun. That there are dozens of things that will frustrate us both and that our lives will be one big, beautiful mess if we're together. But I want that. I want the perfect imperfection of *us*. So please, will you give me another chance? Can I…can I come home?"

She cried through my whole speech and now her face had crumpled as she nodded and threw her arms around me.

"Yes," she cried, "yes, yes, yes!"

CHAPTER TWENTY-THREE

ANDROMEDA

My lips crashed onto his as I jumped up and wrapped my legs around his waist. I'd been starving for him, my soul languishing half alive without his touch these past few weeks. I'd feared that maybe he realized with some distance that we were too different, that we'd just end up hurting one another again. The thought had left me in a devastated, ice cream bingeing state for days. So when I saw him pacing outside of my flat, hope had bloomed hot and desperate inside my soul.

Luke's hands were everywhere as our mouths devoured one another. He griped my ass, my waist. He pulled my hair as he angled my mouth so he could slide his tongue deeper. I didn't care that he was rough, that his tusks scraped a little too hard against my skin. He was here, he was with me and I was never letting him go again.

I let out a gasp of shock when my back collided with the wall, Luke's strong body pressed against me so I felt every hard plane of muscle. My fingers found the edge of his shirt and I tore it off him, desperate for the feel of his skin under my hands.

My fingernails scored his back as I ground down onto his hard length like a sex crazed lunatic. But Luke was just as desperate as I was and thrust his hips up to hit my clit just right.

"I missed you," he breathed against my throat as he bit and sucked the skin. "And I'm sorry for this."

"For what?"

I barely got the words out before I heard a rip and looked down to see my yoga pants split right down the middle. I didn't even get a chance to complain before Luke jerked my panties aside and plunged two fingers into me.

"Oh…oh fuck…" I whimpered.

His palm pressed against my clit as he pumped hard into me, his fingers finding that perfect spot. With that one moment, Luke unleashed a ravenous hunger inside of me. I mewled and cried out as I rode his hand, chasing a release even as I longed to keep this going because I could not stand the thought of Luke not touching me. I was completely, wonderfully at his mercy, as he built the crescendo of my orgasm like maestro with an orchestra. I came with a scream that he consumed with his lips pressed tight to mine.

He was still kissing me when he pulled me away from the wall and laid me down on my couch. The bedroom was a few feet away but that was too far. I needed him to drive into me, to fuck away the past and all the fear and pain it had left us with.

"Take off your pants," I demanded as I shed my shirt and panties.

"Yes, ma'am," he grinned at me as he dropped them to the floor.

I fell to my knees and gave his cock one long lick that had Luke hissing in pleasure.

"Usually I'd let you play, but," his huge hands grabbed me and lifted me from the floor, settling me astride his lap as he sat down on the couch, "right now I need to be inside of you, Andy. Please, baby."

"Yes, I've missed you so much. I thought you'd left me."

"Never again, I can't breathe without you. You're the missing piece of my soul."

Our hands skated over one another, frantic and desperate. It wasn't just reacquainting ourselves with one another, it was memorizing him, drinking him in and trying to satiate my body and soul.

His cock pressed against my wet slit, so beautifully thick and leaking precum. I reached between us and ran my thumb over the exposed head of his dick as I rubbed my pussy up and down his length. He stared, mesmerized by the sight of it, and that only made me do it more. My hand drifted to my breast and I rolled my nipple between my fingers as Luke's eyes seared me.

"That's mine," he growled, and seized my breast and brought it to his lips.

His tusks pinched around my areola while he sucked my sensitive peak between his teeth. He worked it mercilessly while I rubbed myself along his dick. My body was a spring, coiled tighter and tighter with pleasure. Everywhere he touched me left pin pricks of fire and I wanted more and more until I combusted.

Luke's hands gripped my hips so tightly that I knew I'd have bruises and I didn't care. Let him mark me, let him leave my body black and blue from his hands and tusks, an outward sign of our sacred promise to one another. I trembled under his hands, so hungry to be joined with him but wanting this to last as long possible.

"Please…Andy…oh fuck…" he grunted, his hips bucking.

Just when I saw his restraint about to snap, I lifted myself up and brought his crown to my entrance.

"Tell me," I whispered, staring into his eyes.

"I love you," he breathed.

"I love you too."

Not looking away for one second, I lowered myself, slow enough to feel every single inch of him filling and stretching me. The muscles in Luke's forearms strained as he grit his teeth and tried not slam me down onto him. It was intoxicating to have this huge male in my control, holding himself back for me. When I was finally seated on him fully, he pressed his lips to mine and I tasted his tears mingled with mine.

"Together," I whispered.

"Forever."

I began to move, rolling dives of my hips as he thrust up into me. Pleasure curled through my body and swept away the debris around my cracked and bleeding heart. I felt it start to mend, warm and sharp, like a blacksmith pouring molten steel to seal a crack. The broken pieces left behind a year ago were melting, filling those empty spaces that had made me so hollow.

It wasn't long before our bodies slapped harder against one another as we both became overwhelmed by twin waves of pleasure and healing. Our mouths and hands grappled, desperate for more ways to express what we couldn't with words.

When the release broke over me I let out a wild sob, my fingernails dug into his shoulders while he bit down on the crook of my neck. It careened through me over and over, stripping everything but my fragile, unending love for Luke.

"I love you," I sobbed over and over.

"You're mine," Luke swore as his lips ran over my face, my throat, my chest. "And I'm yours. Forever…I'm yours forever, Andy."

We spent the rest of the weekend fucking, eating, sleeping and talking.

About what broke us apart and how we'd do it better. About silly things like how much better Thin Mints were when they were frozen. About the Archive and Luke's new position.

He told me I was his first choice for his department and, after one phone call to the director while I took a quick shower, I found myself as Luke's co-director of the artifact research part of the new Medical Research Department.

Which is how I now found myself walking into a part of the Archive I'd never been before, a giant to-go cup of coffee in my hand as I stifled a yawn. Luke had kept me up late last night, feasting on my pussy until I was a sobbing, cum soaked mess.

It was wonderful.

"Welcome, Agent Kane," said a very tall Mothwoman at the security entrance. "Here's your new badge and clearance. Professor Turner is conducting a staff meeting down that hall, first door on your left."

"Thanks."

I was nervous as I made my way to the conference room. Our relationship, and subsequent divorce, wasn't a secret around here and I wondered how everyone would react to us working together again. There were a few faces I recognized as I stepped through the door. Three of the medical research staff that had left a year ago were now sitting at the table together, whispering amongst themselves as they looked around. There was a clear delineation between them and the new crew, all fresh faced and excited as they chattered animatedly.

Then there were the three other archival researchers who would assist Luke in finding artifacts that could be used in the creation of the cures. They all looked hung over and grouchy at being up at this hour. One had dark sunglasses on and I'd bet even money he was sleeping with his chin on his chest. The other was a huge, frankly gorgeous man with a beard who stood off in the corner and was shoving a ham croissant into his mouth. And the third was a woman sporting a shaved head covered in tattoos who was scowling into her coffee cup. I could feel a spark of energy from her and guessed that she was a Witch of some kind.

Besides me, there were two other Agents as part of the acquisitions and security part of this whole circus.

I didn't recognize them so I introduced myself. One was a Gargoyle by the name of Zach, and the other was an Ephemeral named Alex. Both were a bit standoffish, not really surprising considering the reputation of the department we were resurrecting.

Luke was making a few notes on a tablet and gave me a smile and a wink that wasn't at all professional.

And I didn't give a shit.

"Okay, thank you all for being here so bright and early and with such short notice," Luke began. "I want to introduce you to Doctor Stephan

Grant, who will be spearheading the actual medical research part of this department."

A gray haired man with a scar running down the side of his face and sitting in an electric wheelchair came whizzing into the conference room and I nearly choked on my coffee.

Doctor Grant was a bit of a legend around here. One of the only people to directly, and publicly, stand up to Francesca and survive it. Though he had spent a year as her prisoner, tortured and left without the use of his legs, Doctor Grant never wavered or gave in. How the hell Luke or Director Dearborne had convinced the man to come back was beyond me, but his very presence seemed to ease the tension of those who had been here before and were a bit nervous.

"Doctor, would you like to say anything?" Luke asked.

"No."

I covered a smirk with another drink of my coffee and Luke nodded.

He went over the project at hand: the Scivias and the cure for Vanquis. He detailed everything he knew about the Scivias and also the holes in his own research. For the next hour, I stood there and watched him talk over possibilities with the medical research team as well as the big brains in the room.

We were currently discussing a necklace that was rumored to have once belonged to a Chinese healer. One of the researchers thought it might be able to help with the creation of the cure.

"There were rumors of the necklace being hidden in the Antarctic," said the woman, who was indeed a Witch by the name of Kat. "I can do an archive search for proof within the last decade."

"Good," Luke nodded, "Zach, you and Kat will be an extraction team on this one."

Zach didn't seem all that happy about the prospect and Kat didn't even look at him.

Oh good, this should be interesting.

Luke had assembled a good team in terms of skills, I could see that just from this first meeting. But the ability for them to work together would require more than just their skills. They'd need to be able to put aside their egos, their prejudices; something he hadn't considered.

And that's where I come in.

Up until this moment I was a bit unsure where the hell I fit in, other than as Luke's brawny half. But as I looked at each of them, took in what I'd heard them say the last hour and what I'd gleaned of their personalities, I knew that I was uniquely qualified to help the agents and the researchers learn how to work together. It wasn't an easy balance to achieve, especially when I suspected they'd all been working on their own for a while. Daunting was a good word for it. But I might've been the only one who could work with Luke in this capacity and bring this team together. At least, on the artifact research side.

When the meeting was over, everyone scattered to go check out their new digs. The medical team went to their fancy labs, and the research teams to whatever offices they had.

"Well?" Luke asked as we walked to his new office.

"I think you've assembled a good team."

"But?"

"We've got our work cut out for us if we want them working together in the field."

"Yeah, I noticed that." He took off his new glasses and rubbed his eyes with his fingertips. "Suggestions?"

I sat on the edge of his desk and thought about it for a minute.

"Well, we could do team building exercises, but everyone hates that shit."

"They'd be united in their hatred."

I nodded.

"True. But I think we need to provide some social opportunities. Let them get to know each other outside of the office. Also, it wouldn't be a bad idea for them each to choose something, a skill they think would be useful in the field, and teach it to the other person."

Luke grinned at me and planted a kiss on my forehead.

"Perfect. Let me know what you need from me for it."

"I will. But," I pulled him to me, "that other artifact you were talking about in there, the Caduceus?"

"Yes?"

"What if that was our project?"

"I'm not sure it exists. And if it did, it would be very hard to acquire."

"Sounds like our kind of mission."

His hands cupped my ass, gaze smoldering.

"It does." His mouth captured mine in a sinful, slow dance that had my knees shaking by the time he let me up for air. "I'll start looking into it."

"Good. In the meantime, Professor Turner…"

"Yes, Agent Kane?"

"Shut the door."

CHAPTER TWENTY-FOUR
ANDROMEDA-SIX MONTHS LATER

The underground corridor was stifling, the sand gritty and slippery under my feet, but I couldn't slow down. If we slowed down, we were dead and I really didn't want to die today.

"They're getting closer!" I screamed, my legs pumping as fast as they could.

"I know!" Luke said next to me as he furiously twisted dials on the silver sphere in his hands.

Behind us, the horde of giant scarabs skittered and buzzed as we bolted down the final corridor that would take us out of the pyramid. One of the bug's razor sharp legs swiped at mine and I felt the sting of it against my thigh.

"Any time, Luke!" I shouted and fired the last of my bullets behind us.

"It's really not easy doing this on the run!"

"Well whose fault is that?"

"Yours!"

I opened my mouth to argue when a rumble sounded ahead of us and I screamed.

"The walls are closing in!"

"Just another...Got it!"

Luke chucked the sphere behind us, picked me up and closed the distance to the exit. We squeezed through and I caught a glimpse of the foam bomb going off behind us, encasing the scarabs and filling the corridor with a purple foam that would neutralize all of them, as well as dry in a solid so that the corridor wouldn't collapse.

"You can set me down now," I said as the walls closed behind us.

"I like holding you."

I laughed and chucked him on the arm. When he finally did set me on my feet, it was in front of the rope we'd dropped down into the underground cavern.

"My fault, huh?" I asked, eyeing him.

"You didn't wait for me to complete the incantation."

"It might've had something to do with the ghost army coming for us, which was *your* fault."

"Okay," Luke nodded, as he started to climb. "I'll give ya that one. But I told you to wait until I was finished. Getting that Caduceus was a delicate process. The scarabs were just doing their job and protecting it."

I started to climb behind him when the wall that used to be the doorway we'd just come through gave a shake.

We looked at one another and then back at the wall.

"The bomb went off, right?" Luke asked.

"Yeah, I saw it."

Another rumble, this time the wall cracked. The next second, four long legs pierced through the crack.

"What the fuck?!" I screamed.

"Did they *eat* the foam?"

"Who cares? Climb!"

"Get on my back, it'll be faster."

I climbed onto Luke's back just as the first scarab broke through the wall. He began pull us up fast, hand over hand and even though we were about to be eaten alive by giant scarabs, I still couldn't help admiring the flex of his bicep and forearm muscles.

Oh my God, I'm going to bite the fuck out of those arms while I ride his giant green cock.

"You're turned on?" Luke asked just before we breached the opening.

"It's not my fault you're fucking hot. And I thought we talked about you not smelling my moods?"

"Kinda hard when it's that strong."

By now the cavern below us was filling up fast with scarabs spilling out of the hole they'd managed to carve in the wall. Luke swung us up and onto the hot desert sand just as one of them climbed onto another and actually jumped up for us.

"Those are some determined bugs," I said.

Luke pulled the spell book out of his backpack and began to recite the incantation to close the secret entrance while I got a different sphere out of the pack.

Carefully, I twisted the dials and pushed the time delay button. Instead of a non-lethal bomb of pretty purple foam, this one had one of the deadliest nerve gasses on the planet inside it. Thankfully, Sprite wasn't psychotic and had a lot of safeguards on it to keep it from going off accidentally.

The scarabs started to climb on top of one another, only a few feet away from breaching the opening.

Though in this kind of situation, I'd take easy over safe.

Finally, I got it unlocked and lobbed it down into the cavern just as the secret entrance started to close. One of the damn bugs still managed to slip its legs over the opening and tried to escape. The stone closed with a crunching snap around the body of the scarab, cutting it in half.

Luke and I scampered away just in case the damn thing was still alive. When it didn't move for a few minutes we both let out a relieved breath.

"That was too close," he said.

I glanced at my watch and hissed.

"Speaking of, we gotta get going or we're going to be late."

"We've got time, the plane won't leave without us."

I started marching off toward our drop zone, Luke hot on my heels.

"And if it's delayed, or something else happens? We have to change before we get there for pictures."

"Calm down, we built in a cushion."

"How can you be so blasé about this?"

"Well, it's not my first one and I don't know, it doesn't have to be perfect. Just as long as I'm with you."

"Aw, that's so sweet," I said giving him a quick kiss. "But your outfit isn't as complicated to get into as mine. Then there's the hair and makeup. I have a lot more bells and whistles so chop chop! Come on!"

"I still don't understand why I can't see you in it before. What's the big deal?"

"It's a surprise, that's what the big deal is."

"But—"

"No more chit chat. Come on!"

I adjusted the skirt and frowned at my reflection in the mirror

"How the hell does anyone move in this thing without showing everything?"

"Question of the ages, my dear, but," Marcus did one final spritz of hairspray, "you look *fuckable*."

I laughed as I did one last examination of myself in the mirror.

The Princess Leia slave girl outfit wasn't as uncomfortable as I thought it would be, but the body tape keeping the cups in place were. Still, my curves and ample chest looked amazing in this thing and I knew without a doubt that Luke would lose his shit when he saw it. I'd kept it under wraps for the last month, getting final fittings for the custom made costume when he wasn't home. Marcus had helped me with the hair and makeup, though I doubted Leia had as much of a dramatic cat eye in the movie as I was now sporting but whatever. I did indeed look fuckable and I couldn't wait to see Luke's reaction.

"So does he know about the other surprise?" Marcus asked.

"Nope," I popped the 'p'.

"Take a picture for me, will ya?"

"Sure."

Marcus gave me a quick air kiss and floated out of the bedroom on a cloud of glitter and whatever designer perfume he was obsessed with this week. It afforded me a moment to get my nerves under control. This was my first Comic -Con, my first cosplay and my first super big surprise for Luke since we got back together. I'd been planning this whole thing for months and now that it was about to happen, I was as nervous as I was excited to see his face when it all happened.

With one last final look in the mirror, I took a deep breath and walked out of the bedroom and into our living room. We'd managed to find a large three-bedroom flat in London that wasn't too far from the Archive. I'd commandeered the spare bedroom the second I'd gotten home and showered off the desert sand to get ready.

Luke was standing with his broad back to me, cleaning his glasses. The Han Solo costume from *Return of the Jedi* hugged his arms and ass in a way that made my mouth water. His holster had a replica blaster that looked pretty damn close to the one he'd given away six months ago. I grinned thinking of the surprise that awaited him in a few hours.

"Hey there, you scruffy looking nerf herder," I said.

"That's not a compli…holy shit," he gasped, eyes wide as they raked up and down my body.

"You like?" I asked.

"I, uh…Baby I'm rethinking going to this thing. You sure you don't want to stay in? Do a little role play?"

"Nope! We are going. This is my first comic con and I am not missing out on winning that cosplay competition."

"If they don't give it to you, it will be a crime," his hands skated up my sides, giving me shivers right before he nipped his way up my throat. "Fuck baby, this is hitting some serious adolescent fantasies of mine."

"Well, anticipation for another few hours won't kill you," I said with laugh. "Besides, there's always the bathroom stalls."

He groaned against my skin and I just barely avoided giving in and letting him fuck me against a wall. If we hadn't been under a time constraint, I definitely would have.

Our phone dinged with the notification that our cab had arrived and I barely managed to get Luke to let me leave the apartment. But the second we were in the cab, his hand crept up my thigh and he rubbed circles just shy of the apex.

"If I have to suffer, so do you," he whispered in my ear.

"You're very grouchy when you don't get what you want."

He kissed the spot just under my earlobe and I shivered.

"I'm going to wind you up so tight that you'll let me finger fuck you in the cab on the way home."

I bit my bottom lip to keep a moan from escaping but I couldn't help the way my legs opened, just a little for him. His pinky finger grazed the black silk panties I wore and I gasped at the contact.

"So sensitive," he purred.

He kept it up the entire cab ride so that my legs shook when we left the cab.

"I'll get you back for that," I promised.

He grinned at me, glamour firmly in place.

"I look forward to it."

We had VIP tickets and just made it past the security guards at the entrance when we were asked for pictures. It was like that for the first hour or so. We couldn't go anywhere without a group of people asking to take our picture, or for us to pose. The attention made me tense, too many years at the mercy of paparazzi at home for me to be completely comfortable with this.

Luke noticed it right away and tried to minimize it until finally we had to get a special badge indicating we didn't want to do pictures.

"Sorry about that," he said. "I should've thought of it."

"It's okay. Now," I took a breath as I led him to a hallway that was guarded with two beefy security guards, "I have another surprise for you."

"Oh?"

I showed the two guards my con pass and whispered a code word to them. They let us pass and we stepped into the hallway.

"What's going on?" Luke asked. "This is usually the area where the special guests are waiting for signings and stuff."

I didn't answer because I was bursting with excitement about this. Instead I led him to the third door on the left and knocked. Another security guard checked my ID and let us in to a room with several couches, a table of water and snacks and chairs scattered around. It was almost empty with the exception of a few celebrities milling about, waiting for, as Luke said, their time to do signings and such.

There was one man sitting off in the furthest corner, his handsomely weathered face accented by thick white hair and glasses as he read a well loved book. He was famously shy and reserved, and although I'd met several times before this at different charity galas my family hosted, this was the first time I had ever asked him for a favor.

"Oh my God, that's—" Luke said, clutching my hand.

"Yeah, be cool okay? He's not big on the whole fan boy thing."

"Okay, sure I'll just tell my inner twelve-year-old boy to not freak out."

"Well, not until we're out of here."

The man looked up and I realized how Luke and I both looked like crazed fans dressed like this. But if he was annoyed, he didn't show it. Instead, he stood up and gave me a warm smile.

"Andromeda? It's been, what, seven years?" he asked.

"Harrison, it's so good to see you again. And I think so, yeah."

"I think it was your mother's black and white ball…"

I nodded, trying not to think about the fact I was wearing significant-ly less this time.

"This is my fiancé, Luke."

"Nice to meet you," Harrison shook Luke's hand, who managed to smile and not scream. "I believe I have something for you."

Harrison reached down beside his chair and produced a black box with a red ribbon around it.

Luke took the box, and I held my breath as he opened it. Nestled inside was a version of the blaster Luke had traded for my Thin Mints.

"I had an extra one, but don't tell anyone or Lucas will have my head," Harrison chuckled.

"Sir, this is…thank you!" Luke said.

Harrison waved it away just as someone came and whispered in his ear.

"I gotta go," he said, "Luke, nice to meet you. Andromeda, so nice to see you again, tell your mother and father I said hello."

"I will, and thank you for this."

He waved it away again and followed what I assumed was a PA out a side door.

I turned to Luke who was staring down at the blaster with tears in his eyes.

"Andy, how…?"

"Harrison is kind of a family friend. When he was a carpenter, appar-ently my grandfather commissioned some pieces from him and he got to know my dad's family."

"You know Han-fucking-Solo?" Luke whisper yelled.

I chuckled.

"Not as such. And it's not something we talk about much. Harrison is very private."

"Putting aside that you're on a first name basis with the idol of my childhood," he held up the blaster, "you convinced him to give this to me?"

"Technically, my dad did but—"

Luke crushed me to him and stifled my words with his lips in a hard, passionate kiss. When he finally let me go I was warm and tingly all over, suddenly wishing we were alone in here.

"Thank you," Luke whispered. "This is…Andy, this might be the most amazing gift anyone has ever given me."

"I love you, and I wanted to give you just a little something to let you know how much."

"I'm buying you all the Thin Mints you could possibly eat this next cookie season."

"Yes," I thrust my fist into the air, "that's exactly what I was going for!"

We both laughed as we left the room.

The rest of the day was a blur. The crowds were huge, and even with our VIP pass getting us through lines faster, I was still more than ready to leave by the end.

"You don't want to stick around for the cosplay competition?" Luke asked.

"No, I'm ready to go. Besides, someone promised me some fun in the cab."

I waggled my eyebrows and grinned at the heated look in Luke's eyes.

"I guess I did. Well, then, your worship, should we go?"

"Yes, you sexy scoundrel, you."

"Okay, I think we need a rewatch of the core three Star Wars movies. You need better Leia lines."

"After the cab."

"Well, yeah."

"And while you eat my pussy."

Luke's eyes took on a feral glint and his fingers slipped just under the low waist band of the skirt.

"Star Wars *and* pussy eating? Baby, I love you."

I smirked up at him.

"I know."

Would you like to read the short story about the mission that started it all? The one where Luke and Andy finally got together? Click here to sign up and get your copy of **"What Happens In Venice..."** Or copy and paste this **https://trishheinrich.com/aban don-bonus-sign-up/** into your browser.

Now read on for a glimpse at the next book in the Monsters & Artifacts series, Sinner: An Orc Bodyguard Monster Romance

EPILOGUE
DIRECTOR
DEARBORNE-ONE
MONTH LATER

I stared at the report in my hand as I sipped my bourbon. It was late, or early depending on how you looked at it. Once again, I couldn't sleep and so here I was in my expensive London flat, a robe thrown over my comfy cotton pj's as I tried to tell myself that I was doing a good job.

Except the paper in my hand detailed the agents we'd lost to the Protectors in the last three months and all I could think about were the mothers who would never see their children again.

It's more than last quarter, as are the number of missing artifacts. This isn't just a minor inconvenience anymore. This is starting to look like war.

I threw the paper and the folder it belonged in onto my coffee table and rubbed my forehead with my fingers. I was never under any illusion that this job was going to be easy. But no one had said a word about a secret war with a group that, lately, seemed to be one step ahead of us.

Maybe if we can find that cave, excavate some of those artifacts…
I snorted and shook my head.

Was I seriously considering using class five artifacts as weapons to stop the Protectors?

That was something Francesca would do.

I used to think she was just hard wired to be a villain. But the longer I was in this job the more I wondered if she'd found herself in a similar position as the one I now did, and if she crossed a line with the best of intentions only to find herself unable to find a way back.

Wherever she'd begun, Francesca was a monster when I killed her. And lately I found myself double checking my decisions to make sure I wasn't venturing too close to that same line she had crossed. The specter of her tenure still hung over everyone I crossed paths with, every department, every decision I made. More than a year later, and I was having to prove that I wasn't her while rebuilding what she'd destroyed and trying to safe guard what was left.

Everyone thinks this job is so damn easy, that the right thing is so obvious. But it's like trying to find a piece of coal in the dark blindfolded sometimes. And all I can do at the end of most days is hope that I'm making good decisions.

The change in the room was subtle, but it was that exact type of thing that Trey had been training me to recognize. I didn't want bodyguards all the time, and for some reason the beautiful Dragon had become increasingly grouchy about my safety. So I'd agreed to training to expand on the self defense I already knew, as well as better skills at knowing environmental shifts.

It was the only reason I was able to reach into the couch cushion, draw the gun and turn before the man behind me had been able to take more than a few steps into my living room.

The male was nearly seven feet tall, exceptionally broad but not for an Orc. He had his hands up, and though half his face was in shadow, I recognized the broken right tusk, the scar that ran from his temple to his mouth and the way he didn't quite put as much weight on his left foot as his right.

"Jesus H. Christ Darius!" I said, lowering the gun and letting out a sharp breath. "I could've shot you. What's wrong with a doorbell?"

"Apologies, Angelica," Darius' gravely voice was soft, as per usual but there was a tension there that made alarms go off in my head.

I jumped to my feet and motioned for him to come closer.

"What's going on? You usually don't come see me at all, much less in the middle of the night."

As he moved into the low light in the room I could see the dark circles around his eyes, the smaller scars on his high forehead and down his throat. I knew that his body was a patchwork of them from his service in an elite group of Orc mercenaries called the Sinners, and later as a bodyguard for the York family, which nearly killed him.

He swallowed and handed me a small envelope of photographs without a word.

As I flipped through the photos my stomach dropped to my toes. I recognized the facility as one that the Protectors had been rumored to control, the trucks coming in and out were armored like we did when we were transporting dangerous artifacts. And then there was the cooling system that was extensive and complicated which indicated that they had huge vats of neutralizer.

"What are they keeping here?" I murmured as I stared at the pictures. "And how did you even get close enough to get these? We've been trying to find evidence like this for months."

When I looked back at him, Darius' shoulders were stooped and he had a hand on the wall, holding himself up.

"Darius, sit down before you drop. When was the last time you ate or slept?"

"I found her," his voice caught at the end. "I fucking found her, Angelica and I...I can't get to her."

It took me a moment to realize what he'd just said and when I did, something awful started to take form in my mind.

The York family was a complicated partner when it came to Archive matters. They knew about us, some of their ancestors had been directors, but in recent decades, their business dealings had become less and less on the moral or legal side. As a result, I'd cut ties with them, unwilling to look the other way when they decided to ship artifacts to black market sites.

Three months later, the family estate in Aspen was attacked. Thadeus York had barely escaped with his life, while his two cousins, his nephew, sister and brother-in-law had been slaughtered.

Thadeus' daughter, Nina, had been captured and Darius had been ripped to shreds trying to save her. It was only by straining the boundaries of my authority that I managed to get Darius transferred to an Archive hospital in enough time to save his life.

The moment he was able to get out of bed, Darius had been trying to find Nina. I had never fully understood why he was so driven to find her, though I suspected that he'd been in love with the young woman. He had said it was about honor, something the Sinners took extremely seriously. When they made a promise, it was a bond and the highest form of dishonor and betrayal to break it. Darius saw his job to guard Nina as one such promise.

Whatever the reason, he had asked for my help in secret to help him find Nina. I owed Darius for protecting my family during the years Francesca was in charge, and so I called in favors, used Archive resources under the guise of other things when I could. But I had never thought he'd actually find the girl.

I glanced at the pictures again and shook my head.

"Are you telling me," I said slowly, "that she's in here?"

"Yes."

"No. I'm sorry but there is nothing I can do."

"I can't get in there on my own and I've already called in every favor I can just to get this."

"Darius, what do you want me to do? This place…look at these guards, at the security protocols in place. And this is just the outside. This place is like a super max prison."

Darius pushed himself off the wall and limped toward me, desperation shone in his eyes.

"Please Angelica. You've used Archive resources before—"

"That was small things. Supplies, intel, the occasional agent to help you get in somewhere but this?" I gave him an incredulous laugh. "It's a full blown op, not an under the table favor."

"Have you heard of Project Phoenix?"

I took a step back and narrowed my eyes at him.

"My sources say it's in the planning stages, still on the drawing board."

"It's not."

"How do you know that?"

He gave me a crooked grin, made all the more crooked by his missing tusk.

"Like I said, I've used my own favors and resources."

"Did they tell you that the premise behind Project Phoenix is turning a living person into an artifact? Specifically one who has powerful Witch talents in their family tree."

His smile slipped at that because he knew as well as I did that Nina had unlocked some powerful magical powers just before she was taken. And that's when my brain clicked over into a different possibility, a less than altruistic reason for taking Darius up on his request.

Another choice to make. Another life to ruin. Another half truth to tell. I wish I'd never taken this job.

"There's only one reason for her to be in there if Project Phoenix is real," I continued as a terrible plan unfolded in my mind, "and I think you know what it is, don't you?"

He closed his eyes and nodded.

I felt sick at what I was about to do. Darius was desperate to save her, he'd do anything.

But I'm desperate too, and I've got more people to protect than one woman. Still, I owe him a measure of honesty.

"If I do this," I said slowly, "if I help you, then this is no longer a few favors between friends. This can't be swept under the rug, or hidden in a few doctored reports. It will have to be an official operation, with accountability, a paper trail, all of it."

He was staring at me with thinly veiled hope that was a dagger to my chest.

"I understand," he whispered.

"Darius, really be sure, please. Because while I owe you a great debt, you have to understand that when the order is given, I am not your friend anymore. I am the Director of the Archive, and depending on what has happened…" I took a deep breath and forged ahead, "…depending on what has happened, I can not guarantee what will happen to her."

He jerked back as if I'd struck him and growled at me.

"You'd kill her?"

"I'm not saying that. There's no protocols for a living artifact, but at the end of the day, she is a person, so no, I don't believe she would come to harm."

His hands relaxed at his sides and he no longer looked like he wanted to throttle me.

"But," I said, holding up my hand, "that doesn't mean she gets to go free either. There are a lot of unknowns here and I need you to be prepared for things not to go however you want them to. For me to not be on your side when all is said and done."

Darius frowned, his gaze slid to the side and I could tell he was taking in everything I'd said. I wasn't entirely sure what outcome I wanted. Because while I knew that the Archive would go in no matter what because we didn't have a choice anymore, I also hoped that Darius wouldn't ask me to do it, that he'd walk away. It would make whatever happened after so much easier if I didn't have to look into his eyes and see betrayal.

But I wasn't that lucky.

"I understand," he finally said, "but I need to save her. I need to know…to know what happened. To tell her…"

He swallowed whatever words followed and I was grateful for it. I could do this a lot easier if I didn't know for certain that Darius loved her.

"Alright," I nodded and started to put up a mental wall between my affection for Darius and my duty to the Archive. "I'll let you know when—"

"No, I'm coming with you."

"What did I just say about this not being a favor any more?"

Darius clenched his jaw and pointed his finger in my face.

"You need me. I've got the schematics, information on the security systems as well as a list of all the artifacts that were recently transported in there."

"And let me guess, you're not giving me any of that if you're not in on the op?"

He grinned.

"Never give it all away at once, you won't have anything to bargain with later."

"Christ, you sound like my son."

"Where do you think he learned it from?"

I pinched the bridge of my nose, already wishing I'd just taken the intel and done the op without telling Darius a damn thing.

"Fine, I'll bring you in as a civilian consultant."

"Thank you, Angelica."

"Report tomorrow…or, today at nine. I'll have a visitors badge waiting for you at the front desk."

He nodded.

"Thank you," he said.

"You might not feel that way at the end of this."

"I will, because she'll be safe. That's all I want."

"Well then, let's get her to safety. Now, if you leave I can get at least a few hours of sleep before I have to go in."

I didn't watch him leave because my mind was already finding ways to compartmentalize the terrible decisions I'd likely have to make before this was all over. I typed out a quick email to the people I'd need in my office, and a request for Darius' badge before heading off to my bed. The last thing I thought of before the sleeping pills finally took hold, was that if I wasn't careful, there would come a day I might not be able to look at myself in the mirror.

Return to the Archive in 2024 with Sinner: An Orc Bodyguard Monster Romance. Preorder by clicking here or copying and pasting this into your browser: https://www.amazon.com/dp/B0C4HWZ9V3

ABOUT AUTHOR

Trish Heinrich's unapologetically naughty romance is fueled by caffeine and panic. A lifelong geek, she's thrilled to at last combine two of her favorite things: kissing books and fantasy/sci-fi. When not daydreaming about the latest book boyfriend she's creating, Trish is geeking out with her two kids about the latest superhero movie, cuddling with her husband or binge watching Lucifer...again. You can find her books on Amazon and Kindle Unlimited. You can also keep up with her on Instagram and Tik Tok where her handle is @trishheinrich on both.

ALSO BY

Craving more books by me? You can find all of my books on Amazon and read free with your Kindle Unlimited subscription! Check out my backlist below!

The Silver City Celestials

Devil's Temptation
Devil's Desire
Angel's Awakening
Angel's Agony

Monsters & Artifacts
Feral: A Werewolf Monster Romance
Bound: An MMF Gargoyle Romance
Abandon: An Orc Monster Romance
Sinner: An Orc Bodyguard Romance (Coming 2024)

Monsters & Artifacts: The MacDonald Werewolf Clan
Broken: A Second Chance Monster Romance
Hunger: A Haters to Lovers Monster Romance (Coming 2024)